The Link

Christ, Christmas, & Santa Claus

The Link

Christ, Christmas, & Santa Claus

April D. Floyd

FLOYD BOOKS PUBLISHING CO.

Dedications

To my husband: Eddie Floyd Jr.
Thank you for seeing my talent and encouraging me to write again.
The support and love went beyond anything normal. I love you with my
all, and I dedicate my written works to you.

To my mother: Carolyn Ford
You always believed in me, supported me and loved me. Thank you,
Mommy. RIH

Contents

Prologue

We live in a world where every story seems separate. Seldom do we realize that all could be linked into one connected fascinating tale. The accounts of religions, global traditions and celebrations, nightmares, Greek mythology, mythological anecdotes and fairy tales are woven from the same Fabric. Every story, acquaint and communicate one foregone conclusion which links them all together—our Creator, God.

Introduction

Sixteen-year-old Jess thought to lose her mother—who was Jess' world—when she was just a little girl, was the worst thing ever. Nonetheless, Jess has given thanks every day that she has been blessed with her beloved grandma; who she calls Grandmau-ma. For most of Jess' young life, her grandma has taken care of her. Now, as life would have it, the tables have turned. Jess is taking care of Grandmau-ma; and, is happy to return the love she and her grandma always shared.

The two also shared a special love for all things Christmas. Jess's life with her grandma was simple; but happy. It was built upon a firm foundation; which included Christ, Christmas—and, the magic of Santa Claus, who many considered a myth. Jess naturally loved all three.

While searching for more Christmas lights in Grandmau-ma's attic, an unexpected journey begins. Jess discovers a mysterious locked box that she's never before noticed. Curious, she can barely scurry down the attic stairs fast enough to find Grandmau-ma and pepper her with questions. Her grandmother patiently sits her down and explains that the box Jess stumbled upon is a very special box; one which cannot be seen by anyone unless they are "the apprentice." Grandmau-ma's explanation only inspires more questions from Jess.

Jess unexpectedly embarks upon a quest, with Divine Guidance, to save Christmas and Santa Claus. She learns that her world is only one of many; and, only one of a kind. Even though Jess is just a 16-year-old girl, Jess quickly realizes that she is "the apprentice" the world has been waiting. With this stunning, new awareness—through Christ—Jess discovers strength she never dreamed she possessed. With her divine gifts and guidance, Jess knows it is up to her to save Christmas and Santa Claus—gradually figuring out how they are all linked.

The teenager defies the odds of the "natural" in battles with witches, demons, vampires, wolves, dragons and more. In accompanying Jess on her remarkable journey as "the apprentice," readers will revel in all the wondrous discoveries of worlds, realms, and lands, as well. They will experience a world saturated with an amalgamation of Greek Mythology, A Creator, Bible passages, and folktales of mythological legends and beasts . . . All mysteriously linked for the sole purpose of destroying Christ, Christmas, and Santa Claus.

1

The Joy Of Christmas

Winters wrath was in full swing, and the condensation moisture from sixteen-year-old Jessica's breath cooling below its dew point made every breath she took visible—she marveled as it crystallized in the frigid air. Flinging her red, shoulder-length, curly hair out her face while she tried juggling two brown paper bags full of groceries and a fist full of keys.

It was Jessica's great joy to shop and care for her extraordinary grandmother (several times over), who had raised Jess since she lost her mother at nine. Grandmau-ma, as Jess called her, had only one child and that child had just one child—and so on; as time permitted they all expected to die off eventually. Jess was the only generation to remain other than her Grandmau-ma. Grandmau-ma loved and raised all the children until her significant decline and was now too fragile to attend to daily needs. For seven years, Jessica enjoyed the abundant blessings of helping her Grandmau-ma.

Finally getting the front door open, Jess spotted her Grandmau-ma, knitting a sweater while sitting in her favored chair as the phone rang simultaneously. Out of breath, and cold—Jessica rushed to the kitchen, hurled the bags and keys onto the counter and rushed to the phone; which hung on the wall near the entrance of the kitchen.

Jessica snatched the phone from its hook; she answered, "Hello," breathing deeply. It was her best friend Haley on the other end of that call.

"Are you all right Jess?" Haley asked with concern.

"Oh, I'm fine. I just ran in to catch the phone. My Grandmau-ma needed some things from the market."

Haley interrupted, "How is Grandmau-ma?"

Jess glanced lovingly over her shoulder at the sweet old lady, cradling the phone under her chin while she unpacked some of the groceries. "She is doing great. It's near Christmas, and every year Grandmau-ma has always been intense on this holiday. I have pulled out every light I can find, and it's still not enough to fit all around this big old house. Well, Kinda have my hands full now. Can I call you later?"

Haley gave a small laugh and said, "Okay Jess talk to you later."

Jess' eyes swept Grandmau-ma's old kitchen as she placed the phone back on the wall and sighed deeply. Nearly everything had been loved extra hard and was in some stage of disrepair. Attached to one side of the kitchen wall were stained, natural, square oak cabinets which held onto doors that were slanted and uneven. There was one window in the kitchen off to the side, and it displayed the same old curtains for many years. They were shabby, had penetrated stains and was unappealing to the eye. Preparing hot cocoa on the ancient-but-still-functional stove, Jessica realized the best part about the old kitchen was the open view to her Grandmau-ma while she cooked their meals. Jess looked at the old round refrigerator and realized she had better get busy putting the rest of the groceries away and getting Grandmau-ma dinner arranged.

After filling the soup pot with the ingredients for a hearty, delicious stew, Jessica poured a mug of the cocoa for Grandmau-ma and carried it into the parlor where Grandmau-ma continued to sit knitting, contentedly. With her soft, gently corrugated skin, but still twinkly green eyes, Grandmau-ma glanced up at Jessica and happily accepted the cocoa.

"Thank you, Darling. Have you been able to start hanging the lights outside?" Grandmau-ma asked.

"No Grandmau-ma, I have run out of lights," Jessica replied,

Grandmau-ma chuckled, "Well dear, there are plenty more lights in the attic. In fact, there is a big trunk up there with old Christmas things I haven't used in years. Perhaps you could take a peek after dinner tonight? Maybe, bring down anything that tickles your fancy?"

Jessica smiled and replied with a sweet, "Yes, Grandmau-ma."

She kissed her Grandmau-ma before returning to the kitchen.

Jessica baked some hot dinner rolls to accompany the beef stew. She prepared a tray for her Grandmau-ma and placed it on the table in front of her knitting chair.

"Smells divine. Thank you, Sweetheart. Aren't you going to join me?" her great-grandma asked.

"You enjoy, Grandmau-ma. I'll have some later. Promise. Right now, I'm excited to check out the Christmas trunk you told me about."

"Alright, Dear... Have fun and be careful up there."

Jessica grinned and practically ran to the hallway to pull the strap hanging from the ceiling. She carefully examined the sturdiness of the ladder it released before ascending upwards, holding a flashlight in her right hand. She made strides up the ladder while watching each step as she climbed into the dusty old place. Once she reached the attic, Jess turned on and waved the flashlight, gratefully spotting the short, metal-beaded string to a bald, ceiling light bulb. She tugged at the twine, and it lit up the attic. Jess had never been up here before and stared in amazement at all the treasures her Grandmau-ma had collected and held onto over the years. She was amazed at the concealed treasures that her Grandmau-ma had kept over the years. She was no expert on antiques, but this stuff looked almost magical. Jess could only imagine the history they held and stories they could tell. After observing the antiques around her, Jess discovers the beautifully crafted, hand-painted trunk Grandmau-ma mentioned. Particles flew everywhere when Jess blew on it to get a better look. She then took an old blanket to wipe some of the dust off slowly revealing a crafty old trunk. After kneeling before the chest, she flicked back its hatch. It crackled as Jess slowly opened it. Jessica coughed while she waved the dust particle that filtered the air. Her eyes as big as saucers—eyeing treasures that lived inside of Christmases of ages past. Jess carefully pulled out lights, bulbs, delicate old Christmas ornaments, ancient wooden toy soldiers, and nutcrackers. Jessica's eyes focused in on this big red velvet closed case. Her thoughts raced through her mind, and she said out loud, "What is this?"

She reached the bottom of the trunk to grab hold of this peculiar case. It wasn't pretty dense, and it had a small lock and Jessica couldn't open it. Jessica saw a thick red sac in the corner of the attic. She thought, 'Santa's sack, perhaps?' She laughed, then hurried and grabbed all the decorations and lights carefully placing them in a red sac first, then she set the large case on top. Jessica held onto the bag tightly and slowly climbed back down the ladder, careful not to drop her treasures.

Jessica pushed the attic steps back up into place and left the bag of decorative and lights on the hallway floor; after taking the special locked case out of the sack—she rushed to her grandmau-ma.

With the velvet case in hand, Jess fell to the floor before her Grandmau-ma's feet—half out of breath as she asked, "Grandmau-ma, I found this beautiful velvet and gold case in the Christmas trunk. What is it? It has a lock on it. I can't get it open."

Grandmau-ma's emerald eyes sparkled even brighter as she said, "I haven't seen that in years. There is a story behind this old case, Jess; one that I have never told anyone, including your mother and grandmother. I wanted to tell your grandmother, but she was never into anything, but your grandfather, so I saw no point of telling her anything, and as for your mother, she had always been a lump of coal person. She never really cared a fig about the magic of Christmas, so I kept my story to myself. The terrible accident that took your mother away from us was a dreadful occurrence, my Darling. But, everything happens for a reason. And, that horrible loss ultimately brought you to me."

Jess expression was a bit sad and stated that she was perplexed with Grandmau-ma's statement, so Grandmau-ma explained more.

Jess' eyes and face lowered in sadness. Grandmau-ma pulled the girl close, cooing, "I know, sweet girl. I know. It's okay. Jess, I must tell you a true story; this story has several reasons it's never been told. Tell you what. Why don't you grab us some more cocoa sweetheart; After I tell you the story, you should be able to open the case."

Jess was so eager to hear the story; she wasted no time retrieving two more steaming mugs of cocoa. She then snuggled into a cozy arrangement of pillows on the floor at her grandmother's feet, ready to listen.

Grandmau-ma brushed her hand across Jess red curly hair and said, "Sweetpea, It all began like this,"

Jess smiled. She loved it when her Grandmau-ma called her Sweet Pea. Soon she became mesmerized by Grandmau-ma's account and faded from reality—plunging into the story as it unfolded.

2

History In The Making

It was the days of old. Long after Christ had gone back to the heavens and civilizations continued to spread throughout the world—a time of hard, cold winters and bright nightly stars. The sounds of horses' hooves and wooden shoes were the norm.

There, in the midst of winter's cruelest cold in a gray, dreadful town, a young musher on his dog-led sled, tugs on his rigging when he spots the most beautiful woman he had ever seen. Her eyes seemed to pierce right through him, and his heart skipped a beat or two. That's when fate, intervened. The lovely young woman's kerchief escaped in a gust of wind. Nineteen-year-old Nicolas mushed his team into action, guiding them in the direction of the scarf, deftly grabbing it with his free hand.

Nicolas released the rigging, allowing the dogs to rest, steps off the sled and bows to the young woman, offering the wandering kerchief. "Milady." Never shy, Nicholas stands straight and looks her directly in the eyes, "My name is Nicolas Claus. And, you are?"

Understandably, the girl was surprised yet equally enchanted by the charming, gallant and handsome Nicolas. She did not, however, hold back, "Yes, of course... Sarah. My name is Sarah. Thank you for rescuing my kerchief, kind sir."

Nicolas intrigued her. She found him to be distinctive having a sled with pulling dogs, instead of horses like others in the town. Nowadays, not many folks believe in love at first sight. But, for Nicolas and Sarah, that's precisely, what it was. From that moment on they were inseparable and married in weeks. Sarah was happy to be known as and referred to as merely, Mrs. Claus. Only those in their inner circle were privileged to know her first name.

Several years before Nicolas got married, he would sit at his special place at the same time every year to watch a brilliant shooting star blaze across the sky. His heart told him it was the same star that shone so brightly on the night Christ was born and the star that led the wise men to the newborn king bearing gifts. Although Nicolas had no explanation why he saw this star every year, at the same time, he was compelled to share it with his new wife especially since he and his wife were believers in Christ. Every year, around the same time, since they got married, the two would sit out waiting to see the bright shooting star. Fueled with exhilaration and anticipation every year, he and his wife remained, wrapped in warm blankets, warm milk, and cookies until they saw the shooting star soar across the sky.

After making their wish, Nicolas said to his wife, "Christ's birth means different things to different people for different reasons, but to us, it will mean a day of remembrance of the Christ. I don't know why I see this star at the same time, every year, but I am sure it has something to do with Him and His purpose for me; however, you see this star also, so I think its purpose is for both of us. So around this time every year we, will celebrate after we see our special shooting star and we will continue to honor, thank and glorify the Christ." Mrs. Claus agreed and joy-filled them both.

— ~

The Nordic winters seemed to grow harsher with each passing year. But, the young Clauses had their love to keep them warm. After seeing many children in the town, they positively wanted children of their own and took great joy interacting with the youngsters in their village, with the fervent hope that God would one day bless them with a child of their own. Both were exceptionally skilled with their hands. As they waited for the divine blessing, they made preparations for their future bundle of joy. Nicolas gathered wood to carve toy soldiers, trains, wagons and miniature furniture, painting them with the juice of multi-colored berries. Gifted with a needle and thread, Mrs. Claus would fashion animal and doll shapes from fabric remnants, stuffing them with cotton from the fields.

Things went on for years this way, and then finally Mrs. Claus had a small child growing inside her. Spring had moved stealthily in, and the sun rays begun to rise glistening off Mrs. Claus cheeks. The joyful secret she held from Nicolas was bursting out through her mother's glow—a glow that every woman has when she's carrying her precious baby inside.

Approaching their home after a day's work, Nicolas quickly noticed that his beautiful Sarah was especially radiant, glowing.

Sarah already has a refreshing cup of lemonade waiting for her hard-working husband, grinning widely and mysteriously as he bounds up the stairs to her side. Nicolas rocks in the chair next to hers, studying his wife's face, questioningly. After what felt like forever, Sarah takes Nicolas' hands and places it on her tiny belly. "God has answered our prayers, husband."

Nicolas' eyes grow wide. Sarah laughs, "Yes, Mr. Claus. We're in the family way. There's a wee one growing inside!"

Nicolas jumped up from his wooden chair and, whooped with joy; he was excited. He went running down in circles, then grabbed Mrs. Claus from her chair and swung her around in his arms, covering her with kisses. Both laughed with joy. He abruptly stopped and put Sara down, concerned. "Oh my, Goodness! Are you ok? I'm sorry. Did I hurt you just now? Here, you should just sit."

This time Sarah laughed, kissing Nicolas. "I'm fine. Better than fine. Don't worry, love. I won't break. I'm just growing a baby!"

Nicolas wanted his child to have toys and making them helped him not to be nervous about Mrs. Claus condition. Mrs. Claus went for eight months wishing Nicolas to calm down.

That sweet spring morphed into the sizzle of summer, a colorful fall, and another blustery winter. By then, Nicolas had made so many toys for the new baby; that there was nowhere to put them all. One frosty evening after the Clauses had watched the blaze of their special shooting star. Mrs. Claus was plenty of tired, and she sat, in her rocking chair while Nicolas happily added logs to the fire in the hearth when he heard Mrs. Claus call for him. It was a painful cry out. Nicolas knew something was wrong. He hurried to turn from the fire to the rocking chair. Pain and panic distorted Sarah's lovely face. He rushed to assist her into the bedroom, added pillows and blankets to make her as comfortable as possible, and then dashed for his sled and dogs as swiftly as he could to the towns' doctor down the road.

The doctor and his assistant followed Nicolas back to the cabin in their horse-drawn sled. After quickly hooking their outerwear to a rack; the doctor and his aid rushed in and began working hard to help deliver Mr. and Mrs. Claus first baby. Nicolas was told to stand outside the bedroom for he was too nervous. He stood there as the doctor's aid ran in and out for clean rags and hot water. Nicolas provided all the hot water and clean towels they requested, pacing the floor outside the bedroom for hours.

When the pained screams finally stopped, Nicolas' heart and face dropped when he saw the expression on the doctor's face as he exited the room. Nicolas stood there frantic wondering what the doctor was about to tell him.

"Nicolas... Mr. Claus, I am sorry. Your wife is okay, but I could not save your baby boy. Your wife lost a lot of blood, and I had to do what it took to stop her bleeding, or we would have lost her too. I am also sorry to tell you, Nicolas because of this; she won't ever be able to have children."

After the doctor and his assistant left and before he went to Sarah's side, Nicolas fell to his knees, crying out to Christ the Lord to be strong enough for both himself and his Sarah.

3

Moving On

That severe winter thawed into spring, warmed into summer, cooled into a colorful fall and was back to winter, the full circle of a year. Mrs. Clause stood in the middle of the cottage, surveilling the mounds of toys that covered nearly every available surface in the spaces. Mrs. Clause said it out loud, "Honey, I don't think keeping these toys would help us to move on from this. I think we should give them away. Our little village is full of children of all ages. Wouldn't they enjoy new playthings?"

Sarah's eyes sparkled as her mind formulated a plan. Nicolas was delighted to see the light return to her eyes and a smile spread across Sarah's beautiful face.

"I also knitted clothing that other children can use please take them also. Do you think you're ready to move on and give the children in town these items?"

Mrs. Claus gave Mr. Claus the sweetest smile he hadn't seen since they lost their baby. He was so pleased with her suggestion he smiles back.

Nicolas pulled Sarah into a happy bear hug and threw back his head, filled with new hope, love and laughter, "HO, HO, HO!"

The heartiness of Nicolas' laugh made Sarah laugh, too.

"So, that's a yes, then?" Sara asked.

"Yes, my love—Yes! What a great idea!"

Still smiling, Sarah placed her hands on her narrow hips, feigning annoyance, "Besides, I'm ready to get back to baking. But, how can I when every single table and countertop is covered?"

She left the sitting room for a few moments and returned with a giant, red, velvet bag.

"Where did that come from?" Nicolas asked.

"I knitted and sewed the entire time I was, well, pregnant and, I was going to fashion a dress for myself out of this beautiful red velvet; but, somehow, it turned into a sack instead. You can see the added material where I made a mistake cutting it and sewn it back together." She giggled at her lousy job.

Nicolas embraced his wife again. "Mrs. Claus, I love it. And, I like where you're going with this—I think it's a great idea. I know the children would love these toys."

Over the next few days, the Clauses carefully gathered, inspected, dusted off as-good-as-new and packed away every toy and piece of clothing into the red bag. After putting in the last stuffed animal, Mrs. Claus gave an exasperating exhale, stood back and said, "Finally, I can do some baking now. My table is free from toys."

Mr. Claus kissed her on the cheek and pronounced, "It sure is. But tonight is the night our special star makes its grand appearance. Are you up for that? I mean, it's only been a year..."

"Of course, my love." Mrs. Clause stated. "That is one of our happiest traditions. Now that I have my table tops back, I'll bake some cookies that we can enjoy with our milk as the blessed star passes."

Nicolas kissed Sarah with a new awareness. "Perfect. And, tomorrow morning, I will distribute the toys. It feels like the right timing, don't you think?"

Mrs. Claus nodded happily in agreement.

— —

Nicolas rose long before dawn the next morning to feed his beloved, furry, blue-eyed beauties an especially hearty breakfast. He snugly fitted the collars and harnesses on each dog, secured the big, red bag in his sled, picked up the rigging and was off!

He got to the town, and it was full of children. Many of the youngsters were woefully underdressed for the severe weather, threadbare clothing and shoes only hanging on. Nicolas braked his dogs, stepped off the sled and wrapped their rigging around a nearby tree. No sooner had he hoisted the red bag out of its seat, all of the children swarmed him.

Nicolas pulled out toys and clothes as quickly as he could. He laughed at the children's delight. Nicolas got off his sled and greeted a man in that town named Ralph. This man had taken a liking to Nicolas dogs and mentions he breeds snow dogs. He also admired the artisanship of the toys Nicolas was giving away to the children in the town. Ralph was a short, plump man. Only standing three feet tall, Ralph was full of energy and moved around quite rapidly for such a small person. Ralph had no children and no wife to cook or bake for him. He and Nicolas became friends right away. No words needed to be exchanged. Both men smiled at each other and deftly continued the gift distribution. The funny thing is, even when Nicolas was confident there wouldn't be enough to go around for every child—somehow there was always more inside the bag. After a few hours, when every single child in town had skipped away happily with a gift, Nicolas and Ralph shook hands, grinning, and went their separate ways.

Back at home, Nicolas couldn't contain the sheer joy and exuberance that still filled his spirit, trying to explain it to Mrs. Claus. He was so flushed with excitement; his cheeks were apple red. "This is it, Dear Sarah—this is my purpose. I know it as surely as I know the nose on my face... or, my love for you."

Tears of joy for her husband filled Sarah's eyes.

"Think of it. We've always asked ourselves what meaning the shooting star held for us—this is how we are to celebrate the birth of Christ. By sharing, giving, and bringing joy—especially to children. If we're going to be ready for next year, then I'd better get started on making more toys right now."

Mrs. Claus packed with the same spirit; replied, "Then we better get to work to make more toys, but not before you taste my gingerbread cookies."

Nicolas obliged by eating half a dozen cookies in succession and washing them down with cold milk. His tummy ticked with its yummy treat and his spirit filled with mirth and hopefulness, Nicolas laughed a jolly, "HO, HO, HO!"

4

A Friend Indeed

Ever since the morning of the toy and clothing gifting, Ralph and Nicolas had become fast friends. It turns out; the joy felt that morning resonated as much with Ralph as it did with Nicolas. With no wife or family of his own, Ralph was a frequent and welcome visitor to the Claus home. Mrs. Claus made sure Ralph had a warm meal and some of her baking goods before he left their cottage on every visit.

One snowy morning almost a year later, Nicolas knew it was time to pay Ralph a professional visit and winter was blistering once again. Nicolas had to leave the comfort of his cozy warm cottage and beautiful wife because he was in need of another snow dog to pull his sled through the harsh snow. Nicolas had to visit his friend Ralph but not before grabbing, the bag of baking goods Mrs. Claus had baked for Ralph. Nicolas kissed Mrs. Claus on the cheek and headed out the door as a blast of winter winds greeted him in the face. He harnessed his dogs, pet them, climbed into the sled and loudly shouted "Mush" to compete with the howling winds.

Nicolas realized that the sled was moving slower these days through the punishing ice and snow, and sadly determined it was time for his beloved Micah, one of his lead dogs, to retire. Not only did Ralph breed the magnificent Siberian Huskies, but he also maintained a "retreat" on his property (acres of land) for the older ones who could no longer pull. They lived out the remainder of their days playing, sleeping, eating and being loved.

Ralph ran out to greet Nicolas upon arrival and show him where the dogs could be released to play, eat and drink while the men visited. The little round man's eyes lit up when he saw—and happily accepted—the proffered bag of Mrs. Claus' goodies.

Nicolas knew Ralph bred, lovingly raised and trained the beautiful Huskies; but, he didn't expect to see many running around Ralph's fenced-in, multi-acre farm and kennel. Dogs were everywhere, and Ralph made sure they stayed physically fit. He trained each dog from a pup to pull sleds with rocks in the saucer. All of the animals were as smart and strong as they were gorgeous. One handsome, young fellow, in particular, caught Nicolas' eye, a look that Ralph immediately picked up on and embraced.

"That's Prance," Ralph offered before Nicolas even asked. "He's two years old, smart as a whip, strong as a bull and protective."

Nicolas rubbed Prance's head, noticing how magical looking the pup's bright blue eyes were. "I'm going to miss seeing my Micah every day. At least, I know he'll be happy, and I'll come to visit him as often as possible. Meanwhile, hello there, Prance. How'd you like to come home with me?"

Nicolas smiled as Ralph put a new collar on Prance and the two men shook hands.

"Wanna see what I've built behind some those large trees?" Ralph asked excitedly and pointed to the other side of the farm. Nicolas said, "Sure. Lead the way."

They both walked between two massive trees, and it was like a different world. Ralph smiled as he revealed a wooden build cabin with an enormous door. He grabbed and lit his lantern that nestled outside the full entry. Ralph pulled a latch and opened the door—it made a crackling sound.

Looking inside—it had no windows for daylight to shine through; the inside was completely dark. At first, Nicolas couldn't see a thing, and everything was pitch black except for the warm circle of light cast by Ralph's lantern. Ralph walked in, and Nicolas followed.

Nicolas mumbled under his breath as he looked at his best friend, Ralph. "All that energy... Where does he get it?"

Ralph had built a wooden workshop in the midst of raising Siberian Huskies. Nicolas was examining only the outer appearance of what he could see. "Now, that's impressive!"

Ralph chuckled, "Hold on just—one-second, my friend."

In a fraction of an instant, Ralph lights up the entire area with hundreds of lanterns he'd engineered in sconces all around the walls of what was a giant workshop, to blaze on one after another—like magical giant fireflies. Nicolas clapped his hands in delight and wonder. In front of him were many shelves and tables overflowing with toys of every make and kind.

"You did all this?" An overwhelmed Nicolas asks, his eyes and mouth wide with wonder.

"I sure did," Ralph skipped through the aisles, arms wide, proud and happy. "Something inside of me came alive when I helped you give all those toys to the village's children last winter. I wanted to help you do that again. It's a feeling that I can't describe. But, the joy on all those little faces made my heart soar. What if we could do that for children in neighboring towns and villages as well?"

A tear slid from Nicolas' eye down his rosy cheek. "We have no children of our own—but, had prepared for a little one with the bounty of toys and clothing which we gave away. Sarah and I decided the most glorious way we could thank God for Christ and celebrate His coming into the world was by sharing and making other children happy."

It moved Ralph to see how thrilled Nicolas was so Ralph circled back to Nicolas and extended his hand. "Partners, then?"

Nicolas took Ralph's hand, shook it and said, "Partners. It's a good plan."

Ralph again smiled ear to ear and said, "If we work together, we can make it happen for the next Christ Day. And, just think—this way, your lovely wife can have the cottage all to herself to continue to bake this deliciousness for me. And, you, of course."

As though on cue, Ralph took a giant bite of one of Mrs. Claus' sugar cookies, grinning from ear to ear and lifting his thick eyebrows.

The sight filled Nicolas with mirth, and he released a joyous, "HO, HO, HO!" He nodded his head, "Guess I'd better round up the boys, who are already well-acquainted with Prance by now." Nicolas kissed Micah and said, "Thank you for everything, Ralph... For all of this—Prance—and making sure my Micah stays healthy and happy for me."

Nicolas made it back home, and as was her loving way, Mrs. Claus welcomed her husband, the new dog, Prance, and the rest of the furry team with giant hugs and a delicious meal.

Nicolas, Mrs. Claus, and Ralph got busy making toys and goods. The eve of Christ Day was fast upon the three. Ralph and Nicolas concentrated on making the playthings while Mrs. Claus centered her concerns on clothing items such as blankets, tops, bottoms, and shoes. She also kept up with baking cakes, cookies, and hot cocoa; this gave Ralph and Nicolas the boost they needed to continue making toys for all the boys and girl in their town and go as far as they could reach.

The day of the magical night for the shooting star had arrived. Nicolas was sure not everyone saw this star. He understood that to see the star meant you had a special privilege with Christ and he had a plan for you. Therefore, of course, invited Ralph to share his and Sarah's tradition with them. So, the trio sat bundled up on a hilltop between the Claus' home and Ralph's workshop, the clearest vantage point. They enjoyed a feast of Mrs. Claus' assorted cookies, hot cocoa, and warm milk.

Ralph hoped he would see the magical star as well, a bit worried that only a chosen few were allowed to witness its magnificence.

At the stroke of midnight, there it was in all its glory as it blazed across the crystal-clear, nightly sky, dotted with millions of smaller stars.

Tears in his eyes, Ralph was flabbergasted and humbled. "'Tis true, my friends—this is no ordinary star, and I feel different! I now know why I exist. Christ has a blessed purpose for me, as well!"

Unbridled joy and uncommon energy bubbled through all three. They gathered the remnants of their feast realizing time was moving forward. Therefore, the three got moving, Mrs. Claus got on the sled with Nicolas to ride back to their cabin to gather the items she had made while Ralph headed to his workshop to assemble the last remaining toys. He knew it wouldn't be long before Nicolas would be back to load.

Once home Mr. and Mrs. Claus loaded all of the blankets, shoes, top for small ones and bottoms too and every sort of clothing she had made went into the giant, red velvet bag. She also made and decorated many sacks that looked like giant leg stocking and placed many baking items of her sweet goodies in it for those that might be hungry. Mr. Claus loaded the stockings of goodies last and into a separate bag. After everything was packed, Mr. and Mrs. Claus stood near the fire, and Mr. Claus led them in thankful prayer.

"It's time." Nicolas smiled as he leads Mrs. Claus to the porch of their cozy home. Nicolas kissed Sarah, rigged his team of dogs, and took off with a merry, "HO, HO, HO!" as he headed to Ralph to load the toys.

MR. Claus made his way to Ralph's workshop, and Ralph was readily filled with joy. All the many toys were carefully loaded with delight into the giant, red velvet bag which miraculously held it all—slightly tilting the sled but Mr. Clause paid that no mind. He was ready to deliver the gifts to all the children in the town for Christ Day. A joyful, "HO, HO, HO" bubbled forth loudly and he and his sledding dog road into town.

5

Keep Going

From that day forward, Nicolas, Sarah, and Ralph made toys, clothes and baked treats every year for children in their village and those in the surrounding area. Along the way, Ralph—who was officially known as a 'little person' recruited many of his little person community members to assist in the toy-making process.

Children began to write to Nicolas with requests for toys or a new pair of shoes or something for their siblings or parents. Nicolas loved each child as though they were his very own, making sure every letter, was read carefully—and twice. He and Ralph enlisted the help of an expanded team to help with the tasks of building toys, gathering the list of children, gathering and collecting needed materials and reading their letters to Nicolas. The noble group became craftier in their skills of making toys, and Mrs. Claus was the best clothes maker and baker in all the land. They all worked to make every child's wish come true ultimately.

Theirs was a noble cause and did not go unnoticed by clergy and holy men throughout the region. Because Nicolas was a humble man, who gave Christ all the glory, maintaining that it was the Son of God who called him to do this work. His actions were seen for what they were—honoring the birth of Christ by sharing, giving and spreading joy to others—he was soon known as "Saint Nick." Word of the miraculous star that streaked through the night skies each year at the same time spread as well. All came to believe that this holy night was indeed the eve of the anniversary of the birth of Christ. Charitable groups and orders of holy men and women began donating the materials needed to continue Nicolas' blessed calling.

During a breezy fall season, one of the eldest religious leaders heard about Nicolas and traveled to visit him and his wife, Mrs. Claus. Upon opening the door to their modest home stood an ancient, thin and tall man who held tightly to a book, introduced himself as Jacob. Hospitality was Mrs. Claus favorite thing to do; and so, welcomed the gentleman in and prepared tea, offered stew and treats. She excused herself so the two men could talk about the subject that warranted the visit.

Jacob asked, "Nicolas how much do you know about his families past?"

Nicolas gave a curious expression and said, "My mother's people died off when I was young. My father moved us to a town to escape something dreadful, but I never knew what it was. I loved being in the wooded area, but we had to move near others. My father name was Nicolas too, and his father name was Nicolas. That's all I know, except, that I am the last of my generational seed. You see, I can't have children of my own."

Jacob was saddened by Niclas misfortune and had a gift for him. Jacob said, "Now, I have a gift for you. In my hand is your family's history. You are from a long line of Saint Nicks! Your forefathers battled for Christ since his existence on earth and giving has always been your mark as Saint Nicks. I'm am truly blessed to be in your presence. When I heard about you; I had to see for myself. I know how you are about receiving praise—your forefather's were the same. All praise must go to thy Lord for we are just a mere servant of God. Read how your forefathers were chosen to honor Christ by the name Nicolas. Read of their bravery until death or the Saint Nicolas who was wealthy and used all his wealth giving and helping others. I'll leave this with you. I can't stay. Please tell your wife I am truly thankful for her wonderful snacks and hospitality."

Jacob handed the book to Nicolas and walked to the door. Sara walked into the room, and Nicolas took his eyes off the man only a second, and upon returning to the door, he was gone. Nicolas rubbed his head in wonderment.

Eventually, the religious leaders faded away, but the name Saint Nicolas or Saint Nick stayed with Nicolas all his days. Moreover, Happy Christ Day became Merry Christmas to all.

— —

Years had passed, and old age sat in on them all, and the toy making business was moving very slow, but the demand for toys increased. The passing of time eventually takes its toll on every mortal being and living thing. As children become adults, new children take their place. More children meant more toys, which always filled Nicolas' heart with much joy. However, his body was betraying him. Aging, sore hands, and aches in nearly every bone, joint and muscle made it increasingly challenging to meet the now highly anticipated toys for Christmas across the land. Oh, how Nicolas wished he had a son to pass on the gift of giving to the many needing children of the world.

Nicolas was also doing his best to care for his beloved Sarah, who was plagued with a cruel illness that left her feverish and bedridden. The local doctor said there was nothing more he could do for her; but, Nicolas remained hopeful.

Even the ever-energetic Ralph was forced to slow down by the physical ravaging of aging on the body. Ralph friends went back to their families to spend the rest of their older days at home for they too were forced to slow down. It was a lack of younger recruits, and every effort seems to go at a snail's pace.

On the Eve of Christmas that year, Nicolas sat alone awaiting the appearance of the brilliant shooting star with a cup of hot cocoa in his hand. Because he had always believed that the star was the glorious heralding of Christ's birth, miracles were associated with it. Nicolas needed a miracle more this year than ever. This time, the star seemed to shine brighter and lit up the sky a bit longer. Nicolas dropped his cup of cocoa upon seeing the star and fell to his knees, clasping his hands in fervent prayer. He asked Christ the Lord to heal the love of his life, Sarah, and to give him the strength needed to make what Nicolas knew was his last delivery of toys to the children he so cherished. He also asked God to bless his faithful partner, Ralph.

When the star had magically come and gone, Saint Nicolas made his way to Ralph's workshop to pack the sled with toys one last time for delivery the next morning. Ralph had thick, gray, eyebrows that seem to stand off his face. He had grown very chubby from Mrs. Claus baking over the years, and Ralph loved making toys, but his hands could no longer grip the needed tools; for making the toys got to be an impossible mission. After the task was complete, the two old men embraced with love and appreciation; each silently saying goodbye to the other. Smiling nostalgically, Nicolas hurriedly left to check in on Mrs. Claus, then to make his last delivery to the town's children. Again, the bag never seemed to be out of gifts until the last child was served. Saint Nick; somehow, knew this was also a miracle provided by Christ. He smiled as he through the giant, velvet bag across his shoulders and headed home.

6

A Dream

Nicolas made Mrs. Claus as comfortable as possible before climbing into bed himself that night, quickly drifting off into an intense dream. Suddenly, he heard someone calling his name several times and sat straight up in bed—looking all around his room for the person behind the voice. Oddly there were no sounds—not the fire crackling, not his wife's breathing—just the jingling of bells and hems of singing voices in the background.

Finally, Nicolas mustard the courage to speak out and answered, "Yes, who is it looking for me?"

"Nicolas, rise," the answer came from a bodiless voice. "Christ, thy Lord has shown you a great favor."

Nicolas pulled the covers off his legs, pressed his feet into his slippers, and stood, but as he stood, he realized that his feet weren't touching the floor; he was floating. A light appeared in the form of a bright shining human-sized star with a voice that Nicolas understood.

Nicolas wasted no time pulling the covers off his legs and swinging them to the floor to slide into his slippers. But, there was no floor there! He was floating. A star-shaped apparition of light shone brightly in front of him. The spirit's voiced words of understanding. "Nicolas, come, there is much to see and learn."

Filled with the innocent wonder of a child, Nicolas almost became one with the light, floating so close to it. Before Nicolas was the vision of his six-year-old self, a chubby little boy who loved staring out the window.

"Nicolas, can you remember why you gazed out that window every winter, every year?" The spirit questioned gently.

It had been many decades ago, so Nicolas had to think back for a fraction of an instant. "Why yes, I do remember. My mum was forever commenting on my active imagination. So, I never told her that I saw reindeer that flew in the sky. She would never have believed me. We were surrounded by deer because we lived in the woods. But, on the day you're showing me, I am certain I heard one of the reindeer call out my name. After that, we moved closer to town, so I never saw reindeer or any other deer—again."

"What you saw, my dear Nicolas, was very real, indeed," the shimmery spirit responded. "They only appear to a chosen few. And, it is an even greater blessing that one spoke your name. More of that later— Now, I need to show you a more grievous time. But, hold to your wonderful faith as you watch."

It was the horrible night that Nicolas and Sarah had lost their only child. Even in her weakened and heartbroken state, Nicolas watched his Sarah struggle to get out of the bed and fall to her knees, tears streaming down her face:

> *"Oh, my Christ, my Lord and my God, please help Nicolas to find the strength to fight our way through this terrible pain and loss. Our hearts and spirits are crushed, oh Lord. My sweet Nicolas loves children. It hurts me so that I cannot give him that precious gift. Please find a way, Dear Lord, to give him the fulfillment and pure joy of children that he so deserves. For, I realize it is not written to bear any of our own. Amen..."*

Tears of mixed emotions spilled from Nicolas' eyes. His Sarah had prayed for him as hard as he prayed for her, despite her heart-wrenching pain. Nicolas received clarity of his mission to love other children of the world as his own and serve them by fulfilling something as simple as a Christmas wish.

The benevolent spirit guide was of one mind with Nicolas, "Yes, Nicolas. But, there's one more place we need to visit for you to grasp the entirety of your purpose."

Next, they hovered in Ralph's workshop in the present. Ralph's crippling hands made crafting toys a painful task, but he persevered. "Lord, give us the strength to carry on. I don't want to stop. Nicolas is my best friend and the best man I know. He's only ever seen me, not my lack of height. If I could, I'd work with him forever."

Nicolas was deeply moved, "Ralph has been a loyal friend and partner from the beginning. It is I who am blessed to have such a friend."

In the blink of an eye, they were back in the bedroom Nicolas shared with Mrs. Claus.

The spirit explained what this all meant and said, "Nicolas, the Lord is pleased with your pure and loving heart and has heard your prayers. As men of God have dubbed you Saint Nicolas for your blessed work, another name is to be bestowed upon you. From now through eternity in the heavens and on earth, you will be known as either Saint Nicolas, Santa Claus or their equivalency in the many tongues of the earth. Your blessed work to deliver toys during the magical space between Christmas Eve and Christmas morn will expand beyond your region to include all the children of this world and beyond."

Nicolas' eyes rounded with awe, his heart full, but wondering how this was to be achieved in one night.

The loving spirit answered before he could ask. "Your beloved sledding dogs can rest and play. You will no longer require their assistance. The special reindeer you observed as a child called out your name because they too also knew of your purpose. That special reindeer and others will magically guide your sled through the skies on Christmas Eve every year."

"And, my Sarah?"

"Mrs. Claus will remain—healthy and whole—forever at your side—making you your favorite treats."

"How can I achieve all of this without Ralph?"

"Since you love the size of your small loyal friend Ralph, he, too, will remain by your side with a special alteration to his ears, setting him apart from other mortals. He will gain larger and pointy ears. His ears will represent how he always talked to Christ the Lord aloud. The Lord loved this quality about Ralph. Ralph will be your head helper always, but others will follow. You will have at your service a jolly army of Eve workers or elves—with the same distinctive ears, and they will assist you and Ralph the year 'round."

"We're going to create toys for the children of the world in Ralph's workshop?" Nicolas acquired more insight for understanding.

The angel slowed to explain and said, "Because your work comes from a place of pure love, a special compound has been created for you and yours in a mystical land known as the North Pole, undetectable by the eyes of mortals. The brilliant North Star you faithfully followed every year points to its location. There is but one magic that makes this possible—the honest belief of children in Christ, Christmas and you, Santa Claus. Without that belief, the magic of Christmas will ultimately dies—as a candle slowly burns out. And, the light of the North Star will extinguish."

The spirit spoke paused and then more boldly and said, "The Lord will always grace people with the spirit of Christmas to guide them. Human beings can strengthen the spirit of Christmas with love and joy spread throughout the season and, with the grace of God, every day. It is the spirit of Christmas that ignites Christmas magic. There is but one rule for you, Santa. Gifts are to be given only to good girls and boys. Children who are naughty will receive a lump of coal in their stockings—this is not a punishment but, rather a reminder and incentive to abandon naughtiness and be good; just as the Lord wants all to repent when they err in ways. Now, close your eyes, Saint Nicolas. And, Merry Christmas—Santa Claus!"

7

A Time To Wake

Nicolas heard bells once again, and they became more defined as he woke until they were almost deafening. He rubbed the sleep out of his eyes and looked over at his wife's bed and notice she wasn't in it. "Sarah?" Getting no answer, Nicolas swung his legs over the side of the bed, sliding his feet into his thick, furry slippers. "Did I get new slippers?" Glancing around the bedroom, he realized it was different somehow, larger. "Where am I? Is this still a dream?"

Nicolas shook his head, as though trying to wake up for real. He shuffled to the unfamiliar window, looked out and, there—they were— eight reindeer with bell-covered collars.

Filled with both awe and disbelief, Nicolas rubbed his chin. To his astonishment, it was covered with hair draping from his chin, "A beard? When did I grow a beard? Dear Lord, how long have I been asleep?"

Nicolas hurried to the full-length, gilded mirror in the far corner of the bedroom, a mirror that he had never seen before. He was never one to be vain about his appearance, so when Nicolas saw his reflection, he laughed out loud, "HO, HO, HO!"

Once reasonably fit, Nicolas had now tripled in size. He was so chubby; his belly shook like a bowl full of jelly when he laughed. In addition to the thick, white beard, his hair was snow white. And, his cheeks were rosy red. "I am awake, right?" he asked his image in the mirror.

Curious and a bit confused, Nicolas pulled on a beautiful a vibrant deep red color robe, trimmed in white fur that was conveniently hanging on a hook near the mirror. He then ran out his bedroom door unto a rail, and as he looked over it, he saw hundreds of small people walking and working. The place was circular in an open format. There were several floors as he looked down. It was so much to take in, Nicolas felt a bit faint. His next instinct was to leave the bedroom and figure out what was going on. There were, however, two large double doors Nicolas opened them. It led to a lovely terrace trimmed with a golden, red and white striped railing.

The scene before him was nothing short of magical. He looked beyond the railing, and the place was circular with an open format. It was a Christmas village with nothing but beautifully decorated life-size gingerbread houses, filled with happily busy little people scurrying back and forth. Nicolas felt faint. As though by magic, there was an overstuffed red chair directly behind Nicolas on the terrace to catch him. "I must still be dreaming; this—this can't be possible," Nicolas said aloud.

"Ah, but, it is possible and very real, my best buddy," Ralph responded cheerfully, popping up next to Nicolas out of nowhere.

He called out, "What is this? I thought I was dreaming; maybe I am still dreaming."

Nicolas utters to himself, "That's it! I am still dreaming."

While Nicolas was yet staggering over his thoughts, Ralph walked up to him, "Hey, there, Saint Nicolas, my best friend."

Before Nicolas could comment on Ralph addressing him as Saint Nick, he said, "Ralph?"

Ralph continued to explain things. "Yep, it's me, Saint Nick. Or, should I say, Santa? It's okay. I know you're confused. I will tell you; I was too when I first woke up. Mrs. Claus and I were prepared and awaken before you to help you adjust faster to your new reality."

"Where is Sarah?" Saint Nick asked fretfully. "She's been so sick. She wasn't beside me when I woke up." Nicolas' eyes began to fill with tears. "Is she, is she— "

"Mrs. Claus is fine. Better than fine, I promise," Ralph quickly interjected, placing both hands on Nicolas' newly husky shoulders to calm him. "We all are. Welcome to our new lives in the North Pole where no sickness exists. Come, Mrs. Claus is waiting for us with her famous hot cocoa in the library. We'll clear up everything for you. I know, this whole thing takes some getting used to, right?" Ralph chuckled.

The magnificent library was majestic and cozy at the same time. Sarah Claus ran into her husband's arms. "My love, isn't it wonderful?"

Nicolas didn't want to let her go. "Sarah! My precious Sarah... It's you. It's really you. Thank God! Oh, Lord how wonderful it is to see my Sara! But, how? You were so sick. I was afraid that— "

"Shhh—" Sarah placed her fingertip to Nicolas' lips before he could continue. "I know, Darling. We have been blessed with favor beyond reason. An angel visited me as well last night. The Lord healed me. As long as we are in this magical land and fulfill our loving calling, we will never grow beyond our years now and will be together forever."

"Praise God," Saint Nicolas rubbed his soft new beard, "but, I'm still not quite grasping it all."

Mrs. Clause sat in a chair next to him and proceeded to give the instructions the angels told her to give. She softly said, "Your work, my love. Our work... Our purpose of bringing joy to children to display the magic of giving and to honor the birth of Christ. God placed us in this magical land to eternally carry out that divine purpose. These great volumes of books in this library contain the life stories of every child who has ever been and every child who will ever be. Ralph, would you please show Santa where we keep the current naughty and nice lists?"

Mrs. Claus escorts Santa to an alcove in the library. "You see, there are two separate books of lists for any given year: one for the nice children, and one for the naughty. Only you can keep up with the positive progress of the naughty ones with this magic pen, and hopefully, eventually cross their names off the list."

Nicolas nodded in understanding.

Ralph walked in, intervened, continued happily, puffing out his chest, and said, "As for me, I'm the head elf. Yessir, I've organized and will supervise our brand new toy workshop operation. And, we've acquired the assistance of an entire village of elves—little people like me— to help us. Ain't it grand?"

Again, Nicolas nods his head, taking it all in, "Indeed."

Mrs. Claus gave Ralph the notion of getting their coats and said, "Let's all take a walk outdoors. There's something important you must see."

They walked down the beautiful decorated curved step to the first level of their new domain. Santa Clause was in awe as the elves all simultaneously stop in motion and turned with respect as Santa walked by. Ralph opened the doors, and the three went out into the winter wonderland of brilliant, snow.

Mrs. Claus pointed and said, "We're surrounded by those snowcapped mountains that are invisible to the rest of the world. And, see that gigantic, crystal waterfall?"

Santa took a deep breath and said, "Yes, it's breathtaking. I've never seen anything like it. The streaming waters are sparkling with all the colors of the rainbow."

Mrs. Claus held her husband's hand then said, "Yes, but it also serves a critical purpose in this land. Its magic both allows the reindeer to fly and measures the spirit of Christmas in the world. Should that spirit dwindle and if children stop believing in Christ, Christmas, and Santa Claus, the waterfall's stream will eventually dry up. We never want that to happen. The angel was very clear about that point. The flow of the falls is our way to calculate the spirit of Christmas. If the stream stops flowing and dry up, Christmas will die and so would our entire purpose."

Mrs. Claus diverts her husband's attention to cheer him up after sharing that critical bit of information, "Don't worry, dear. We're never going to let that happen." She addressed his head elf. "Ralph, take my husband to see the reindeer. I need to get back to the stove. I'll have some nice hot cocoa for you two when you get back."

Mrs. Claus hugged Santa her husband and excused herself. Ralph said to Santa, "Did you, by chance, notice the beautiful reindeer outside our window this morning, Santa? I'm sure you, at least, heard them. You're going to love them. Mrs. Claus named them all." Now, at the outhouse for the reindeer, "There they are!" Ralph pointed to each as he said their names. "Their names are Dancer, Prancer, Cupid, Dasher, Vixen, Comet, Donner, and Blitzen. The little one, off to himself, is Rudolph."

"Listen, guys," Ralph interrupted, "I'm going to dash and leave you two alone. You're in the best hands possible," Ralph winked at Nicolas and chuckled. "Welcome home, good buddy. See you later." And, he was off!

Santa spent time learning more about the reindeer. He loved them all immediately. They display their different personalities to him right away. Santa knew Rudolph was different—unlike any of the others and was particularly special. Santa made it back to his new dwelling place called home.

Upon his return, Sarah kissed her husband on the cheek, "Oh, and Nicolas, just wait until you see the kitchen. It's enormous and fitted with everything piece of equipment and supplies any baker or chef could ever dream of!"

As she spoke, a beautiful wisp of an elf with long, dark hair, star-bright blue eyes, and an even brighter smile appeared at Mrs. Claus' side.

"Would you and Santa care for extra marshmallows for your hot cocoa, Ma'am?"

"Why, thank you—Khausna, dear... That would be lovely. Nicolas, this is Khausna—my talented sous chef and executive assistant in the baked good and delicious meals department."

Nicolas extended his beefy hand, "Lovely to meet you, Khausna. Do you mind if I ask a question?"

"Of course not, sir. Please ask anything you would like to know, and I will answer to the best of my abilities."

"Thank you. Where do you and all the other elves come from?"

Khausna's tinkling laughter was musical. "We come from two places, Santa. Some of us are born from the intersecting dance between evening star beams with the rays of the Northern magical lights. Some of us were born from the magic in our hearts from other worlds and brought to the North Pole by angels. Like you and Mrs. Claus, we were bestowed with special names and specific assignments."

Santa pinched himself. "Ouch!"

"Nicolas?" Mrs. Claus exclaimed. Khausna giggled.

"Just making sure this is really real, Mrs. Claus."

"Aw, my love, this is all as real as our faith in Christ and our love for each other. Every soul here has been shown favor and have a special purpose."

Santa threw back his head with a merry, "HO, HO, HO!" He kissed his wife and happily accepted a giant mug of steaming cocoa, filled with marshmallows, from Khausna.

"Time for me to get to work, then." Santa Claus drained his cup, rubbed his belly and was off!

8

Tired Grandmau-ma

Jessica stared at her Grandmau-ma and asked, "Grandmau-ma, are you drained and ready for bed?"

Still curled at her Grandmau-ma's feet, fixed to the story, Jessica took a loving, long look at the old woman. "Grandmau-ma, we can stop for tonight. You look worn out. How 'bout I help you to bed now?"

Grandmau-ma bent down and kissed her sweet granddaughter on the forehead. "No, Sweet Pea, I'm fine. Better than fine, in fact. This Christmas season is the best that I've had in a long time. I wouldn't dare want to sleep. I've waited a long time to reveal this story—most of my life." Grandmau-ma lifted with an eye-opening moment. She continued. "I now know, why—I never found the right person to tell. It wasn't meant for me to tell anyone. You, my dear, are special and I knew you were as soon as your mother put you in my arms but to be 'the Chosen One' just makes my heart rejoice in a way; it hasn't in years. No, my dear... I don't want to waste time on sleep... 'the Chosen One' has arrived!"

Grandmau-ma kissed her sweet granddaughter on the forehead and responded, "No, sweet pea, I'm okay. I have been waiting to tell this story most of my life, but the truth is that a person can only see this case if they have the magic of Christ, Christmas and Santa Claus in their heart."

Jessica's eyes widened, confused, "The Chosen One?"

Grandmau-ma smiled radiantly, "Sweet child, it is written that only those who truly hold Christ, the Christmas spirit and the magic of Santa Claus in their hearts can even see this old case. Just like Mr. and Mrs. Clause and their elves. When you brought the case down from the attic, what I always believed to be true was affirmed. You, my darling girl, are 'the Chosen One.'"

Jess anxiously questioned, "Chosen for what?"

Grandmau-ma answered, "Jess, I am not sure, exactly, that part wasn't revealed to me. Now, how about you get your old Grandmau-ma more hot cocoa and I'll tell you the rest of the story."

Jess hurried off to the kitchen again and soon returned with two more steaming cups for them both. Jess could hardly wait to see what was in the case. She nestled back in her spot under her grandmau-ma waiting to hear the rest of the story. Grandmau-ma took a satisfying sip and continued with her fascinating tale.

9

The Naughty & The Nice

Christmas magic thrived throughout the earth for centuries, and beloved traditions passed down from generation to generation. Parents almost always teach their children to be good; but the eventual knowledge of Santa's naughty and nice list and his penchant for checking it twice provided extra incentive for boys and girls to be on their best behavior—at least, most of the time.

Word got around from the beginning that Santa loved milk and cookies. So, on Christmas Eve every year, plates of cookies and glasses of milk were left on tables or hearths for the jolly visitor before bedtime. At some point, nearly every child in every land tried to stay awake to catch a glimpse of Santa and his reindeer. But, Christmas magic always lulled them into a profound, sweet slumber.

As Nicolas had been instructed by the spirit, good children received presents; naughty children found a lump of coal in their stockings. Over time, Santa's 'naughty' list began to grow longer than his 'nice' list; this greatly saddened Santa Claus. He hated delivering coal, wanting every boy and girl to be good and kind.

Three children in particular just seemed naughty by nature, receiving coal year after year—until almost grown.

The first was a mean little boy, Chris Norm. Chris' cruelty surfaced at age seven when he first found twisted pleasure in hurting small animals. Chris' taste for torture blackened his heart. Chris would hurt innocent defenseless animals for his fun. One year, Chris focused his evil intention on the sweet, little dog of a neighbor named Rebecca. Everyone in the neighboring town knew Rebecca's funny, happy, little Toby. One day, Toby wandered off to a nearby lake. Seeing his opportunity, Chris spotted Toby and lured the little dog close to him with small bits of meat, gaining Toby's trust. As soon as Toby was within reach, Chris kicked the helpless, innocent animal repeatedly with all his might. The more Toby whimpered, the louder Chris laughed. After beating the Toby, he couldn't walk Chris walked away snickering, leaving Toby to die.

Rebecca had been frantically scouring the neighborhood for Toby, screaming his name. Reaching the lake a few blocks away, Rebecca heard weak whimpering. Her heart broke when she spotted Toby's broken and bleeding little body by the water and cried out for help. Other children arrived and quickly constructed a makeshift stretcher for Toby with cardboard, sticks, and blankets, afraid to move him more than necessary.

Luckily, the town veterinarian was still in his working—even though it was Christmas Eve—when Rebecca and her friends arrived with little Toby, who was barely holding on to life.

Dr. Wells assured Rebecca he would do what he could to save Toby, but couldn't make any promises. Too many bones were broken, and there was excessive internal bleeding.

Utterly heartbroken for the pain her little Toby was suffering, Rebecca was thankful it was almost Christmas so after pressing her small hands together and giving glory to God through Christ—as she was taught, she addressed Santa looking to the sky. "Please, Santa. My best friend is hurt and needs your help. I have only one wish this year—help Toby. I don't want toys—just Toby. Please, Santa."

Dr. Wells did what he could to clean and bandage Toby, falling asleep beside the little dog's quilted crate that night. The next morning, Toby was up, jumping around, yipping and happily wagging his tail inside the box. Rebecca rushed in just as Dr. Wells awoke and burst into tears of joy. It was a Christmas miracle! Santa had granted her wish.

That year, Chris' entire stocking was filled with several lumps of coal—as well as every Christmas after that. Sadly, Chris never changed, growing into a cruel, miserable adult.

Then there was Nefari Bass—another Child who stood out on Santa's naughty list. Nefari came from a selfish, wealthy, and globe-trotting family, but her heart was evil as her name shortens for nefarious.

Nefari's greedy parents owned every piece of property in the town where they lived and bled their tenants dry with excessively high rent and ridiculous taxes. Neglectful and selfish absentee landlords, the Bass' poorly paid "managers" to oversee the properties as they frequently traveled around the world—without Nefari—leaving the evil little miss with an endless line of nannies and governesses. After a brief time, the childcare giver inevitably quit. Nefari strategically tortured everyone, giving them no choice. No Nanny— meant time with Father for Nefari and she loved it. Nefari was like him—evil. He would take her into town with him and watch her as she teased the poor kids with food and toys; this was her joy as her father collected unjust money from the townspeople.

And, every Christmas, Nefari's elaborate, personalized stocking was filled with coal. For that, Nefari hated Santa. Every year she was determined to stay awake and catch him.

One Christmas Eve, Nefari's mean spirit was powerful enough to shake off the sleep that Christmas magic cast over children because the naughty list was longer than the nice list and the magic was lower than usual.

And, there they were, two elves, stuffing Nefari's stocking with coal.

"Ah Ha! Elves are doing Santa's dirty work." She said to her self. As the Elves tended to their duties of coal stuffing, they began discussing her. "If kids like this Nefari continue to increase in number, outweighing the good, we're toast. When the belief stops, the Christmas Spirit and the magic of Santa will die. So will we."

Wicked Nefari couldn't believe her good fortune. Hiding in the shadows, she learned the secret to Santa's magic was the belief. Nefari rubbed her hands together with evil glee, instantly devising a plot to bring down Santa and all this Christmas hooey. Realizing that all she had to do was destroy people's belief in Santa—and, she would unmistakably stop Christmas, thinking, 'If I can't have Christmas, no one will.'

Each year onward, Nefari patiently listened for more secrets to be revealed by the sloppy elves. Santa was troubled by Nefari—unlike no-other and continued allowing lumps of coal in her stockings.

Another child who found himself consistently at the top of Santa's naughty list was Andrew McGillicuddy. Sadly, Andrew lost his father at age seven; so, he was surrounded by women—his mother and four sisters. While being the only "man" in a house of women can be challenging and maybe annoying—sometimes—it is never an excuse for being mean. Andrew was angry with his father for dying and grew to resent being stuck in a houseful of women. Rather than being protective of his mother and sisters, his anger and resentment deepened into a hateful rage; and, he turned that rage on them.

Andrew disrespected his mother and destroyed whatever his sisters loved—toys, clothes, sentimental trinkets. Andrew's mother would be in a constant argument with him about the girls' things. Some days his quarrels with, and disrespect for his mother became physical. Andrew hit her often. Once, he struck his mother so hard; one of his sisters sent for the local doctor. The decision was made. Andrew was impossible to handle and was sent far away from his family to a home for boys who were difficult.

Receiving coal in his stocking was no big deal to Andrew. He couldn't care less—until he'd been in the boys' home for a couple of years. The boys there bullied, taunted and tortured him just as cruelly as he had treated his mother and sisters.

One day, in the few moments at the group home when Andrew was able to find alone time, he broke down, cried and begged God to forgive him for his mean-spirited ways. He wanted his mother and sisters back in his life. Close to Christmas that year, he even apologized to Santa, promising to be good if Santa would just reunite him with his family and he promised to take care of his family. That was his only wish. For the first time in Andrew's short life—he was sincere.

God heard Andrew's prayers, and Santa felt the depth of his wish but still—a test of faith ensued. Andrew received a lump of coal anyway for Christmas. Andrew saw the coal and fell to his knees, placed both hands together, prayed and said, "Dear God, is it too late for me to fix all the bad that I did? I now know, how much my mother and sisters need me. I am sorry that I have been on the naughty list for so long. I only wish to fix what I broke. I want Christmas again with my family." God has shown favor and allowed Santa to grant Andrew's wish. Santa magically scratched Andrew's name from the naughty list and inscribed it on the list for nice children. That Christmas morning, Andrew was reunited with his family and was a changed boy. The family cried with joy and thanksgiving.

Many Christmases came and went. Andrew was the only person to have changed from the naughty-to-nice list. He and his sisters grew up to be kind and loving young adults, always keeping Christ and Christmas in their hearts. They were the opposite of the now also grown-up "lump of coal" kids. These were children who too received lumps of coal and resented Christ, Christmas, and Santa Claus. Their feet were in a hurry to badness—and so, followed Nefari—their ringleader.

Nefari's family's property empire grew. Nefari succeeded her mother and six months later her father. The realm was left to her although she had a brother. Nefari's empire included giant toy stores in theirs and neighboring towns. Nefari had never forgotten the conversation between Santa's elves that she had spied upon as a child—and, never abandoned her mission to destroy children's belief in Christmas and Santa. Nefari's family toy stores were the way to do it. In marketing for the toy stores, Nefari worked unceasingly to convince little ones that there was no such thing as Santa Claus; that any toys they received were purchased by their parents from her toy stores. She convinced many parents, her toys were of real quality and unless the toys came from her stores—parents were neglecting the genuine needs of their child's play time.

Nefari's arch-enemy in her war against all things Christmas was the former lump of coal kid-turned-do-gooder, Andrew McGillicuddy. With the help of his sisters, they worked just as tirelessly to spread the love of Christ and the spirit of Christmas-giving year-round to young and old. However, Nefari, materialism, selfishness, and greed seemed to be winning the battle. As they increasingly tried to spread the Christmas Spirit, the more parents bought toys for their children at Nefari stores.

Andrew knew that he and the side of right needed help. He and his closest sister, Lizzy, joined forces and wished together with all their might that Christ and Santa would send them a holy weapon or divine intervention to help them save the spirit of Christmas and Christmas magic.

Their prayers and wishes were answered. The very next Christmas morning, Andrew and his sister discovered a beautifully crafted wooden trunk settled under their window. Even though the chest was oversized, it was amazingly lightweight. Andrew lifted, and carefully carried it to his tabletop.

Inside the trunk were two large velvet cases, with a handwritten notation on top. Andrew handed one of the velvet cases to Lizzy and read the note aloud. It was from Santa himself:

> Dearest Andrew, you have proven to be one of my most joyful surprises. The way you turned your life around is proof of Christ's abiding love for us. You and your sister, Elizabeth expressed pure love with your unselfish Christmas wish and will always be my special helpers. It is Christ Jesus who gives me the powers I have to make children happy; and, it is He who gives me the ability to grant your wish. The enclosed gifts for you and Elizabeth are what you'll need to help keep the spirit and magic of Christmas alive in the hearts of children—young and old—everywhere.

Each locked velvet case contains a magical, crystal snow globe; one for you and one for your sister. Not everyone can see the globes or its box; that grace is only bestowed on those chosen few who possess the purest of hearts, love for Christ and Christmas, belief in the spirit and magic of Christmas and me—Santa Claus. No one can see or unlock the case to your globes unless they process the love of Christ, the Christmas Spirit of giving, Santa Claus and has been shown favor.

The cases and enclosed globes are to be kept safely guarded by the two of you in separate locations. Know that when the globes unite, each feeds on the other's power from the Almighty and possess the magic of Christmas which alters time and space—granting the ability to visit all lands and many worlds in one night. Yes, this is how Santa Delivers toys all over in one night—Ho-Ho-Ho.

So, in time—I bid each of you; go your separate ways, as far as different worlds and spread Christmas Spirit. Take heart in knowing that no matter where you are in the world, all, either of you has to do is touch your particular globe on Christmas, and you will be together. Neither of you would sleep in death until your case is revealed to a person chosen by Christ. After the cased globes are appointed; the appointee will be led to do what they are assigned to do. When the next Chosen One is selected; you will both awaken to a new life in death and be with me. Also, the chest holds my first toy delivery bag that Mrs. Claus made for me. Elizabeth, keep it and the trunk with you—it would assure and comfort the next chosen one. Be Blessed and Merry Christmas, Santa.

Grandmau-ma's gentle, gnarled fingers lovingly smoothed Jess' fiery red curls as she finished her story, understanding the confusion on her granddaughter's face, "Ah, yes. Such a special time and glorious gift from the Lord. Now, that favor is passed on to you. Every year, I've climbed up the ladder into the attic to touch the globe and spend Christmas with my brother, Andrew. To us, it felt like an entire day; but, in the natural world, it was a mere few seconds."

Jess tilted her head, trying to put the pieces together.

Grandmau-ma continued. "That's when your mother decided I shouldn't be alone all the time in this big old house and dropped you off to visit for a spell. It was a dreadful winter. No one could possibly know what would happen next. I miss her, too, darling; but, I've had the honor of raising you from that day till now. I enjoyed every moment of being with you. And, now, because of you, I'll be able to see my brother again and not just for Christmas."

10

True Identity

Suddenly, it all made sense to Jess; she ran to take a good look at the bag she put the Christmas decorations in and examined the error Mrs. Clause made when making it and ran back to her Grandmau-ma.

"Grandmau-ma, that's Santa's first toy Sack! And, your name is Beth—which, like Lizzy, is short for Elizabeth! Are you saying what I think you're saying?"

Jess jumped up, her head spinning. The information was coming together too quickly, "Omigod, Grandmau-ma! You're the Lizzy in the story! And, your brother Andrew— My Uncle Andrew— Are the same! Wow! Are you Santa's eternal helpers? Am I—am I the one you've been waiting for because I can see the case? What does that even mean? But, why does it sound like you're saying goodbye?"

Grandmau-ma's smile radiated across her face, "My smart, wonderful, strong and brave Sweet-pea. Yes, Darling, you are the one to bring back the Christmas magic. But, there is nothing to fear. You're old enough now; and, the spirit will lead you throughout this journey, just as it led Andrew and me so long ago. I saw my brother every Christmas, until eight years ago when his case was revealed to a "Chosen One" in his path."

Jess' eyes filled with tears.

Grandmau-ma pulled Jess to her and cradled her like she was still a little girl. "There, there... No need for tears—this is a magnificent mission. And, it's time. Your Grandmau-ma is so much older than anyone human could fathom. I've lived and served through nearly an entire millennium. And, I'm ready. You just need to know that I love you very much. Inside the box, you'll find everything you need to know for the journey you will take."

"Are you leaving me?" Jess sniffed.

Grandmau-ma lovingly stroked Jess' wet cheek, "I will always be with you, my love. Just not physically—all is as it should be. It is your destiny to open the case. And, I promise, my Jess, I will never leave your side."

Jess fights with the idea of her grandmau-ma leaving—she wipes her tears again. "You'll disappear just the way Uncle Andrew did when I was little? No one explained to me where he went; he just came up missing." Jess stated somberly.

Grandmau-ma nodded, "Yes, Jess. I would physically disappear—remember it's only physically."

Grandmau-ma kissed and hugged Jess one last time, pressing a tiny key into the girl's hand, "It is the appointed time, Sweet-pea. Remember, I love you and am with you forever. Open the case."

A single tear fell from Jess left eye as she gazed into her grandmau-ma intense green eyes for the last time. Jess unconsciously wiped her tears as her eyes are now drawn to the old crafted case.

Grandmau-ma whispers again, "Jess, open the case."

11

A Special Meeting

ess placed both hands softly on the case and slowly unlocked its lock. She looked at her Grandmau-ma once more. Grandmau-ma gave her assurance with a head nod. Jess opened the case, and bright lights busted from it while drawing Jess into a wintery white setting. Jess blocked her eyes for it was bright and everything around her was white. As her eyes adjusted, Jess noticed a man resembling Santa Claus with his chubby, jolly belly, red rosy cheeks, red suit and black boots.

Jess glanced back at Grandmau-ma with tear-filled eyes. After a last, lingering, loving gaze between the two, Jess gingerly placed the key into the case's lock.

She was momentarily blinded by a light brighter than the sun and somehow felt physically sucked into it. Jess blinked. Suddenly, everything around her was unfamiliar, white and wintry, yet she wasn't the least bit cold. In the distance were a roundish man with a white beard, red suit, black boots and the rosiest cheeks she'd ever seen.

The round man laughed, "HO, HO, HO! Welcome! Hello Jess, come to me."

Next to him was another figure, a man who possessed an extraordinary glow—a man who reminded her of all the stories she'd ever been told about Christ. He spoke in a loving voice, "Hello, Jess. Come to me."

The man with the glow had to be Christ, she told herself. Jess remembered in her Grandmau-ma story—Christ was always first. Although Santa appeared to Jess first, she walked toward the resemblance of Christ first. Jess obeyed, walking to the glowing man-like apparition of Christ. She wondered if she had died and gone to heaven. As she got closer, the image spoke again; surrounding her with the most wonderful feeling of warmth and unconditional love, "Be blessed, my child." Then he disappeared.

Jess whipped her head back in the direction of the Santa Claus image. He smiled, nodded his head, 'Yes,' and with a twinkling of his eyes, he projected her value before backing into the winter white disappearing from Jess sight.

Suddenly, Jess pulled her face from the case and Jess eyes adjusted once more, and the light was drawing back into the case; revealing a large hand designed magical snow globe. Her attention next was drawn to her Grandmau-ma who was no longer in her chair. Jess was now all alone. Jess allowed reasonableness to crowd everything she had just experienced. Tears fell from her eyes, for she needed her Grandmau-ma's comfort.

In an instant, Jess was pulled back into Grandmau-ma's sitting room, but for a brief moment, the brightness surrounded her face. The bright light moved from her face and began swirling around a giant, intricately designed snow globe like nothing Jess had ever seen. Her eyes automatically tuned in on Grandmau-ma's chair. But, she wasn't there.

Jess was all alone and frightened. Fresh tears fell, "This can't be happening," she cried. Trying to hold on to reason, Jess ran to Grandmau-ma's bedroom. There was no trace of the old woman—just the belongings of her sweet Grandmau-ma. She ran back to the sitting room and collapsed on the floor, sobbing. The grandfather clock struck 10, and it was two hours until Christmas. Although, time continued to pass while she was in transition her life seemed to be changed in an instant. She longed for her mother who had died and now a grandmother who had disappeared.

"What am I supposed to do? I don't want to be alone for Christmas, Grandmau-ma! Come back, please!" She cried.

Just then, the snow globe glowed brilliantly. Jess remembered Grandmau-ma's story about touching the snow globe to be with her brother for Christmas. "Maybe if I touched it now, I would be re-united with my Grandmau-ma." She thought as her eyes lit up with hope.

— ◠ —

Jess closed her eyes and wrapped her hands around the snow globe, pray-ing fervently, "Please, God. I don't want to be alone for Christmas."

Suddenly, the globe was gone, and Jess' hand was gently taken by a masculine one, "I know what you mean—me neither..."

Jess is startled. She snatches back her hand as her eyes pop open, "What? Who are you? Where am I? Where's my Grandmau-ma?" Jess glanced around. It was as though she'd been dropped into the middle of the beautiful Christmas snow globe. She stood in the middle of a crowd but didn't recognize anyone. She did, however, acknowledge her favorite Christmas hems that they were singing with voices so beautiful—she'd almost danced. Her eyes widened as they followed the largest, Christmas Tree she'd ever seen—decorated to perfection.

Then she got a closer look at the tall, movie-star handsome young man with the Mediterranean-blue eyes who had taken her hand. He was smiling, tickled, "Hi Jess, I'm Jose. Welcome to Christonia a magical Christmas town in a magical world. I know it sounds weird, but I've been waiting to meet you for eight earth years."

Jess' jaw dropped. Jose retook her hand, "Yeah, I know. Like I said, weird. But, tell you what. Why don't we stroll on over to Merry-Land? The café there has some of the best hot cocoa ever—and, I'll explain ev-erything. Okay?"

"Uh, yeah, sure..." Jess stammered, still in a state of disbelief. This place looked like a Christmas card she'd seen in her grandmau-ma's attic. The atmosphere bubbled with Christmas Spirit and joy. Gloriously bright Christmas lights and ornaments, decorated Christmas trees, giant candy cane street lamps and cheerful red bows were everywhere. The people either walked the streets laughing with bags stuffed with gaily wrapped gifts or were ice skating in the middle of the town like professionals. It was pretty dark out; so, Jess reasoned that all of the children must have been tucked away in their beds.

Taking it all in, walking alongside Jose, holding his hand, Jess was in a daze. 'Magical' was the only word that came to mind. When they reached the picturesque café, Jose gentlemanly opened the door, gesturing for Jess to start first. Jess was gazing as she entered the shop. Inside, Jose led her to a cozy corner table, where they could talk.

A kind woman in a Santa suit with a tablet of paper and pen in her hand, came over to them and asked, "May I get you and your friend a cup of Santa's cocoa or would you like a cup of coffee? We also have Santa's cookies and hot bun rolls."

A cheerful server dressed in a Santa suit appeared at their table, tablet and peppermint-striped pen in hand, "Hello there! How would you two like a steaming cup of Santa's special cocoa or coffee? And, we have hot cross buns, fresh from the oven!" Her eyes twinkled most merrily as she spoke.

"Seriously?" Jess blurted out loud, skeptically and unintentionally, "Wait! There's a happy waitress—is in a hot Santa suit, that does nothing for her figure—smiling asking do we want Santa's cocoa. How much is she being paid? It must be a lot for her to wear the get-up. Now, I know this place is different."

The waitress tilted her head, puzzled. Jose cleared his throat and smiled apologetically, "Sorry. She, uh, is not from around here. New kid in town. Tell you what. The cocoa and buns sound great. And, how about a batch of Santa's chocolate chip cookies for later?"

The server looked puzzled. Jose cleared his throat and intervened, "I'm very sorry. She's not from here. We will have two sweet bun rolls and two cups of Santa's cocoa and send a batch of Santa's cookies for later."

"You can't say things like that." Jose explained with sheer concern and continued to say, "It's mean, and there is no mean here. Can't you tell? Everyone is happy. It's Christmas."

Jose turned his attention back to Jess, "Uh, yeah. About that—I should've warned you to check any Scrooge-like vibes or skepticism at the door. There's no skepticism or mean here. This is where Christmas lives always. Joy, peace, and goodwill toward every life here—all day, every day. Especially, now..."

Before Jess could open her mouth to respond, the cheery server was back with their order. Part of Jess was delighted; but, the little girl in her who was scared and missed her grandmother, broke down in a deluge of new tears, "I just want my Grandmau-ma back. Can this magical place do that?"

The server looked away briefly and quickly dismissed herself. Finally, the two were in the clear to talk. Jose continued and expressed his concern, "You must be something special to have the privilege that's been bestowed on you. I understand it's hard right now, but look around. It's Christmas, and you're not alone."

Jose glanced around to make sure no one else saw Jess sadness, and he tried to hurry away, Jess tears and said, "There's no crying on the best day of the year."

Jose looked again at Jess and saw her pain. His beautiful eyes were brimming with compassion, Jose took both her hands in his, "Please don't cry, Jess. I can tell by the expression on your face you're stressed and terrified. You don't know how all this works. But, I also happen to know how special you are—stronger than most humans in every way—even if you don't yet know it yourself. You possess unshakeable faith in Christ and Christmas and Santa Claus and have the purest heart. That's why you're the Chosen One. The Creator doesn't make mistakes."

Jess sniffed, took back her hands to dry her tears and blow her nose, "Why does everyone keep saying that? I'm just a regular kid! Chosen for what...? And, again, what is this place? Nothing about it seems real. Go ahead, explain."

Jose was worried. The chosen one spoke with little faith. How to convince her... Jose wondered and hoped he was up to the task bestowed on him.

Jose took a deep, satisfying gulp of his cocoa. "This is Christonia. And, it is magical. However, it's also just as real as you, me and the delicious hot cocoa that you haven't even tried yet."

Jess smiled in spite of herself and lifted her colorfully decorated, over-sized mug to take a sip. "Whoa, that's amazing! I've never tasted hot cocoa, or anything—so delicious."

"I know, right? That's because it's Santa's and Mrs. Claus' own special recipe."

Jess' incredulousness was melting; but, not entirely just yet, "Santa? Mrs. Claus? Like—they live here? Is this the North-Pole?"

"Not exactly... But, the Pole is not far," Jose laughed, "And, it's the most magical place in all the worlds."

"Okay, buddy. Pump your brakes. Did you just say, 'worlds,' as in—more than one?"

"I did. You see, there is so much more to life than meets the mortal eye in your world. Yes, there are many worlds, many lands, and many realities. I was chosen by Santa himself to help you strengthen your faith—making it stern. I must convince you of the special privilege that has been given you, to make sure you understand it all, direct your journey, and help you ultimately to accept the journey as the Chosen One—only then, would she be the Apprentice everyone, everywhere has been waiting. I am also here to help you locate the second globe, which was left in the safe-keeping of your Uncle Andrew's apprentice many years ago." Jess shook her head, disbelieving yet believing.

"Yes, it's true," Jose continued. "Even though I appear not much older than you are, I assure you, I am quite capable. Time and space move differently here. In actuality, I am several hundred human years of age."

Jess' mouth dropped wide open.

"I know. It's a lot to process. Centuries ago, in the physical world, I worked for your Uncle Andrew. Nearly all my time in that realm, really, since I was seven. My father died when I was a baby; and, there were my mother, Estonia and three sisters to care for—we had next to nothing. What you might call dirt poor. Even as a young boy, I knew my responsibilities as the 'man of the house.' Your uncle hired me for menial chores when I was small, then gave me greater responsibilities on his farm and property as I grew up. My sisters were older than me, married and left home, never looking back. Sometimes they would appear in my dreams as evil witches. I loved all things Christ, so they had no love for me at all."

Jose slowed in an emotional state, only for a moment and snapped back, "Anyhow, my beautiful God-fearing mother, Estonia died. My sisters didn't even return home for her service. I was heartbroken. That's when your uncle first took me in—I was so alone. He thought I was taking care of him, but the truth—he was taking care of me. It always seemed odd to me that although he was an older man... he never aged. One day, I learned why. The Creator had shown him favor, and Santa helped alone side God. Andrew had many interests; but, his life was devoted to demonstrating his love of Christ, Christmas, and Santa Claus."

Jose smiled as he continued. "While living with and working for your Uncle Andrew, I met your cousin, Judas. He'd also come to the farm to help out Andrew. For a while, the three of us were like family. One year, while we decorated the farmhouse for Christmas, Andrew asked Judas to fetch some additional Christmas ornaments from the storage shed. He carried a box of ornaments and a red velvet box back into the living room. Even though I wasn't a blood relative, your uncle always said he saw something special in me and allowed me to see the box as well physically... And, its contents."

"The globe," Jess nodded, hanging onto Jose's every word.

"Exactly... It was a miraculous honor. Both of us listened to Andrew's story and our ensuing instructions to save Christmas."

Jose took another deep sip of cocoa. "Right after Judas accepted his journey and became the first apprentice—an Angel sounded a warning for your uncle, Andrew."

Jess interrupted, "A warming! About what?"

"The Angel warned about, the safety of the globe. He was told that he had to leave the physical world. Leaving was painful for your uncle because staying near his only sister gave him comfort. He was instructed to take the globe, Judas and I with him."

Jose sat up straighter while continuing. "After we came here and made Christonia our new home; Judas was entrusted with the globe for safekeeping and spiritual missions. Here is where I learned much about my mother who died in the physical world. It turned out that in this world my mother had surviving members and I come from a blessed bloodline also. My mother, Estonia assignments linked into many worlds... the physical world, magical worlds, and mystical worlds. My moms had a previous life and a purpose. Truth is that until her purpose is met, she simply transition to another world. I'll tell you more about that later. Anyhow, sometime afterward, Judas betrayed the Christ and your uncle. The details were never shared with me; but, I'm pretty sure it involved the 'lump of coal' gang, and their obsession with destroying the meaning of Christ, Christmas, and Santa Claus."

"Yeah, Grandmau-ma told me a bit about them. That ringleader, Nefari, sounded 'pure evil.'"

"And, then some," Jose agreed. "Actually, we're gonna talk about Nefari more a little later. But, right now, I want you to finish your cocoa and a bun. You're going to need their warmth and sustenance."

After finishing their snack, Jess was curious about no currency passing hands or tab paid; just an exchange of smiles, 'Thank you' and "Merry Christmas!"

Outside, Jose took Jess' hand and walked her to the center of the village. "You trust me?"

Jess nodded, "Yes."

"Then close your eyes. Engage all of your other senses. Listen, though, with your heart; not just your ears."

After a few moments, Jess smiled broadly, and a single, happy tear slid down her cheek. Her entire, being was filled with light, and overwhelming joy, the kind of pleasure that took away any and all hurt and the sound of magic was like flying with magical glittering powder. Jess heard caroling that sounded like angels singing, laughter, and bells ringing. Jose smiled too, recognizing that Jess was feeling the Magic of Christmas. There was another feeling, also, as Jess opened her eyes. She was empowered by the abiding love of Christ and Santa.

"Cool, huh?" Jose grinned. "C`mon... I've got a lot to show you before we get to the specifics of your mission. Like I said, time and space don't move here at the same rate as in the physical world. But, by earthly measure, we're on the clock. There are only two hours left before midnight and Christmas. You up for a tour?"

The next stop was magnificent natural caves bordering the town. The interior of each was magically covered in Christmas twinkle lights. All the sounds and smells of the season echoed in and around the cavernous wonders.

"All of the people who live here are beings with the purest hearts of Christmas Spirit. There are no worries, only joy, and peace. We all have exactly what we need, work that we love and we love each other. That's why there was no money exchanged at the café. Yeah, I caught that look on your face," Jose laughed. "This is a magical land, a sort of neighbor of the North Pole. It is also a holy land, the foundation for all that is good in other worlds and realms. For now, it's the only world that hasn't been corrupted or touched by evil."

Jess was impressed. "Wow, bad hasn't sniffed this place out yet? What, is there some kind of special protective barrier surrounding it? One thing, I know is that everything good has an enemy lurking."

Jose facial expression turned from joyful to fearful. He knew why Jess was the chosen one. He then said, "No, not yet and that's where you come in, Jess, you are a fighter aren't you?"

"Yes, why did you ask?" Jess, lifting one brow.

Jose placed both his hands on each of Jess' shoulders and said, "You're here because you are the Chosen One. You touched the snow globe. Here, maybe we should sit," Jose guided Jess to a candy-red, lacquered bench.

"Uh-oh, this can't be good," Jess swallowed, taking a seat.

"Well, hopefully, it ultimately will be, Jess. Let's get back to Nefari. Listen, as much as I would like to; I can't sugar-coat it for you. Nefari waits for you."

Jess jumped. "What! What are you talking about? Why me!"

"Nefari discovered more than a millennium ago in human years that Christmas magic is, indeed, real. And, good... And, that it ultimately comes from Christ. Perhaps it wasn't her fault because her father was evil and she was birth into it, but Nefari was an evil little girl and now an evil villain. Instead of inspiring her to be good, the coal only made Nefari evil manifest more. She then pursued an army of children and parents who felt as she did. The elves were worried that the growing number of mean-spirited children in the world would destroy belief in Christmas, Santa, erase the truth about Christ. That's all Nefari ever wanted."

"Is that why she started the 'lump of coal' kids?" Jess asked, wondering where Jose was going with this.

"Yes, sadly, she grew into an evil, twin of her father. She's gained power beyond the worlds and is determined to crush everything and everyone associated with Christmas, Christ, and Santa Claus. They say that water always seeks its own level; so, Nefari sought out and practiced dark magic. She literally and figuratively sold her soul to the beast, the Dark One, Satan. Some call him the Devil. Others know him as Lucifer, who was cast out of Heaven by God at the beginning of creation. Nefari's family was already rich. But, with her evil pact with the Dark One, she gained earthly wealth beyond measure, immortality and the Key-of-Death."

"Again, what does Nefari have to do with me?"

"Jess, as the Chosen One, you have the power to rid all worlds of her evil."

Jess' eyes widened with panic. She practically jumped off the bench. "Are you kidding me? I'm out of here! Wait—which way is out?"

Jose gently grabbed Jess' arm. "Jess, wait... please, you are the chosen one, I am sure. It was said throughout generations that an Apprentice (you) would be the only person to rid the world of Nefari's evilness. You just need to remember how strong you, your faith and your love of

Christ and Christmas and Santa Claus. Your Grandmau-ma and uncle Andrew believed in you also. And, if it's any comfort, it was never meant for you to do this alone. You will be guided and supported every step of the way. Your Uncle Andrew entrusted me with a special book. It's called The Book-of-Knowledge. I was instructed never to attempt to open it but to hide it until the Chosen One from the other snow globe appeared. That's you, Jess... You're finally here. There's more I must tell you, this holy place will have evil in it for the first time. Nefari follows the magic when it's used. She knows you're here and because of her severe hatred of Christ, Christmas, and Santa Claus. She followed her father and sold her soul to the beast—the one called Satan and Devil. She learned and practiced that evil dark magic. She used the dark magic to punish all that loved Christ, Christmas, and Santa Claus. She used it to gain riches to gloat over everyone. The worst thing is she used it to gain the Key-of-Death and used that key for mortality. Your uncle, Andrew, gave me understanding about the Book-of-Knowledge that you must see. It was passed to me, and I promised your uncle to take care of it and you. Come with me?"

Jess acquiesced, but rolled her eyes, sighing, "Do I have a choice? Lead the way."

"Wonderful, it is hidden from curious eyes by a special magic. All you have to do is read its contents before Christmas Day is over. It explains everything you will need to know. Let's go get it."

12

Overtaken By Fear

Jess followed closely behind Jose, "Why before Christmas Day is over?" Jose stopped running. They'd reached their destination. "Tell me you didn't hide something as important-sounding as the Book-of-Knowledge in a barn? Anyone could find this place."

Jose grinned, "This is a land of magic, based on faith and belief, remember? And, to answer your first question, according to your uncle, Andrew, once the one that holds the first snow globe enters this town, the evil Nefari, will enact her vengeance on Christ, Christmas, and Santa Claus, immediately after Christmas. She has already locked in on you're being here. It's time; the book is here. Open the barn door, Jess. Please?"

Jess pulled on the rusted handle. The door creaked so badly; she thought it might fall apart in her hands. Inside, the barn's dirt floor was covered with hay and old tools but no animal. "Okay, we're in—Now what? I bale all the hay to find the book?"

Jose ignored Jess' cracks, held her by the shoulders and said, "I see; you really don't understand the power of the globe in your possession." He asked her to once more close her eyes. "Remember, Jess, everything here exists because of faith, belief, love and Christmas magic. Look inward and know that what I speak is the truth. Believe! Then, open your eyes with unmovable, unyielding faith."

Jess saw the seriously concerned expression on Jose's face, sighed with a deep breath, then, closed her eyes and believed within her soul. The moment she opened her eyes, the hay began spinning into a funnel. The funnel morphed into a swirl of snow, then a blizzard, accompanied by howling winds. Jess' eyes widened; but, she was not afraid. She screamed above the uproar, "Now what?"

Jose grabbed her hand, "We walk into the blizzard. Told ya the warmth of the cocoa would come in handy."

Laughing, Jess realized the cocoa was magical also. They both walked in hand-in-hand. As soon as they walked in—the blizzard went away.

Inside was night, with a Christmas tree adorned with one bright star. They were drawn to it, and they saw it as very beautiful. Underneath the tree was a beautifully wrapped gift box. Jose and Jess dropped to their knees on the softest grass to get a better look. Jess reached for the package and glanced at Jose. He nodded, for her to go ahead and open it. Jess quickly unwrapped the gift. Inside was a thick book covered in lush dark green velvet with gold trim. Jess softly stroking the fabric of the book activated it, and in the blink of an eye, the pair were back in the barn again—warm.

Jess spoke first, "Mission accomplished."

"I'm afraid this was the easy part, Jess. Now, the real mission will begin. But, you have been graced with everything you need to defeat Nefari. Like your snow globe. You know by now that it's not just a pretty toy. Its magic is powerful. You should have it with you at all times."

Jess shook her head, "Are you kidding? Do you know how big that thing is? How am I supposed to lug it around? And, how am I supposed to find the other one?"

Jose repeated, "Jess it's magical, and I don't know where the other globe is, and I don't know where or what happened to your cousin, but the Book-of-Knowledge will lead you to your cousin and the other globe. Let me show you something."

Jose pulled out a chain from under his shirt. Attached to it was a small, red and white, enchanting charm. "This used to be gigantic, too. This charm was given to me by my mother before her transition to another life. She taught me how to use it. It instills knowledge in me ahead of time. That's how I knew all the details of your arrival. It too was big, but now it's a charm that I keep with me and safe."

Jose winked, removed the charm from the chain and waved his hand over it. The intricately woven white gold and ruby encrusted candy cane were restored to its original size, which was almost too heavy to hold. Jose waved his hand again to reduce the charmed talisman to its tiny form.

Jose looked Jess in the eyes, "Jess, you have everything you need to defeat the wicked Nefari. You will be the one to help children of every world and every land to believe again. And more so, you will be the one to save Christmas in every world and every land! You will make the Christmas Spirit complete again. One more thing Jess, the biggest deception is trusting things or situations you think you know. Trust no one to this information. Protect the Book-of-Knowledge and the snow globe. Quickly find your cousin and the other snow globe."

"Your book and your globe are far more powerful than this. I just wanted to demonstrate how you will keep the treasures with you at all times. Jess, you have everything you need to defeat the wicked Nefari. You will be the one to help children of every world and every land to believe again. And more so, you will be the one to save Christmas in every world and every land! You will make the Christmas Spirit complete again. One more thing; evil's greatest weapon against you is deception. Not everything or everyone is as they seem. Therefore, trust no one in your world with this knowledge. Quickly get understanding from the book, find your cousin and the other snow globe. Look, I know that sounds scary; but, it's very important, Jess. Okay?"

"Got it. Jose, thanks for all your help, but, I'm not sure how... "

"No buts... It's all inside of you. My purpose was to lead you to fully believing again and to lead you to the 'Book-of-Knowledge.' You are the

Chosen One, not me. However, if you need me, I'm only a wish away. I promise that I will be here to aid you in anything you need. Jess, it's time, you need to start reading. Remember, Nefari already knows you're here. Open the book and start reading."

Just as Jess placed the book in the lap to open it, a deafening howling filled the air, startling her and Jose.

"It's Nefari," Jose screamed, competing with the obnoxious sound. "Jess, open the book! Open the book!"

It was impossible to hear. "Jose, what's happening?" Jess tried to scream back.

Jose tried to exaggeratedly mouth the words; but, it was too late. Jess had run out of the barn, drawn to the threat. Outside its doors was a giant black cloud, complete with bolts of lightning and claps of thunder. Jose was right behind her, knowing that evil was making itself known.

Using both hands and mouthing the words again. "Open the book!"

Jess stood, mesmerized never taking her eyes off the wicked cloud. The howling—like an F-5 tornado gave way to dead silence. The wind no longer had a voice and a drop of a pin onto cotton presented no sound—for a time, leaving extreme fear in both Jess and Jose.

The foreboding black cloud began to separate and swirl, releasing a threatening, snake-like, coal color ribbon. It slithered around Jess' aura, examining, probing her. Before it could coil in the air back to its origin, Jess couldn't resist, she had to touch it. She reached her slender fingers toward it and grabbed the tail. Nefari shrieked in pain, as though someone had burned her; all the while, snatching back her probing ribbon. Jess stared in wonderment for she felt no pain from the touch of the strip but her it branding her with coal-blackened scorch mark.

She was correct in her thinking. Everything about Nefari sent a message that she was evil and not one you want to stick around. Nefari less intimidating image was six three in height with a slender built; with a long neck. She had dead piercing black eyes, curved hips, small breast, razor sharp and pointy nails that were black, cold black hair that wrapped upward adding several more inches to her height. She had on a black bodysuit with a black, long overall coat with a very long stiff collar.

Jose unfroze and ran towards Jess to get her out of Nefari's trance. Upon seeing Jose's efforts, Nefari turned only her long slender neck and gazed her evil black eyes towards him, putting him in a spell. The spell allowed Jose to know what she had done to the jolly Christmas town. Jose stood there still, frozen in time, with a horror expression and unable to move. He and his appearance were stuck under Nefari's spell as he watched in horror what the jolly Christmas town had endured.

The shape-shifting cloud morphed into a frightening image that resembled a woman. 'Nefari!' Jess alarms went off, and everything about Nefari sent a message through Jess' spine that this was the work of pure evil and she did not want to stick around. Nefari hovered just above the ground; she stood well over sixteen feet in height with a slender built; with a long neck, piercing dead black eyes, small curved hips, small breast, razor-sharp teeth and pointy nails that were blood-red in color. Her coal-black hair was tightly wrapped on top of her head like a horn—adding several more inches to her height. She had on a black form-fitting garment and long black overall coat with a long stiff collar.

Jose lunged toward Jess to snap her out of her shock. With one blistering gaze, Nefari turned only her long slender neck, gazed at him, casting a paralyzing spell, rendering Jose frozen in place. The spell's most vicious feature allowed Jose the terrible ability to observe the havoc Nefari had wreaked on Christonia, while unable to move a muscle.

In the vision, just as a tornado formed and dropped its vengeance on a city full of unexpected tourist, Nefari dropped her revenge on Christonia. Jose watched in horror as Nefari's evil scourge upon Christonia demolished buildings and homes. The large towns Christmas tree—for gathering had been cut and every bulb crushed. All the Santa suits, Christmas lights, toys, gifts and all other Christmas decorations have been thrown into an enormous fire burning—fuel with coal. Her poison coal dust-choked to death many of the village's residents, who retired; dead in the streets. Many parents cried with a heavy heart as their children lay in bed dead on Christmas Eve—Nefari had poisoned the cookies. The excellent coffee and cocoa shop was depleted and it workers scattered and some lay inside dead from Nefari's poison coal—dropped in the coffee, cocoa so that all who drunk died. Nefari's dark magic brought a dormant volcano to life, spewing its boiling lava through the streets and toward the Christmas caves. Adults ran screaming, clutching their crying or dead children. Tears slid down Jose's frozen-in-place eyes.

The undead monster threw back her head in satisfied, evil laughter; then turned her attention back to Jess. The girl clutched the Book-of-Knowledge to her chest.

"Ah, yes, the Chosen One," Nefari hissed. "You reek with horrible purity! If you think you can save your precious Christmas; think again. I may not be able to touch you in this magical world, you ridiculously weak child. But, mark my words, Little Girl, I will cut you down before all is said and done. You're only the Chosen One, for now—clearly you haven't accepted Apprenticeship yet, so disregard this futile mission— go on your way, girl." Nefari words and death gripping black eyes bore through as she slowly teased the girl. "Oh... Maybe; just maybe, you're prepared to die. Are you, Jess? You know—ready to die!"

Part of Jess was paralyzed with fear, her mouth dry, and her throat unable to swallow. But, the influential part of Jess that made her the Chosen One stood her ground against the monster, Nefari, staring her down.

"Are you?" Jess managed to fire back, resolute.

Nefari's wicked laugh was bone-chilling. She was angrier than ever, and she vented—her plans. "I will enact my vengeance upon you in a world where I possess all of my powers. I will not rest until I end Christmas for good—every world and every land will feel my rage! Any that try to stop my plans of killing what I hate, Christ, Christmas and Santa Clause, will die. That includes you and all you care about!"

Nefari looked over at Jose—still unable to move.

Tears immediately fell from Jess innocent eyes and the utmost fear possessed every inch of her body. Her legs stiffened, her tongue laid flat in her mouth dense and dry, her throat lost its power to swallow, and the answer to Nefari question was, "No! Please! No! I didn't ask for this!"

Nefari smiled—hearing her thoughts. With a wave of her hand, Nefari vanished, but her wicked laugh echoed a bit. Her departure released Jose from his paralytic spell. Jess collapsed to the ground, emotionally spent, clawing at the dirt and fighting for breath.

Jose saw Jess on the ground and ran over to her, and immediately dropped to her side, "You're okay. Don't listen to her. No matter what, Jess, you can't let Nefari win! Focus, Jess—if you open the book you can release its power and guidance; it has similar power as the globe. It will take you home, but I think you should read the book here because Nefari's power isn't as powerful here and she won't be back. With the newfound information from the book and the power from the globe; you will be able to handle Nefari in the physical world. With both Globes and the book, you will be able to save Christmas in all worlds and all lands, both physical, mystical and magical. Therefore, read it, and then proceed to the physical world to find your cousin with the other globe. Accept the mission—become our Apprentice and save us all! Get up, Jess! Let's go."

Internally, Jess was still fighting with herself. Part of her wished that she wasn't the Chosen One. But, the more significant part of her accepted her destiny. Jess loved Christ. She loved Santa Claus and, she loved all things Christmas. She would not let Nefari win. She also knew, no matter what she did; Nefari wouldn't rest until she was dead. She had to fight. While still on her knees, she looked at Jose's desperate face and said, "Hurry, get me somewhere safe."

Jose happily said, "Sure thing. I must tell you… While in a trance, Nefari showed me what she did to Christonia. It's horrible but be encouraged—everything but death can be fixed because magic exists here. Christ will handle the loss of our members in the town."

"I need safety," Jess said firmly.

Jose knew Jess was ready to accept her mission and battle. Jose and Jess ran to the Christmas caves, thinking they might be safe there. Upon arrival, molten lava and popping lava sparks made it impossible to get close. They both dodged popping lava sparks and lava balls that seem to understand that they were there to destroy it.

"Watch out!" Jose yelled at Jess—a lava ball had dashed out for her.

Amazement sprung from Jess' eyes, "Oh my God, Jose. That one almost got me. I don't know what I'm supposed to do to fix this."

"Hold on to your faith, girl. You cannot and will not defeat Nefari if you continue to be oblivious to the power of the book, which you hold, to the power of the two globes, and to the power that is within you. You are special, and you have no time and no room for uncertainties. Not, now! You have an evil monarch after you. You have Christ, Christmas and Santa Clause that is backing you with a multitude of angels and people who believe."

Jose reached under his shirt for the charm, kissed it and held it to the sky, declaring, "As it was. I believe!"

13

Jess Have Faith

ess watched in awe as the lava abruptly stopped flowing, and its sizzling balls froze in mid-air. In an instant, the lava and its damage evaporated.

Jess turned to face Jose, "I believe, too!" And, just like that, the cave's twinkling Christmas lights lit in unison, as though nothing had ever happened.

Jose smiled with relief and gratitude, "Now, let's get you someplace safe."

They walked to the very back of the cave. There was an opening to the left of Jess that only those who believed would be able to see. Jose held his breath.

Jess spotted it, looked at Jose and said, "So, I guess this is the way, huh?"

Jose smiled, "Sure is. You go on in there and read. I'll use my charm to cast a shield of protection around you. Meanwhile, I've got to get to Christonia—I must help fix the damage Nefari left behind."

Jess hugged Jose with gratitude and a determined smile. He held up his enchanted candy cane charm to cast the shield over her, then ran as fast as he could to Christonia. He knew his people needed all the help they could get from Nefari's wrath.

With the charm's powers, Jose was able to restore the town and its contents back to its beautiful, physical glory. But, the charm had no authority to bring the dead back to life. Only Christ Jesus, God Almighty could breathe life into the dead. Nefari's attack had taken the innocent lives of three men, eight women, and twelve children.

Jose trusted that Christ would heal the people of Christonia, and stood on a Christmas-festive gazebo in the center of town square, to tell them so. He encouraged his neighbors never to lose faith, to stand firm in their belief. He reminded them how Christ died for us all. Then he talked about Christmas. He told the people how important Christmas was and how it honors what Christ had done for them all. It helps us to remember the blessing of giving. Then he spoke about the loyalty of a man Christ trusted, Santa Clause. He pointed out how loyal Nicolas was before his transition into Santa Clause, stating why God loves him so. Last, he told them about Jess, the Chosen One, who was now in their midst, sparking a bit of newfound hope.

All cheered, and praises went out to Christ, Christmas, Santa Clause and now, Jess—the Chosen One soon to be their Apprentice who would rid all the worlds of Nefari's Evil.

14

Book of Breadcrumbs

On the cave, Jess grappled with the references to her physical world and magical worlds. To her, this place felt as material as her hometown in woods. So, why distinguish them as different? She wondered. Jess knew the book would answer most of her questions and she was ready to explore it for understanding. First, she wanted to test the book's power. This cave was pretty and a unique feature for the towns people and tourist but, it was just a cave like any other—cold, damp and mildew-smelling. It had no comforts of home at all. Therefore, reading the book would be quite uncomfortable.

She closed her eyes, made a wish, held the book in the air, and declared, "I believe." She opened her eyes and before her was a lovely, crackling fireplace—glowing with warmth; a thick rug; a comfy sofa; a comfy throw blanket; beautiful flowers all around giving a pleasant aroma; a cocoa-maker machine that made Santa's cocoa—fresh with every cup, and a buffet filled with cookies.

"Wow!" Jess exclaimed, clapping her hands with delight. She poured some cocoa, packed a mound of cookies onto a plate and snuggled into the couch with the book, "Ahhh, now this is more like it!"

Hungrier than she'd thought, Jess, shoved an entire cookie in her mouth, washed it down with cocoa and opened the book, at last. The first page held instructions in embellished, dark gold cursive:

> The holder of this book will receive written secrets that cause success through their life's missions. The power of this book comes from its ability to hold written secrets. The books' pages are written as you go and throughout your journey. You can unlock its power with every mystery you unfold and every successful challenge you pass. Make sure you protect the book of knowledge secrets. Never allow anyone to open it. Because the book hasn't the ability to distinguish, whom or what has unlocked it. It will reveal secrets to the wicked as well as the righteous. The book and the globes work on the amount of faith you possess. Unlike the book, the globes only work with someone who maintains the Christmas Spirit, but the one that holds both the book and the globes will have ultimate power in all worlds.

Jess turned the page. It was blank—in fact, they all were. She closed her eyes, breathed in deeply and focused inward, as Jose had reminded her. She was brave and strong. She had complete faith and enduring love for Christ, Christmas, and Santa Claus. She believed with all her heart. Suddenly she had no fear, and she turned the page again. This time was different. At that moment, Jess could feel the empowerment and protection. She was fearless!

When she turned to the second page of the book again, all Jess could say was, "Wow!" She starred in amazement—the dark golden writing was searing itself onto the pages right before her eyes. This time, the message was personal:

> Hello, Jessica, you are reading this, so it means you have taken your fate to defeat the evil Nefari and her heinous plan to rid all worlds of any trace of Christ, Christmas or Santa Claus. You have accepted Apprenticeship!

The love of Christ, Christmas, and Santa Clause has always been active in your family—you are from a noble lineage. You are fused with the perfect combination of pure faith, belief, and love—the first in your family to cross all other worlds—this is the secret to why you were the Chosen One.

Jess, as you know, defeating Nefari and all evilness, will not be an easy task, but all depend on (you) to complete it. The battles that you are about to fight will span several worlds. There are many worlds—magical, mystical and spiritual—many lands, and many realms. Two of these worlds' paths have crossed many times—Spiritual and Physical. Your most challenging battle starts in one world, the physical world. The spirit world has many gifts within it realms such as, life that doesn't end, no questions about who is it that they serve. In the spiritual world, no one but the Creator (GOD) and all whom he allows may ever enter into the spiritual realms. The physical world has magic that God gives and black magic which comes from the devil. The physical world continues to ignore what they see every day, God. The physical world people die and time exists there so immortality can survive there. The magical worlds are like this Christmas land filled with magic, wonderment, and surprise. Also, there are mystical worlds. In these worlds, it defies logic and nothing makes sense. Creatures of these world posse abilities for unknown mystical reasons. In the magical and mystical worlds, time doesn't exist (except Christmas days), and evil powers are limited, so immortality doesn't work in these worlds. Find out as much as you can about these worlds and this book before returning to the physical world. Finding the second globe will make your overall agenda doable, but obtaining that globe will open hurtful doors. While physical and emotional pain is transpiring— REMEMBER WHO YOU ARE AND WHOSE YOU ARE... and, you will be provided with all that you need for Victory.

Jess turned the page—it was blank. Jess stated aloud, "That's it! There has to be more! I need answers."

She re-read her introduction over and again until Jose returned.

He glanced around the cove inside the cave, "Jess, I've gotta admit, you give a whole new meaning to the phrase, 'Make yourself at home.'"

"Yeah, I guess I did." Jess closed and placed the book on the sofa next to her. She looked dazed and a bit confused but determined.

Jose remained hopeful for the Christonians. "I did all I could for Christonia. The rest must be done by Christ—He will fix this. Hey, they all know that the Chosen One is here to rid them of Narfari's wrath! For now—I had to come back to take you to a lady that will further explain the powers of the Book-of-Knowledge."

"Great! I have many questions—so let's go!" Jessica said as she snatched the book of secrets and abruptly stood up.

As they trotted out from the cave, its original form took place. The cave regained its outer beauty again with wet and cold elements. Jess felt a shift. She turned back to see that it was restored to its original state, "Wow, outstanding." She then turned toward the opening of the cave and continued her trot behind Jose.

15

Fix A Wrong

On their way to visit the mystery woman, Jose stopped abruptly. "Jess, I don't know to say this; but, there's something I've got to tell you."

He had learned from both his mother and Andrew the importance of listening to the spirit inside and being obedient to it. He had to explain to Jess about the damage Nefari had done the part he and his magical charm couldn't fix. He was unsure if he should tell her—he didn't want to revert her faith.

The expression of heartbreak on Jose's face was unbearable. She looked intently into his eyes and said, "Jose, what is it? You look as if you've seen a ghost! What happened?"

Jose blinked back tears, "Not a ghost—Nefari. Her evil ravaged Christonia, killing men, women and children alike. My magic allowed me to repair the physical damage. But, there is nothing I can do about broken hearts or lost lives. My neighbors are begging for help, and I don't know what to tell them."

Jess tilted Jose's chin with one hand, gently placing the other on his shoulder, "Hey, what about that faith you preached to me about and, helped me find? It was you who convinced me that as the Chosen One, I could right the wrongs that have been waged against Christ, Christmas, and Santa. So, that faith and belief tell me that Christ will right this terrible right as well, in His time. Pray for them and trust in He that sent the Christ and He who sent me. By-the-way, I'm no longer the Chosen One... I am THE APPRENTICE. Tell them; I have accepted my FATE!"

Jose eyes lifted and he nodded with venerating faith and tears of Joy. "Thank you, Jess. Ms. Apprentice! You're right. Okay, I'm good now. In fact, this news will make the entire town rejoice! We have a mystery lady to find. Let's race."

Both ran as fast as they could with new power from above.

16

Lessons Learned

While Jose wasn't the least bit tired, climbing up and down the sparkling magical hills of snow and hurdling over whispering logs, Jess was exhausted. Ever the gentleman, Jose extended a helping hand whenever she needed it, pulling her along. Jose had forgotten that Jess was from the physical world and hadn't discovered the natural magic in his world.

Jess stopped at a gigantic tree log that had lost its glorious stand. Jose jumped on top of it—playfully. Sometimes Jose would deliberately slow down just to observe the sparkling, childlike wonder in her eyes. He saw that Jess wasn't used to all the magic. It made him happy. Jess laughed at the beauty of everything—including the small creatures that would be called insects or animals in the physical world. But this magical world, instead of pests to be squashed, they shimmered in every color of the rainbow, as did the small animals that populated the forest. All of the chirping, clicking, and buzzing was melodious. They all were aware of her presence there and seemed to be overly joyful.

As joy and play go hand in hand, the two took advantage of a glistening, frozen pond that stood between them and the forest they needed to reach. Of course, that meant sliding, skating and racing each other across the ice, laughing until their cheeks and noses were rosy red. Jose ran fast on the ice and pretended to fall. He lay there completely still. Jess slipped on lousy footing until she reached him. He reached up and grabbed her by her hand, pulling her completely down onto the ice with him. Jess saw that Jose was joking and begun laughing with him.

"You should have seen your expression. You really thought I fell and hurt myself." Jose laughed aloud, "Jess you're not in the physical world here. Magic is all around us. It's not as powerful as the magic in the book or the globes, but the magic of this place allows us to stay healthy and young way longer than in the physical world. We don't die here unless we're killed, but we transcend to a different life force. I am taking you to a person who will explain more. However, for now, Jess, use the magic and we'll get there a lot faster."

Jess, gazed into Jose sincere deep-sea blue eyes and said, "You're right about me. I've always had a hard time letting go. I need to let go of the physical world for this world to embrace me. I'm ready. Let's go."

Jess stood and took Jose's hand and snatched him up with no concern for losing her footing on the ice. She then got up, slid across the ice with ease, and circled Jose in fun and said again, "Okay, let's go."

Jose loved the fact that it never took Jess long to learn what he was trying to teach her. Jose gave a dazzling smile and turned his head slowly away from Jess, but his eyes were fixed on her attractive face. His eyes finally caught up with his head, and he allowed his hand to release itself from hers. Jose pointed in the direction of the forest. "This way," he said.

Jess followed behind Jose intensively and paid close attention to every word he uttered. She had realized he was there for a reason also. He was her guide in everything, and if she wanted to fulfill her purpose, she had to pay attention and remember everything he would say.

Stepping off the ice, they began their journey and there it was—a majestic, breathtakingly beautiful forest. Ahead of Jess and Jose, in their path were the most massive trees Jess had ever seen. After a few minutes, a giant, fallen, magical tree blocked their way. Before climbing over it, Jess examined it lovingly. Jess looked puzzled while approaching the base of the tree. Jose was walking a few steps behind her and too saw the tree in their path.

After looking at Jess, he said, "This tree is huge, and we must cross it. Are you ready?"

Jess glanced up at Jose with quizzical eyes, "I don't understand."

"What? We can just jump over it." Jose was unaware of her expression.

"Well, from all appearances, this tree is perfectly healthy. Although magical, it still resembles features of trees in my physical world. The bark is still fresh and moist. Here, take a sniff. It still smells like vanilla. If it were dead, it wouldn't have that lovely scent anymore. And, see? There are no fungi; there's no large holes or cracks, its bark isn't loose or peeling or insect infestation. This tree isn't stressed because there's no wilting from lack of water, overwatering, too much or too little sun, and the roots are in great shape, yet it lay here and has fallen from its graceful stand. Why?"

Jose looked at Jess in amazement. He briefly closed his eyes with his pointer finger in the air and said, "Wait! How do you know so much about trees?"

Jess smiled and said, "When I was with my grandmau-ma she lived in the woods, and I just loved the trees. I relaxed under them, cried to them and revealed my secrets to them. Even though I have a best friend, Haley, not too far away, the trees were my closest confidantes. Somehow, I took notice of them, and I felt as though they listened to me; which, of course, is crazy, 'cause trees don't have ears." She laughed.

Jose marveled at this beautiful, sensitive girl, "Doesn't sound crazy to me. You see, these trees here are magical just as the whole town is. We need wood for firewood, paper, and other things, but we will never kill anything including the trees. Everything cycles here and when a tree is down, we use it for our needs. Its spirit was ready to cycle into its purpose, whatever that purpose may be. I suspect that this handsome fellow sacrificed itself so that it can be repurposed and live on in some other form—maybe for a new house. The magical circle of life is really another blessing from the Creator. It seems you have a special bond to the trees; maybe there's a reason why. Let us go—we're almost there."

"Awesome," Jess whispered, almost prayerfully.

Jess hurdled over the large tree and followed closely behind Jose. It was getting dark, and they were hoping they would make it to their destination before dark. All their efforts were to no avail—it wasn't enough daylight.

Jose was first to admit defeat, "We're not going to make it." Jose rubbed his hand through his hair, "So, how do you feel about camping out?"

"The darkness is fast approaching, huh?" Jess questioned.

"Yes, it is but the ground here is dry. We can make a little fire and sleep under the trees. You don't mind roughing it, do you?"

Jess chewed on her bottom lip, "No... but, do we have to? This book can do some pretty cool stuff. Like back in the cave."

"I don't know, Jess. That was pretty cool. But, do you think you should be using its magic for personal gain?"

"Gain? How about personal survival? We're in the middle of nowhere."

Jose shrugged his shoulders. Jess clutched the book, closed her eyes and declared, "I believe." By the time she opened her eyes, two sturdy tents had popped up, complete with blankets and pillows, along with a warm meal for them both, a cooler full of cold drink and a lovely, warm fire. "See? So, you're welcome," she teased. "Let's chow down then grab some sleep."

"Yes, Ma'am," Jose grinned, still uneasy about Jess using the book as her personal wish lamp.

Jess and Jose ate, campfire-style, swapped stories about their lives, prayed to God to give thanks for His blessings and grace, then retreated to their respective tents.

As she promised, Jess kept the Book-of-Knowledge close. She held it to her as she slept. Sometime in the middle of the night, it began to glow. At first, it startled Jess, as she forgot where she was. Then, she sat straight up, worried that maybe this personal gain stuff wasn't a good idea, after all.

Jess took a deep breath and reached for the book. She then touched it, and the glow dimmed a bit. She opened it, and the light faded away, but another note was writing itself on the second page:

> *Dear Jessica, the trees will protect you from Nefari's wrath in the magical world, as they comforted you in your physical world. But, know too, that when the power of the book is summoned, the evil one can hone in on the use of magic, and your location. Be ever vigilant and discerning of the book's power. Watch out for the evil one—she is lurking near.*

Jess could hardly breathe, and she peeled the covers from her legs. "We have to get out of here!"

Suddenly, a loud, threatening, oncoming presence disturbed the quiet of the night. Jess and Jose scrambled out of their tents at the same time, momentarily panicked.

Just as Jess stiffened and her mouth went dry, she remembered what she had just read. A surge of courage and uncommon knowing ran through her being.

In the distance was a mighty tree that somehow held an expressed face within its bark that said, trust me. Holding the book, Jess grabbed Jose's hand with her free one and started running in its direction. Jose trusted Jess' instinct and asked no questions. As with the cave, all evidence of their presence at their make-shift campsite vanished when they did. Jose then knew that her wishes for comfort were the reason they were running.

The loud rigorous uproar continued firmly behind them as they ran toward towards the distinctive tree. Neither Jess nor Jose knew why they were running in that direction, but Jess had a hunch and Jose frighten, followed her lead. A three-dimensional, and wicked male voice called out from amongst the trees as the uproar noise settled a bit allowing its message to be heard. Approaching them; the sinister male tongue demanded, "Give us the book!"

"Us?" Jess asked out loud. "There's more than one evil entity after me?"

In magical lands, trees can stimulate and express feelings, and three menacing-looking ones were moving through the bristle of the settled trees toward Jess and Jose right now. Suddenly, the wooden threats froze in place; but, their terrible intent was still evident. Before this could be a relief—they quickly realized why the trees had stopped with their pursuit. It was Nefari, who had successfully pinpointed Jess and Jose. Her appearance—completely coal and wicked affected Jess. She handed the book to Jose so she could run faster. Once again, fear caused her to forget

Jose screamed, "Jess! You're not in the physical world—use your powers! You are more powerful than Nefari here." Jose threw the book, and Jess immediately felt its power, and she guided it through the evil winds. It glided directly and quickly into her hand. Her spirit led her to the tree that she had somehow connected with and Jess clutched the book, felt the words she spoke with all her heart, "I believe."

She pressed her back against its mighty trunk, becoming one with the towering tree. Together, they grew taller than all other trees in the forest. Jess' face became the tree's face; and, her arms, its branches.

Her voice was one hundred times stronger than when she stood alone, calling out to Nefari, "Be gone, Nefari. Yours is a wasted battle. You will not win. Christmas will always win because Christ Jesus will always win."

Jess captured Nefari using all of her branches, and she then used the power of the book to hold her in place.

The evil trees that once displayed an evil expression on its bark now resembled a joyful appearance with pleasant voices. Jess held onto her while she caused all the trees to sing. Jess, added tone and balance as the forest birds and animals joined in the singing.

Nefari laughed wickedly, seemingly amused by Jess' words and powers. Her arrogance led her to entrapment by Jess' branches, holding her in place, no matter how ferociously she thrashed about.

The menacing expression embedded in Nefari's evil tree soldiers' bark, changed into unmistakable joy. Jess, spoke again "Let this night be Silent and Holy!" She held on tighter to Nefari and caused the trees gained pleasant singing voices. Jess, added in with tone and balance as the forest trees, birds, and animals began to sing in unison:

> "Silent night, Holy night
> All is calm; all is bright
> Round yon virgin, mother, and child
> Holy infant so, tender and mild
> Sleep in heavenly peace,
> Sleep in heavenly peace.
> Silent night, Holy night
> Shepherds quake, at the sight
> Glories stream from heaven above
> Heavenly, hosts sing Hallelujah.
> Christ, our Savior is born,
> Christ, our Savior is born.
> Silent night, Holy night
> Son of God, love's pure light
> Radiant beams from thy holy face
> With the dawn of redeeming grace,
> Christ, Lord at thy birth
> Christ, Lord at thy birth."

The singing, reverence and pure joy all around her tortured Nefari. She shrieked with agony the whole time, but could not cut herself loose from the tight grip of Jess's branches. The entire forest became as one while swaying and swinging to the tune of joyful Christmas spirit as it filled the air. Jess started another song to bring even more agony for the wicked Nefari. Every tree in the enchanted forest was ordered to sing and sway to another song. The trees lifted it's branched in singing, We Wish You A Merry Christmas, but before the song was complete Nefari mustered up enough magic to cut loose of Jess branches—this was too much for her wickedness to take.

Nefari nearly exploded, mustering forth enough magic to slither through Jess' branches. Her wickedness simply couldn't take another moment of that which she hated above all else.

"The battle has just begun, little girl," she howled at Jess. "This is not over; I will make people doubt Christ, I will make them forget the existence of Santa Clause and anything that even remotely stinks of Christmas! Trust that we will meet again—soon. You have been warned."

After Nefari disappeared in a puff of black smoke, all in the forest went back to normal. Jess simply stepped out of the loving tree. She lay her head against its bark and hugged it, thanking it for helping her. Then, released the trees from the magic of the book and they instantaneously became as they were.

Then she turned to Jose and walked into his open arms. "You are indeed the Chosen One, Jess. I'm so proud of you, and kinda in awe. You are just 16 in the physical world, right?"

"Yup... And, thank you. Of course, I had a really good teacher," Jess winked, grinning broadly.

Jose smiled full of pride. He thought how Jess was brave and it didn't take long for her to realize the power she possessed. Because of the trees; he now, understood that she recognized things from the physical world were preparing her for every battle. Jose quickly reminded her of something that they both may have forgotten.

Jose looked her in the eyes, "Jess, it is still my responsibility and obligation to get you to the Woman-of-Wisdom because she possessed more knowledge about that book and the only one that can tell you everything about the book, and its history in multiple worlds. Remember, you need this information to win before you return to the physical world."

Jess nodded, "I understand."

"Speaking of which, it's daybreak. I don't think our destination is much farther. Jose tapped the friendly tree, gestured thanks."

Jess, with more confidence, held her book tighter, "I'm ready. Lead the way."

17

A Charmed Lady

Jess and Jose soon found themselves in an even more charming part of the enchanted forest. The trees were singing and swaying to beautiful unknown tones. Slowly Jose and Jess approached, the tonality quality became clear, louder, and stronger—as if it was sending an alert warning to someone near or ringing a doorbell. Every living thing and every inanimate object came to life. Jose assumed it was because of Jess's arrival—being the long-awaited apprentice. The branches of every tree, every bush, and even the snow—hummed in harmony.

And, there it was—past the winter's dust—this had to be the place. The pretty little gingerbread cottage was surrounded by Christmas snow that glistened from the sun—like beautiful bright crystals. The smoke that rose from the chimney even whistled Christmas melodies; the entire surrounding areas smelled like cinnamon and sugar. The charming the little birds who chirped, in tune were circling Jess—saying welcome. Jess and Jose held hands, soaking it all in and smiling with delight and soon, they were singing and dancing to the Christmas music. Their spirits overflowed with absolute joy. The two were so mesmerized by the

Christmas magic surrounding them; they didn't even notice when a thin older lady. She stood only five feet tall, with dark caramel skin, long neckline, beautiful long lashes, tightly waved white hair, and the most beautiful bold round shaped eyes that peeped out now and then from her partially covered by a wide-brim Christmasy hat stepped onto her porch.

The woman's musical laughter got their attention. "Hello, welcome," she called. "The forest told me you were here, Jess. I was wondering when you were going to pay me a visit with the book. Please, come in."

Mrs. Wisdom's outfit matched her voice. Even though she wore overalls, they shone as white as snow and were bedazzled with red and green crystals, making her almost look like a walking Christmas tree—especially with the hat.

Mrs. Wisdom entered her cottage first, leaving the door open for her guests to follow.

Jess had second thoughts because the woman knew her, but she knew nothing about this woman or the place they were standing, and so bombarded Jose with questions, "Wait, you're the one who warned me that my biggest challenge would be evil's weapon of deception. How do we know this old lady is the real Lady-of-Wisdom? She's been waiting for me? And, the book?" Jess nervousness wouldn't allow Jose to answer any of her questions—continuing to whisper loudly. "I mean, this is weird. How do we know this isn't one of Nefari's tricks?"

Jose finally was able to speak, "Jess, calm down—he smiled to reassure her. She can be trusted. Look, I'm happy you're listening. But, let me ask you this. How did you feel when we got here?"

Jess said, "Powerfully, Joyful... Like Christmas was coming out of my pores." Her expression showed she saw where Jose was going with his question.

Jose continued, "Exactly... That's called Christmas Spirit. And, it lives wherever good and belief reside. This spirit comes directly from Christ—a gift to help us know the difference between good and evil. Now, let's go inside. It's not polite to keep Mrs. Wisdom waiting." Jose playfully gestured, "Ladies first."

Jess looked at Jose,　in front of him, and trotted up the few stairs. Jess was immediately at ease, feeling warm and right at home, as soon as she walked in the door. Mrs. Wisdom had a cozy fire going and a spread of hot cocoa and cinnamon rolls on the sitting room table.

"Help yourselves. I know you've traveled far and might need to warm up a bit. So, Jess, I perceive you have questions for me?"

Jess sipped her cocoa and said, "Yes, Ms. Wisdom I do. I am no longer the Chosen One—I am the Apprentice now, and I must know all the things that are essential for me to complete my journey. I really don't know where to start."

Ms. Wisdom tilted her head peeking at Jess, "First, you should always trust your instincts, your spirit."

Jess sipped her cocoa, a little embarrassed, "Yes, Ma'am. Sorry, that I was unsure; upon my seeing you. All of this magical stuff and different worlds are all so new to me."

"Ah, yes... Well, It's a lot to take in within a brief life-span. Happily, I can help you with all of that. Jess, I am blessed to have been graced with special abilities in this magical world. Yes, I possess the wisdom of the ages, but more than that, I feel emotionally all the things I inquire to know. These gifts were bestowed upon me by the Christ because of an extraordinary promise between Christ and my family's bloodline. May I have your hand, darling?"

Jess complied and extended her hand to the wise, old woman. As soon as their hands touched, Jess caught her breath. She felt wrapped in love and comfort, as though she'd known Mrs. Wisdom all her life. She just wished she could see Mrs. Wisdom's entire face underneath that Christmas hat. Jess wanted to get a better look at her eyes.

Mrs. Wisdom took a deep breath and closed her eyes while holding on tightly to Jess' hand. She moaned lightly as a stiff gust a wind blew the cottage's door wide open. Jose jumped up to close the door as quietly as possible, not wanted to break Mrs. Wisdom's concentration.

After what felt to Jess like forever, Mrs. Wisdom opened her eyes, released Jess' hand and said, "My dear, I must first tell you about a world that was destroyed because of evilness, a world that I originated. It was a magical place, much like this one. However, there were no seasons to change, which meant no rain or snow. And, we didn't speak orally—we communicated through expressions, mind reading, and emotional attachment. It's critical that you realize that Christ and the celebration of his birth, Christmas, are celebrated in whatever world or realm one may be from, and the demonic enemy of Christ and Christmas has targeted this belief in numerous in over many lifetimes.

When I was a small child, my world was under attack from the sinister one determined to destroy our faith, our belief, and our world. My people were slaughtered. All of our large libraries which held volumes of knowledge from the ages were ravaged, as well as those who were charged to protect them. The caretakers put up a valiant fight, but evil was the victor. Our world was obliterated. My mother fled our world with me, my sister, and her Book-of-Knowledge—the only book to survive from our world. My sister was sent to the physical world to fulfill her purpose. I was brought here to this magical world with my mother and her Book-of-Knowledge. Sadly, the escape took its toll on my brave mother. She died shortly after our arrival. The separation of my sister and I was very heartbreaking. I never spoke her name again since—it was painful. Now, I can say her name because touching your hand has allowed me to see it all."

Jose and Jess appeared confused. Ms. Wisdom turned to Jose and said, "My sister name is Estonia." Her eyes watered as she continued, "You are my bloodline! You are my Nephew! Jose!"

Jose was shocked, yet overjoyed that he still had a family member whom he could gain his history. He got up and examined his aunt and hugged her. "What do I call you now? You have always been Ms. Wisdom to me."

"You can call me by my name, given to me at birth from my mother. My name is Sapience. I am Auntie Sappie for short."

Jess, smiled and said, "Tell me more."

"Sure..." Ms. Wisdom tuned back to her abilities, and Jose sat back down so that his newly found aunt could continue.

Ms. Wisdom closed her eyes and reopened them and said, "Transformation to this world from mine was more than a notion; there were side effects, and I grew up fast. In your world, it goes on time, but in all other worlds, time cannot be measured. If time existed here, an infant turned into an adult only took me fifteen minutes. During that, I learned to speak orally and understood my purpose. Now, it time you learned everything about your purpose. Let me explain the importance of the Book-of-Knowledge that is now in your safekeeping. It belonged to my mother, then, to me. I was directed by Christ to make sure the book landed in the hands of a special soul, Jose, to keep it in hiding for the Chosen One, Now Apprentice. Jose, in turn, has obeyed and brought you, to me. It's only a bonus to learn who he really is to me."

Jess glanced at Jose, who diverted his gaze, blushing as Ms. Wisdom continued.

"My people were slaughtered, and my world is nonexistent now. This book must never get into the wrong hands!"

Jess a bit overwhelmed, "Yes, Ma'am... Wow, this is a lot to process. But, what does the Book-of-Knowledge want me to do now?"

"As Jose may have shared, now you use the power of the book and the magical snow globes in your physical world to defeat Nefari's evil. Not just for humankind, but for all worlds who long to be free of her malevolence and destruction, and her army of followers. With both, you can easily cross worlds and realms. However, it is of utmost importance that you locate the second globe. You will then have the advantage of the united power of the globes."

"But, Mrs. Wisdom, how do I begin?" Jess pleaded.

"You must return to your physical world now. My Christmas magic can only ward off Nefari but for so long. She sent her calling card in the wind that burst through my door after you'd entered. Jessica, lastly and perhaps most importantly, be very careful who you trust in your world. All are not as they appear. Nefari and her followers are masters of deception."

Mrs. Wisdom somewhat continued to hide under her hat but managed to kissed Jess on both cheeks, "Now, go with God. Once all your battles are won, you will return the Book-of-Knowledge to me, its owner. The final battle will occur in this magical world. Know that you were chosen because you are extraordinary, Jessica. I will be here waiting for news of victory and the book. Now, when you're ready, open the book, concentrate on home and you will be there. The book will guide you every step of your journey."

Outside the cottage, Jess and Jose said their goodbyes.

Jess tears fell, "I wish you could come with me. How can I accomplish this without you?"

Jose hugged Jess tight, rubbing her back, "It's just like My Aunt Sappie said. You're extraordinary. My place is here. Christonia needs me. I believe in you. You can do this!"

Jess smiled through wet eyes, "Goodbye, Jose."

He kissed Jess on the forehead. "No, it's not goodbye... It's—see you later. Right? Remember, I believe in you. Now go."

Jess opened the book, closed her eyes and focused on 'home.' When she opened them, she was right back in Grandmau-ma's sitting room with the book in her hand and the snow globe, sitting in its red velvet case, right next to her.

18

Prepare For Battle

Jess sat on the floor next to her Grandmau-ma's favorite chair in deep thought as quiet tears fell from her eyes. She could not stop the agony of missing her Grandmau-ma, and she wondered if her Grandmau-ma was watching over her. She needed some assurance that she wasn't alone, but as she sat there on the floor she realized that's how she felt; completely alone. Jess wiped her tears with her bare hands as she realized Christmas in her world has come and gone. She knew just as Santa had one year to prepare for Christmas, she too, has one year to before the next Christmas vengeance of Nefari's wrath. She sat up and wiped her eyes, feeling alone and lost, and so, prayed:

"Dear God, please help me." Jess prayed to herself. "How will I defeat the evil in this world with no magic? How will I know deception when it's staring me in the face? I know you will guide me about, but I also ask for comfort."

Jess, looked around and everything was as she had left it days ago. Amazingly, the fire was still burning in the fireplace. If Jess hadn't just returned from a world of magic, she would have thought that was impossible. The Christmas lights were left plugged in, so, it made sense that they were still blazing bright. Christmas was over, and she still had three beautifully wrapped gifts from her Grandmau-ma under the tree, snuggled in the lovely red tree skirt Grandmau-ma had made. She scooted closer to the tree.

Inside the first box was a soft, fluffy red and green sweater crafted by Grandmau-ma's loving hands. It was warm as usual but more substantial than average. Jess asked her grandmau-ma a million times to sell her work because it was astonishing. Grandmau-ma never cared about money; so, Jess dropped it.

The teenager cried fresh tears of joy blended with the loss when she picked up her next gift—wrapped in Jess' favorite colors, royal blue, and gold. "Grandmau-ma remembered." She cried. Inside was a gorgeous patchwork quilt that was also exceptionally thick and heavy. Jess said aloud, "Grandmau-ma must have used different materials in her quilting."

The last box was flat and smaller than the first two. It was also beautifully wrapped with shiny red paper and a black ribbon tied around it. Inside was Grandmau-ma's will and her official financial records. Jess' eyes grew wider, and although being alone, she spoke aloud. "Grandmau-ma wasn't poor at all; according to this, Grandmau-ma was a wealthy landowner with properties in eight states and several out-of-state bank accounts. My Grandmau-ma just shunned material things." Because Jess was the only beneficiary, she realized now—she was wealthy, too. 'And, I'd exchange it all in a heartbeat for just another day with Grandmau-ma,' Jess told herself, sadder than ever.

Sitting on the floor cross-legged, Jess glanced up at the tree's ornaments and spotted an envelope hanging from a branch. She jumped up and grabbed it. The note was addressed, *'Sweet-Pea.'* Jess couldn't get the note out fast enough:

'My Darling Jess, my Sweet-Pea, I love you more than words could ever express. Each of these gifts holds a purpose for your journey, so please keep them with you at all times. I will never leave you. You are not alone. Remember, Sweet-Pea, always hold on to your belief in Christ, Christmas, and Santa Claus; the three major spirits will guide you through this important journey. And remember, these three gifts will shield you. I love you, Sweet-Pea. Be courageous my dear and may the Creator of all things see you through. Forever yours, Grandmau-ma...'

Jess, didn't understand how a sweater, blanket, and money would help on this journey, but she was determined to be obedient.

Suddenly there was a thump at the door, and a concerned voice cried out. "Jess, please open the door! Where are you?"

Haley asked while trying to peer through the slightly opened curtains. Jess snapped into her battled mode only thinking about protecting the globe and the book.

"Jess, I know you're in there. I can hear you. Open up!" Haley screamed.

"Just a sec. I was asleep; you do know it's late." Jess called out.

The Book-of-Knowledge began to glow. "Be right there!" She yelled towards the door again. Jess opened the book to its newest page to quickly read. Jess knew she had to open it before answering the door. She turned its large page, and it read:

Jess, remember, things are not always as they seem. In your world, magic doesn't rule, but deception does. On rare occasions, trickery can work for good. You are the Apprentice, and you must use what you've learned, and you must listen to your spirit.

Jess remembered Jose's neat trick with his charm. She hoped it would work as efficiently for her. She swept her hand, with belief in her heart, over both the book and the snow globe. They shrank into beautiful Christmas charms. Jess carefully slipped them on the gold chain around her neck, asked for protection from Christ. Jess jumped up quickly and said, "Now that ought to do it." She then wrapped her new quilt around her—realizing she was supposed to have been sleeping.

She opened the door. Haley stood there shivering in skinny jeans and a tight, cropped sweater. "Jeez, it's about time. It's freezing out here," Haley complained.

"Then why aren't you wearing a coat?" Jess rolled her eyes, "Come on in, Haley. Seriously, did you leave your coat in your truck again?"

Haley had already run over to the fireplace to warm her hands, "Girl, you know me. I'd rather look good than be comfortable. Besides, I didn't expect you would take forever to open the door!"

After getting satisfactorily warm, Haley finally looked at her friend. "Wow, you look worn out. How was your Christmas? Where's your grandmother? Sleeping? Hope I didn't wake her up."

Jess turned away from Haley, "Grandmau-ma passed on Christmas Eve. She was buried in a special burial spot with the rest of my family."

Haley turned Jess around and grabbed her hands, "Buried! Already? I didn't have a chance to say goodbye."

Jess lowered her head, "Yes, I know—but our family doesn't believe in holding a body longer than three days. I'm sorry."

"Still, I wished you had at least called me? I know, I said I'd be busy with my mom; but, Jess, this was an emergency. I would have dropped everything. Oh my goodness! I am so sorry for your loss. How are you? What are you going to do now?"

Jess sighed and said, "I really haven't planned anything. My Grandmau-ma left me everything, and I have no financial problems or bills to worry about, but this loneliness is killing me."

"Jess, I have just the thing to help keep your mind off things." Haley offered excitedly.

Jess raised one brow and said, "Your ideas usually lead us in some serious trouble."

Jess cocked an eyebrow, plopped on the sofa and crossed her arms, "Hmmm, your ideas usually lead to trouble."

"Not all of them!" Haley protested.

Jess thought back to a time that Haley got them into a jam and said, "Remember that time when we were ten or so? You thought it would be a great idea to go on a treasure hunt. What you didn't mention was that the treasure hunt meant stealing other people's stuff."

Haley raised her hand in defense, "Totally not my fault. My cousin tricked us both. He made it sound like a game. How was I supposed to know it was stealing?"

Jess chuckled, "Yeah, a game that got us both in deep doo-doo, literally."

"Thank goodness, my uncle, put it all together and got us out of that mess." Haley smiled.

"Yeah, but, we still had to clean the trash and the animal poop out of the yard for a month," Jess whined.

"You know what they say." Haley shrugged, "Character building—all that."

"Character!" Jess laughed hard. "To build character—you need something positive. The only positive thing, I got from that was the beautiful Christmas ornament I found when I fell into the stinky ole' compost bin behind the shed. I kept it, too. Reminded me of our botched 'treasure hunt.'"

"Ewww, that was so gross. You—stank—so bad..." Haley tilted her head, noticed the charms around Jess' neck. "Hey, speaking of treasure, those are pretty. New?"

Jess fingered the precious miniatures, "Yes, my gifts from Grandmau-ma. They were under the tree, wrapped before—you know, she died. They will always remind me that, somehow, my Grandmau-ma is always with me; in my memory, heart, and soul." Jess turned her head, her eyes welling up again.

"Hey, no more tears. That's a good thing—now, back to my idea. Come hang out with me."

"What, now?" Jess moaned.

"Yeah, now... There's an entire area is being super-developed and a party. It doesn't require travel. In fact, it's only seven miles once we're out of these woods. Jess, we will be able to live near a town again. It turns out that they are even building a school. So, we can finish our senior year there! Isn't that awesome? Well, if my mom lets me stay here."

Haley appeared very excited about the new local town coming, but it didn't sound impressive to Jess. She loved living in a peaceful, wooded area. And, she'd learned to enjoy being home-schooled. She didn't like being intruded on, and the secluded woods gave her that. She loved the animals and the trees.

Jess frowned and said, "Haley, I don't want to be near a town, and I thought you moved from your mother to get away from the town living. We both did. Trouble seems to be all we got into, and that's why your mother sent you to live with your aunt and uncle in these private woods. It has been all good since we've moved here. We haven't gotten into any trouble at all and homeschooling was the best thing ever. Who wants to spend all day with a bunch of ungrateful teens who don't know anything? I don't! I like things the way they are, Haley. And, sorry—I don't want to go to a party. I just want Grandmau-ma back."

"Sorry, Jess... I know you do. But c'mon... Don't make me beg. I don't want you staying here alone. Just change clothes. We'll do a little something with that wild hair; I'll fix those circles under your eyes, add a pop of lip gloss—and, bam!"

Jess with a firm expression, "No! No, No Party! I don't want to go, Haley."

"Okay, okay. Fine. Well, you're not going to stay here." Haley grabbed Jess by the shoulders. "Listen, I know grown-ups think we're still just kids. But, we're both old enough to know that life is all about change. Nothing stays the same. You must accept that, but I also know that isolating yourself isn't healthy! I'm not going to have it. You're not alone because I'm here and I love you, Bestie. Plus, I'm not taking 'no' for an answer. So, get to packing. You're coming with me!"

Haley had her hands on her hips, so Jess knew she wasn't going to win this one. On the way to her room, Jess asked, "What did you mean if your mother allows you to stay?"

Haley sighed, "Jess, that's what I really came over to talk about."

While Jess threw a few things into a duffel bag and her backpack; Haley stretched across Jess' twin bed—rubbing the soft, colorfully, crafted quilt that Jess Grandma had made and said, "My mother has gotten rich from her toy stores. Her new husband aided her in building those toy stores everywhere, and they are moving to another location. She's got it stuck in her mind that I need to be around her more so that I can learn the family business. You know how in love she is with her chain of toy stores. Loves them more than she ever loved me. Now, she claims she needs my help. They're opening the newest store in New Hampshire; and, Mom wants me to move there with them. I can't live without being close to my only friend. My mom is so Intense and unreasonable. I don't want to go. Why not just kill me now?"

Jess stopped packing and sat next to her. She leaned her head on Haley's shoulder, "I can't live without you either, but I can't move. My life is here Haley. What are we going to do? Your mother has always been hard to reason with, but we must try."

Haley groaned stressfully and said, "We will try. I don't know exactly how we will convince her that I am better off with my uncle and aunt."

Jess wagged he head, "We will both tell her that we won't be separated and that's that. If your uncle allows you to stay, then it shouldn't be a problem because I'm sure your uncle doesn't want you to go either."

Haley sat up quickly, "Wait, I know. Why don't we drop your stuff off at Uncle Bob and Aunt Renee's? Then, we can take a little road trip into town to see Mom. And, since you're the level-headed one, maybe you can convince her I'm better off with my aunt and uncle. C'mon, Jess... I don't want to move so far away from my best friend."

Jess pulled Haley into a hug, "That's not going to happen! Well, maybe it is worth a try, a try, I guess. Your mom has always been impossible. We just can't take no for an answer."

"True that. Maybe we could butter my mom up by promising to let her show us off at one of her fancy New Year's parties? Oh well, that's still a few days off. Ready?"

"Yup..." Jess stuffed her new sweater and quilt into the bag. "Let's go."

Haley placed her hands on her narrow hips again, giving Jess the side eye, "Uh, you know, we do have blankets and quilts at our house."

Jess was somber, "Yeah, I know. But, none of them were made by my Grandmau-ma. This one was just for me..."

"Oh, Jess... Of course. I'm so sorry. I'll miss sweet grandmau-ma too."

Unlike Haley, Jess pulled on her warmest puffy jacket. Jess told Haley to lead the way. Jess slowly looked at her Grandmau-ma's cabin while walking through the hallway to the front door. She remembered the memories and locked the door behind them. Once outside, Jess looked once more with one tear freezing on its way down her cheek.

Before Jess climbed up into Haley's truck, the moonlight produced an unusual, supernatural sparkle in Jess's necklace. Jess looked at Haley to be sure that the spark was seen only by her. She tucked the necklace into her sweater, fully understanding that it was a message to remind her to remain vigilant and Jess knew she was to pay close attention to the events that would follow.

Haley's truck had large snow tires and was fully equipped for the harsh weather in the winter and the muddy dirt roads in the summer. Jess sat quiet, deep in thought and withdrawn. She thought how unpleasant Haley mother had always been and she didn't look forward to seeing her at all. Haley saw Jess mood and turned on the music louder than usual, and they were off to Haley's aunt and uncle house first, after that, they planned to take the drive to her mother's location to convince her that Haley's fine where she is.

Jess always loved Bob and Renee's gorgeous, two-story, log cabin country home. It had plenty of space and a huge fireplace. Jess loved the green roof, window frames, and front door. It also had an oversized beautiful stone chimney. When they arrived, Jess mused at the good times she and Haley had shared in this lovely house over the years and how she had thought Grandmau-ma was poor, by comparison, when she was little. At their cottage, where everything was old and falling apart, if Jess even brought up the word "repair," Grandmau-ma happily ignored her to sew, knit or bake something.

Inside the polished stone foyer, Haley yelled, "I'm home, and I kidnapped Jess!"

Uncle Bob appeared immediately, kissing both girls. "Hey, Jess... Always good to see you, Sweetheart. Haley, baby, have you been out in that weather without your coat again? Speaking of weather, I've been watching the skies, and something awful is baking—a blizzard... Something— So, let your mom know you're going to have to postpone the visit. I don't want you driving in this."

Both girls were relieved. Haley winked at Jess, "Sleepover!"

Jess smiled but thought how she'd much rather stay there than trek into town to hang out with Haley's mom at her temporary digs to try and convince her of anything. Jess couldn't quite put her finger on it, but Haley's mom always made her skin crawl. She was distant and self-absorbed, bossy, and mean. To Jess, it seemed Haley's mom only cared about her businesses and her hand-picked bunch of husbands. Rather than making Haley her number concern—building an empire took first place so, it was a kinda no-brainer—Jess was not a fan. Now Haley mother wanted to move Haley away—nothing felt right about that to Jess. Besides, she wondered to herself if she should follow Haley? Or should she stay focused on her mission? Ultimately, was that part of the Mission? Jess was officially confused. She decided to take one step at a time and pay attention to any signs given her.

Jess then snapped back into what Haley was excited about and asked, "A sleepover will be fun; however, we are getting too old to be excited about a sleepover. Don't you think?"

Haley chuckled and said, "Naw, I could never tire of our sleepovers. I guess the blanket will come in handy. We had better grab it with the rest of your things."

After tossing her bags into Haley's pretty, teenaged girl room, Jess joined Bob, Renee, and Haley in the great room—the expansive and cozy family room extension of the kitchen. The fire was crackling in the over-sized fireplace. The wall-mounted, photos of Christmas was joyful to the eye, and Aunt Renee was preparing a feast of assorted pizzas, popcorn, brownies, and hot chocolate.

When Jess entered the room, both Bob and Renee rushed to wrap their arms around her. "Oh, Baby... We are so very sorry to hear about your grandmother. Haley just told us," Renee shared, holding Jess close. "Your Grandmau-ma was such a sweet, wonderful woman."

Bob agreed, "Yes, she was. And, Jess, you know our home is your home. You can stay with us as long as you like. And, please, let us know whatever you need or want. We're here for you, Honey."

Jess loved Haley's Uncle Bob and Aunt Renee so much and was so grateful that they loved her, too. "Thank you. Just being here with you guys now makes me feel a lot better."

"Good... Anyone up for game night?" Aunt Renee suggested.

Bob Jumped up from the sofa and said, "Not me... I need to get more firewood. The coming storm is strong, and we need to be prepared."

Uncle Bob put his coat on and went outdoors. Aunt Renee, Haley and Jess settled into their positions in the large couches and chairs, in the great room.

Uncle Bob came back with wood, fighting strong winds to shut the door behind him, and dropped the logs near the fireside. After placing two timbers in the fire, he too sat down to catch his breath.

Just as they settled into their positions on the massive couches and chairs, a powerful wind blew open the heavy front door. Bob jumped up, "Woe! I knew it!" He closed and double-lock it. Then the electricity went out. "Hurry, Light the candles lined on the mantle," Bob instructed.

Renee, Haley, and Jess quickly got busy lighting them all. Jess took a single candle up to Haley's room to get her special quilt and duffle.

The blizzard and its accompanying winds were so loud and whipped so hard, everyone could feel it. Even though the house was sturdy, it felt like the walls were trembling. Two front windows shattered on the upper level. Jess came running down to tell her uncle the windows are blown out.

Renee and Haley were terrified. Uncle Bob and Jess remained calm and steady, deftly grabbing whatever they could to cover and secure the windows upstairs. Jess knew this house as well as she knew her own. She and Uncle Bob grabbed flashlights, hammers, and nails and ran upstairs to secure those windows.

On their way back down to join Haley and Aunt Renee, there was a loud pounding on the front door. Bob opened it, struggling to keep the fierce winds from taking it off its hinges.

A small man with a Siberian husky rushed in. The man helped Bob to close and lock the door. He was out of breath, "Thank you so much, Sir. We were half-way home when this storm came out of nowhere. I've never seen anything like it! I'm Ralph, by the way. So sorry for the intrusion; but, may my dog and I hang with you guys until it blows over?"

Leaning against the door and sweating from the effort, Bob extended his hand. "Hello, I'm Bob. Good to meet you. And, of course, you can stay. No one needs to be out there right now. Beautiful dog—I'll bet he could use some water. C'mon, let me introduce you to my family."

The Renee and Haley welcomed Ralph and his furry friend as Bob introduced them. Jess walked in with her bag attached and looked at Ralph—he somehow seemed familiar.

Bob then introduced Jess, "This young lady is my niece best friend but more like another daughter to us. Jess this is Ralph."

Jess, examine Ralph and his dog inquisitively, "Hello, it's very nice to meet you Ralph and your dog too."

Bob wondered if Ralph knew more about storms and asked, "How long do you think this storm is going to continue?"

Ralph was looking up at six foot Bob, "I'm not sure, but I don't think I've ever seen it this bad before."

Bob was curious about Ralph, "Where do you—."

Before she had a chance to ask any questions, more windows blew out, glass flying everywhere.

"That's it!" Bob yelled. "Everyone grab a flashlight and head for the cellar. Now!"

Renee and Haley grabbed food and go to the underground cellar. Ralph took hold of his dog's leash and followed to the basement. While the others headed downstairs, Jess ran to grab her backpack and quilt before joining them. Her mind was racing. 'This little man resembled a persona like the Ralph in Grandmau-ma's story, as Santa's best friend. But, that didn't make sense. That was hundreds of years ago. And, wouldn't Ralph be in the North Pole making toys for next Christmas?' She passed through her mental intrusion and took the storm as a sign the journey had begun.

In the cellar, it sounded like a train was roaring through the house upstairs. Haley and Renee were huddled under a blanket, holding each other and crying. Bob was busy trying to secure the entrance of the only shelter they had. Jess sat in a corner wrapped in Grandmau-ma's quilt. Ralph and his dog sat next to her.

Ralph leaned in to whisper in Jess' ear, "What you're thinking is true, Jess. I was sent here to help you with your first battle. You probably can feel that this is no ordinary storm and if you want these people to survive—you need to use your power right now and make this stop!"

"What? How," Jess answered, her eyes wide with panic. "The book doesn't give a recipe on how to stop a blizzard, tornado or whatever this is!"

"Take my hand." Ralph held his hand out.

"What?" Jess expressed confusion and fear.

Ralph insisted. "Take my hand and close your eyes. I am going to take you away for a moment, and we'll be back."

Jess sarcastically said, "It's a storm Ralph where would we go now?"

Ralph grabbed her hand tighter and again instructed her to close her eyes. Jess complied. When she opened her eyes, she was on a boat on a stormy night. She stood up, looking around while the ship was being tossed into the air like a toy by the roaring sea. Jess jumped because it was also several men on the boat panicked over powerful winds, and taking on water. The men on the boat were struggling to keep it from capsizing. Despite the fact, that all the other men on the boat were frightened to death, Jess noticed a man sleeping, then she could hear shoes hitting the wood surface on the ship fast approaching the sleeping man.

One of the frightened crew ran to the man to shake him awake, "Get up! We are about to perish!"

The sleeping man awakened. "Why are you afraid, o' ye of little faith?"

Then, he got up, rebuked the winds and the waves, and it was utterly and perfectly calm.

The men were stunned, asking, "What kind of man is this, that even the winds and the sea obey him?"

Jess gasped. This was Jesus and his disciples!

When she blinked her eyes, she was back in the cellar with the others, and the present storm was winning. She understood, why Ralph showed her the message of Christ. She had to embrace her faith, so she wrapped her hand around the charms and said, "No storm can beat the maker of storms, God. Storm I rebuke you in the name of my Lord, my savior, my God, Christ!"

The roaring stopped immediately. Haley, Bob, and Renee stared at Jess, dumbfounded as they wondered was that sheer luck? On the other hand, was there something going on they didn't know? They took it as sheer luck—happy that it stopped. However, Ralph and Jess knew it was Christ who stopped the storm.

They all slowly climbed up from the shelter. Upstairs, glass, trash and tossed furniture were everywhere from the rare winter tornado. Everyone except Jess and Ralph stood in shock.

Ralph held on to his dog's leash, taking Jess aside and whispered, "Jess, it is of utmost importance that you always remember that you are the one person on earth who possesses both spiritual and magical powers. The worlds are depending on you. Remember! Remember who you are. Always embrace your faith and use it."

Everyone stood outside amidst the fallout from the vicious storm and waved goodbye to Ralph and his dog.

Within minutes, neighbors were milling about, ready to help one another clean up the collective mess and repair damages in any way they could.

19

Becoming Aware

Haley's mother had heard about the storm and frantically rushed to make sure her only child was okay. Bystanders could listen to the screeching from the tires as the car quickly stopped on the dirt road as she pulled up to Bob and Renee's ramshackle home. Her chauffeur-driven, black, luxury car tires had smoke coming from them, and so did its passenger. When her driver opened her door, Jade stepped out onto to the snow, dripping in diamonds, wearing ridiculously impractical stilettos, a tight fitting dress, red designer dress and full-length sable coat. It looked as if she had diverted from her original plans.

Stumbling through debris and mud holes, Jade screamed, Bob eyeballed his sister, "Haley, Haley, where are you? Mummy's here, Darling! Haley!"

Bob ran around to the front of the house to meet her. "Calm down, Jade Spinous. Haley is just fine. She's out back."

Before Bob could finish his sentence, she had already entered the broken-up home yelling bypassing Bob as if he was non-existing. Haley was in the backyard trying to pick up some of her things out of the debris. Haley was still shaken by the severity of the storm and certainly didn't expect to see her mother here.

Haley snapped out of her mental coma when she heard her mom's panicky call. "It's okay, Mom. I'm fine."

Jade touched Haley's face and seemed to examine her body to make sure the girl was, indeed, unharmed. Once Jade realized everything about Haley was okay, she put her arms around Haley. "I was afraid. You're all I have, and the thought of anything—" Jade appeared to be choked up. "I'm happy you're okay."

Bob didn't know how weak the storm had made his home and said, "I think it's best to stay out and clear of the home. Not, sure how long it can stand."

They all stayed in front of the home sitting on things the storm had tossed about to and fro. Jade kissed Haley on her forehead and led her out to the front yard of the house.

Jade looked around at everyone and said, "This storm had an act of vengeance in these woods. That's it," she declared. "You're coming with me right now. This place is a wreck. Bob, you're going to have to rebuild from the ground up. Perfect time to take my baby from this forsaken place!"

"Mom, no! I don't want to go. I need to stay here and help Uncle Bob and Aunt Renee." Haley whined.

Bob abruptly said, "Come on, Jade. Haley is perfectly fine here. We have our cottage down the road, and it wasn't harmed at all. We will stay there until this place is back. It could have been worse, but it wasn't. Thank God we are all safe."

Jade threw her head back, laughing cynically, "That's a good one, brother. God? Really? Who do you think ravaged this house and these woods in the first damn place? What, with one of his tests of faith? Yes, let us thank God for bringing that godforsaken storm near my baby. God is the one that controls storms, and then you go and thank him for sparing your life. That's ironic! When will you people see if there is a God, he's playing games with you, and he uses things like storms to see what you will do if he did this or that!"

Renee overheard everything and chimed in, "That's enough, Jade. Now you have God all twisted. God is not testing us, 'Let no man say God is trying them.' That's what the good book tells us. Storms happen. Bad things happen. But, they are not sent by God. He gives us everything that we need to endure and overcome the hard times' life throws at us. Jade, will you go to church with us? I'll like to introduce you to the one who helped me understand God."

Jade nearly folded over in laughter as she circled her sister-in-law, eyeing her up and down. She walked a few feet away and said, "Bob, remove your goody-two-shoes wife from my sight. She makes me want to retch."

Bob wanted to spare his wife's feelings. He knew how horrible his sister could be. He walked away—to talk and gesture Jade to follow.

Jade said as they walked, "You never told your bible-toting Step-ford wife that the three things I loathe most in this life are anything having to do with God, Christ, Christmas or that ridiculous Santa? In Fact, I've noticed you haven't explained to her why you never get sick. You'll never die, like your mortal wife. You never told her about our father! Have you? Why married Mortals if you can't tell them the truth? I'm the smart one! I sided with our Father. You sided with your mortal mother. Shameful when a person deny who they are."

Bob angered, "I haven't denied who I am. I am my mother's child. I only accept that part because she was good. Our Father! He was unnatural—and has had many names, a son of evil—fallen angel—wicked giant, and you put this curse of eternity on me! I never wanted it or asked for it. I serve your purpose somehow, and that is why you sacrificed for us to be immortals. I only had one request, and that's to protect my secret of immortality, don't bring it up again! Ever!"

"Fine!" Jade spun around to eye him. "Never allow that wife or anyone ever to mention anything having to do with God, Christ, Christmas or that ridiculous Santa to me! Ever!"

"I can agree to that but you're in my house, and you will not speak to my wife about anything. It's time you leave now, Jade!" Bob ordered, furious.

"Oh, don't get your panties in a bunch, Bob. Fine. I feel pity for Ruth, Rita, Renee—whatever her name is. Poor girl doesn't know that you'll outlive her." Jade, laughing, "I'm ready to blow this dump, anyway. But, I'm taking my kid with me."

Bob thought of Haley and calmed himself, "Jade, wait! Why now? She's safe. We all weathered the storm. Isn't she scheduled to visit you for New Years? That's still days away. What are you really up to?"

"She's mine, and I said I want her now!"

"For what? Slave labor? Yeah, I heard about your new store in the town they're further developing a couple of miles away. It seems to me a toy story would be at the bottom of their priority list."

Jade chuckled, spewing venom, "You think I give a damn about any opinion of yours—about anything? You'd better think again. If you must know, I'm renting a charming, luxury suite in the only decent hotel within a 100-mile radius. Haley and I will stay there for a few days while I supervise my latest store's opening; then, we'll return to my fabulous new home in Windham, New Hampshire. We won't be so far away. Perhaps I'll even let you see her once a year."

"You should be ashamed of yourself, Jade. We've raised that girl since she was six years old. Where were you all that time?"

"Well, busy. Duh? She was an inconvenience then. But, I want her back. Now— Do I make myself clear, Bob or shall I call you Robert? Name changing won't slow folks awareness about your extended existence. Eventually, you'll find, this physical world isn't big enough to hide, and you'll need me again. Poor fool! Tread lightly—my brother."

Bob begged, "Think of Haley for once. Her life is with us. She's happy here. She has a best friend. You know Jess. They've been inseparable since they were eight. Those two girls are more like sisters than friends. Do you honestly want to rip Haley away from everyone she loves and everything she knows? And, Jess just lost her grandmother. She would be totally lost without Haley. Do you really want to devastate them both by tearing them apart?"

"Absolutely!" Jade's threatening eyes were growing darker, denser and pierced through him.

"Jade, please, listen to reason."

"Reason? Wow, you're really more pitiful than I thought. When have I ever listened to so-called reason? Look at you! A paunchy, balding, middle-aged man who still whines like a baby. You really are your mother's son! Sickeningly, sentimental—she coddled you and never taught you anything about the real world—just those stupid myths about God, the Christ and on and on—making me nauseous.

That's why Father passed down to me, everything he had learned from his father—how to be tough and take what you want from this world benefits my kind—strengthening us within. I will teach these values to my child.

You and Mother were weak. The two of you made me puke with 'Christ this and Santa that.' If you've invested any of that crap in Haley, trust me, when I tell you—I'm going to rip it all out. Whatever it takes..."

Bob grabbed Jade's arm, "Our mother is dead. How dare you talk about her like that! She was wise, and she had your number the minute you were born. She always believed something was wrong when she birthed you. She told me before she died, why she named you Jade Spinous. I called you by your first and middle name only. Have you ever wondered why? Your first name means a broken-down, vicious, or worthless horse, a disreputable woman, and a flirtatious girl. Your middle name means difficult or unpleasant to handle or meet. She referred to you as thorny many times because it means very difficult or complicated. You are all those things and worst. Mother knew you well. She may have appeared weak to you, but she knew who you were from the moment you were born and wisdom makes you the strongest person alive. She wasn't weak, Jade—just full of wisdom."

Jade focused her eyes on Bob's hand wrapped around her arm with a withering glance, practically growling, "If you want to keep that hand, brother, I suggest you move it. Right. Now!"

Bob released Jade, staring her down. "If you love that girl, you do not want to do this."

"I'm taking my daughter because I love her and as for your mother, what did wisdom ever do for her? She's dead isn't she?" Jade gave a haunting laugh and shouted, "Haley Let's go!"

Jade continued to ignore Bob's pleas, dug into her expensive bag and pulled out her fancy checkbook, "Here, I know what will make it all better—this should cover your years invested in my child; and, cover the damage to your—um—residence."

She ripped out the check, handed it to her brother and screamed out. "Come on, Haley. It's time to go my dear."

Bob tore the check to shreds without even looking at it, tossing the pieces at Jade.

Jade rolled her eyes, "Whatever. Idiot..."

Haley walked over to them and stared at her uncle in tears, "Uncle Bob? You and Aunt Renee don't want me here anymore?"

Bob pulled his niece tightly against him, "No, Baby... That's not it at all. Of course, we want you. We love you. I'm very sorry. Jade is your mother. And, we have no legal rights."

Haley sobbed now, "Please, please. Don't let her take me."

Bob was crying, too, "Oh Sweetheart, it's gonna be okay. Just remember, trust in God. He has a plan. Remember and trust in everything we've taught you. You're a good girl, and we're so proud of you." Bob kissed Haley on the forehead.

"But, what about Jess?" Haley thought of Jess'. "But, Mother, Jess' grandma just died. I want to be with Jess."

Jade reached out and grabbed her hand leading her to the car.

Haley cried louder, "Mother wait! Jess needs me now more than ever. I can't leave her now. I won't!" Haley snatched her hand away from her mother. "I don't care what you say! I won't leave my only best friend."

Jade's skin blazed an angry red. Her eyes were inky black because Haley was disrespectful. Jade was embedded in the teachings of her father and never should a child talk back and express anything. Jade was bursting with hate for all that her brother had put into her daughter's upbringing, Christ, Christmas, Santa Claus and now disrespect.

Jade back hunched over a bit as she continued to penetrate her sayings to Haley. "Little girl... Who—Do—You—Think—You're—Talking to? As long as I am your mother, you will never talk to me in this manner again! I decide what will happen to you! And as long as you're alive you will only do as you're told. No whining, No debating, and No disrespect will ever exist between us again! My words are final. Do you understand?"

Miserable, frighten, and fretful, Haley hung her head, nodding 'yes.'

This behavior infuriated Jade even more. "Look at me when I'm talking to you. We are leaving. So, get your self in the car; and, do not make me repeat it!"

Jess heard the commotion, dropped her trash bag and ran from the back to the front. She saw Jade forcing Haley into the backseat, sliding in beside her and screamed, "What's happening? Where is Haley going?."

Jess inside knew what was happening. Eyeing Haley's river-of-tears as the chauffeur stood by the door allowing them to get in seemed to slow down. She realized she could be seeing her best friend for the last time. "Wait, Ms. Jade! Please!"

Jade looked as if Jess was making a fool of herself. She dipped to sit in her car, ordering the door shut and told her driver to go and the only thing she left behind was the dust from her vehicle as it sped out of sight.

Tears still streaming down her face, Jess watched after her friend being driven away in what felt like slow-motion. She turned to Haley's uncle, standing with tears rolling down his cheeks, too, staring at the car. "What just happened? Will Haley be back, Uncle Bob?"

"I don't know, Sweetheart. I just don't know. My sister is as stubborn and willful as she is mean." He looked at Jess for the first time. "Let's talk about you now. What do you want to do, Jess? Renee and I don't want you to be alone at a time like this, either. So, please know that you are more than welcome to stay with us. If you want to..."

Jess sniffled, "Thank you, Uncle Bob. I might take you up on that. But, first, I think I'd better go and check on Grandmau-ma's house. Let me go in and get my bags."

"Whatever you want Jess. I'll—wait— the storm destroyed our cars. How are we going to get you home?"

Neighbors and friends filled the woods and roads, picking up branches, car and house parts. A slender, older man in jeans, checkered shirt, a beat-up leather jacket and interesting pointy-toe shoes was walking by and extended his hand, "Hi, I'm Joe. Sorry, didn't mean to eavesdrop; but, if the little lady here needs a ride home, I'm happy to assist."

Bob extended his hand, "Thanks, Joe, I'm Bob, Jess' uncle. Haven't seen you around here before."

Joe laughed, "That's because my son & I just came by to help some friends. We've got an all-terrain vehicle that navigates the snow pretty well. In fact, Rufus is the one who'll be driving you, Miss Jess, if that's all right with you and your uncle. I'm going to hang back and assist with the clean-up."

"Thank you, Mr. Joe, I appreciate it. I'll be right back, Uncle Bob. I'm going to grab my stuff and find Aunt Renee."

Renee walked back out with Jess, clinging to Bob in tears. "Oh, Jess... I hope you really do come back. It's going to be empty in this house without Haley."

Just then, a tall, muscular young man with rusty brown hair, green eyes and the most extended nose Jess had ever seen. In fact, if it weren't from that nose he would be a total package. Bounded out of a red 4-wheeler, he introduced himself. "Jess? Hi!"

"Yes, hi... You must be Rufus. Your dad said you were coming. This is my Uncle Bob and my Aunt Renee." Jess tearfully kissed Bob and Renee good-bye, promising to be back soon.

A gentleman, Rufus opened the door to his truck for Jess. She was mesmerized by that nose, which was red as a beet. Maybe it was just allergies, she thought.

"Your father seemed really nice," Jess opened the conversation. "He seemed to be a person you'll love to have when you're in a sticky spot—very reliable."

Jess was surprised that she felt so comfortable around Rufus, a stranger she'd just met.

Rufus nodded, "He is. Good perception because he is very reliable."

Jess continued, "I live in those woods to the left. It's a little tricky with all these downed branches; but, I'll show you the way. My friend, Haley, once tried to visit me in a car and..."

Jess stopped in mid-sentence and burst into tears. The sadness of losing Grandmau-ma and the relocation of Haley was swallowing her, and she'd hoped she didn't lose her Grandmau-ma's house too. Worst, Jess feared she was losing track of her mission.

"Hey, Jess, please don't cry. I'm happy to drive you to see your friend whenever you'd like," Rufus offered comfortingly.

"That's so sweet, Rufus; but, I couldn't ask you to chauffeur me around."

"Why not? It's what I'm best at, and I love doing it!"

Jess now curious, there was no real need for chauffeurs in such a small town and was it her imagination or was Rufus' nose getting even redder? "Thanks for the offer, but right now, I just need to make sure my Grandma's house is okay and fix whatever needs fixing."

"Well, I can help with that, too. My father was—is—a carpenter and taught me everything he knows."

"Wow, thanks, Rufus. I'll take you up on that one 'cause I have no idea what I'm doing."

Arriving at the large, old house, Jess and Rufus walked the perimeter. It looked untouched by the storm.

"How is this possible?" Jess asked out loud. "Don't get me wrong. I'm happy the house is still intact; but, there was this weird blizzard-tornado combo thing last night."

Rufus scratched his head. "Well, that's kinda how tornadoes work. They touch down in some parts of an area, leaving the rest unscathed. Clearly, some things are just in God's hands. Sometimes there's an answer. Sometimes you just have to let it go and walk on faith."

Jess smiled, stunned that she was actually smiling. Her heart was still aching, but Rufus successfully took her mind off of her sorrow for a few minutes. She liked this guy! "So, tell me more about you and your family."

"Deal! If you let me chauffeur you around a little just for fun."

"Fun?" Jess squinted.

"Yes, fun... F-U-N, fun!" Rufus insisted.

Jess said, "Wow, I don't even know what that is anymore."

Rufus grinned, "Then, my mission is to absolutely change that. My dad always says fun reminds us to be joyful, which is, by the way, our natural state of being. And, sometimes, it helps us to see things more clearly. If you don't mind my saying so, Jess, you really need to see things clearly right now. Am I right?"

There was her smile again, nodding 'yes.'

"Then let's go have some fun." Rufus ran to his truck and opened the passenger side door for Jess. "Hop in!"

Before Rufus started the ignition, Jess reached for her seat belt.

"Oh, you won't be needing that," Rufus laughed. "Open the glove compartment and grab ahold of those straps."

Straps? Jess' mind questioned, wandering off into some dangerous places. What the hell is he going to do with belts?

Sensing her anxiety, Rufus reassured her, "Jess, I need you to trust your instincts about me because your perception of people is established within your personality. What are you feeling about me right now?"

Blunt much? Jess initially thought. Then she let the question sink in. When she did, a sense of calm washed over her. "I like you. I feel comfortable around you. I know it sounds crazy; but, even though we've just met, I feel like I've known you for ages. And, the strangest part is, I trust you—a perfect stranger. Who does that nowadays? Plus, my Uncle Bob didn't tackle you; so, he must have sensed that you weren't a psycho."

They both laughed.

Serious for a moment, Rufus responded, "Good. Trust your feelings, your instincts—that's very important. Pay attention to your perception of people—especially now. Now, close your eyes and hold onto the straps as tight as you can!"

Jess did. The next thing she knew, the wind was blowing through her hair, and she could smell damp earth. She slowly opened her eyes. She was flying! She was high in the sky, above the clouds on the back of a sturdy reindeer with a shiny red nose! Filled with mirth and excitement, Jess threw back her head and laughed. "It's you! Rufus, you're Rudolph! That's why your nose is so red." She hugged him. "Wow! This is so much FU-UU-UU-N!"

Rudolph dipped up and down and back up again like a roller coaster, tickling Jess' tummy. Even though it was morning in her Hemisphere, it was night in moments, elsewhere. Rudolph wanted her to experience how he, Santa and the other reindeer covered all the world in one night. Jess needed to know that for sure to succeed in her mission.

The necessity of her destiny was now unalterably seared into her heart, mind, and spirit. Jess closed her eyes again, savoring the feel of the wind on her face and hair. When she opened them, she was back in the truck with Rufus, not Rudolph.

Rufus took Jess' hand, "Still wanna know about my family?"

Jess enthusiastically nodded her head up and down.

"I am a blessed being." Rufus turned facing Jess. "I've been a dog twice, a man and a reindeer. I will continue to reincarnate until I have fulfilled every purpose and job assigned to me by the Creator. My first earthly father was a carpenter. I was his loyal companion, a big, slobbery, happy pooch. I watched his every movement, taking great pride in and happily completing every task given to him. I loved that quality in him, so it's what I strive to do with everything. My father was one of God's most faithful followers. God so loved him; He entrusted my father to raise the Son who would sacrifice his life for us all."

Again, Jess gasped out loud, "I get it! I totally understand! Your father was—is Joe—short for Joseph! If we are blessed by and entrusted with a special task by God, we can move between worlds and times but more than that—we can transition to different beings! Whoa, that's why glory belongs to Him; I understand now. Creation is so, well, infinite. And, until now, I could only see my teeny-tiny portion of it. Thank you so much, Rufus. This was awesome. You're awesome! Gotta go. I finally know what I have to do now."

Jess jumped out of the truck, then whipped her head around to ask, "Hey, how do I reach you when I need to catch that ride?"

Rufus laughed, "That's easy. Just sing my song, and I'll be there."

"Thank you, got it! See you later." Jess' didn't have to ask what this song was because it could only be one; plus, she could see everything plainly. She happily ran to her Grandmau-ma's house. Rufus was gone. She thought she'd test out the calling card and broke into song:

You know Dasher and Dancer, and
Prancer, and Vixen,
Comet, and Cupid, and
Donder and Blitzen.
But, do you recall
the most famous reindeer of all?
Jess, upbeat tone expanded as she continued the song.
Rudolph, the red-nosed reindeer
had a very shiny nose
and if you ever saw it
you would even say it glows.
All of the other reindeer
used to laugh and call him names.
They never let poor Rudolph
play in any reindeer games.
Then one foggy Christmas Eve,
Santa came to say,
"Rudolph with your nose so bright,
won't you guide my sleigh tonight?"
Then all the reindeer loved him
as they shouted out with glee,
"Rudolph the red-nosed reindeer,
you'll go down in history!

Before Jess belted out the last note, Rufus was knocking at the door. Laughing again, Jess threw open the door, "Wow, that was quick!"

"Not really, I was already here after the first mention of my name but had to hear you sing the entire song. You don't sound so bad. Do you need me?"

Jess laughed again and threw her arms around Rufus' neck, "No, this was just a test drive. It so-ooo works."

Rufus gently pulled away; and, took Jess' hands in his, "I have three 'never-dos' for you. First, doubting yourself should never be allowed. Two, never doubt the power of God. And, three, never challenge the power of magic. Okay?"

Jess smiled, "I understand, thank you. You're the best."

Rufus winked and left. Jess shut the door, realizing she was exhausted. She wanted to get a good night's rest so she could start fresh on her mission to save Christmas. Instead, she could only think of Haley. Wondering if she was okay. Jess missed her so much. Sometime during all of that thinking, Jess drifted off to sleep; and, she dreamed.

20

An Unlikely Home

Jade loved nothing more than collecting new things. She was almost excited to show Haley the luxury of the latest home. On the ride there, however, neither mother nor daughter spoke a word. Upon arrival, Haley noticed the pavement change and they were riding on rocks. A curved trail was leading them somewhere she was sure she'd didn't want to go. Haley looked up and out the car window. Wondering, was it possible that this piece of sky was darker than the darkest night she'd ever seen? Why are the clouds were thick like smoke? She shook with fear upon seeing the most significant trees she had ever seen—they looked to have thousands of eyes on them, watching her and piercing into her thoughts. The vehicle slowly got closer and ahead of her was what looked like a creepy, old castle—concrete and stone. 'Perfect, just perfect,' she thought. 'I'm on the verge of a new prison.'

"We're home" Jade announced dryly after the car came to a complete stop. Haley's misery was etched on her face. "Oh, enough with all the pouting and boo-hooing. I'm sick of it. You should be grateful. But, no worries. I'll whip you into a polished business mogul in no time. The first lesson is to stop hunching over."

Haley tried desperately to plead with her mother one more time. "Jade Spinous, this is your dream, not mine. I never said I wanted to be a business lady! I don't want your stores! I don't want your doomed castle or your evil ways! I don't want it! I don't need it! Please take me back home. Please!"

How Jade hated her ugly—yet accurate—middle name. She angrily thought, 'Bob has used it before. Now, my child is using it! Thorny, difficult, yes I am! But no one is allowed to call me that! Especially, not my child!'

Yes, she was undoubtedly more thorn than rose but didn't want to be reminded of it. She angered, and the rage produced a hard slap over Haley's face.

Jade was breathing heavily then said, "You, you will never call me by that name again, ever! Do you understand?"

While still holding on to the side of her face, in silent tears. Jess mustered the ability to speak, "Yes, Ma'am." Jade chilled Haley to the bone, "Much better," Jade snapped. "If we are to get along, Haley, we must have an understanding and remember, you are mine to do with as I please. I will not tolerate disrespect, talking back or anything else that pisses me off. I speak; you obey or suffer the consequences. And, you will address me as Madame. Are we clear?"

Terrified, Haley held her tears as best she could, "Yes, Madame."

"Here, use my handkerchief and wipe those tears dry. It's time we go inside."

Haley reached for the door.

"Wait!" Jade scorned. "I see, I absolutely have my work cut out for me. We don't open our doors, Dear. The chauffeur does that. I signal, and he opens. Don't worry; you'll eventually get how things work."

The chauffeur came around the car and opened the car door. Haley hadn't noticed before how much he looked like a werewolf—super hairy and super scary.

"Right this way, Mademoiselle," hairy guy gestured.

The castle reminded Haley of a death walk. She observed the enormous, menacing stone and metal statues populated the cold, concrete entrance: lots of half animal, half human monstrosities—like the bird-man creature with a rolled up document in its mandible. A ginormous, unworldly globe like no earth Haley had ever seen, propped atop the head of a gargoyle, made her jump back. These would scare any unwanted visitors off, Haley thought: to top off its menacing look, the castle's giant, blood-red double doors featured scary lion's-head knockers with the handles sprouting through the flaring, angry nostrils. 'No warm and fuzzy vibes here...' Haley thought. Haley wondered what it all meant, the image stuck, and soon fear followed. She remembered Jess' advice to remain strong. She turns from looking at the sculptures and waited to enter the castle home.

A butler straight out a bad dream—opened the castle's massive doors for Haley and Jade. He was unnaturally tall with strong jaw lines, sharp pointy teeth, and really long fingernails. "Welcome back, Madame," he bowed to Jade. Turning to Haley, he politely nodded his head, "Welcome, Mademoiselle."

Haley didn't like the look of her mother's workers but continued walking in slowly. On the first floor, the stunning contrast of the interior of the castle to its exterior took Haley off guard. It was luxurious and beautifully appointed. Haley stared from the gleaming burgundy and white marble floors in the massive vestibule to the regal, split, polished mahogany staircase. At the rear-behind, the considerable split staircase—were wide hallways with large archway entrances leading left and right.

Her mouth must have been hanging open because her mother popped her gently under the chin with her fingers, tipped with pointy, red nails.

Haley's thin build would never suggest that she had always had a voracious appetite. She didn't even show the slightest hint of a pot belly. Haley chose her words carefully, "Madame, may I see the kitchen?"

Jade's mouth turned up into a semblance of a smile, "Now, there's the child I know. Believe it or not, Haley, you're my baby, and I love you. So, I made sure my servants stocked the kitchen with everything you could possibly want. My cook can whip up your favorite dish within moments."

Before heading to the kitchen with Haley, Jade turned to the butler, "Please take my daughter's things; and, make sure her room is ready while I show her around."

They'd left Uncle Bob and Aunt Renee's in such a hurry, Haley didn't have the chance to bring very much with her. Jade would have thrown everything out anyway. She held particular standards, which she was sure Bob and Renee never instilled in Haley.

Haley's eyes darted everywhere as she followed Jade to the kitchen— shimmering wallpaper, giant archways, and doors, elaborately decorated statues that sent a chill up Haley's spine. "Now, that's strange," she noted.

"What's that, Dear?" Jade blushed admiring her child's intellect.

"Well, all of the doors and entryways look as though they were built for giants. But, the kitchen door seems to be normal sized."

"Excellent observation," her mother praised. "When these kinds of structures, oversized doors were de rigueur."

Jade noticed an expression of confusion on her child's face and rephrased her wording for de rigueur. "It was the way of fashion and meant to express you have entered a prestigious home," Jade observed Haley's expression and knew she understood and agreed. Jade silently realized Haley's education wasn't up to part, but she would fix that too, but she continued to explain. "Eventually the cooks and servers found the heavy doors prohibitive to doing their job. So, the kitchen doors were altered to make allowances for frequent entrances and exits with arms filled with food and dishes. Also, that's why they the door to the kitchen are swinging doors."

Jade hooked her arm through Haley's, "This is nice, hmmm? I love your inquisitive mind. Bonding together is what I wanted for us. The chance to teach my only child everything I know; so, that one day I can bequeath my entire legacy and empire to you."

Seeing Jade appearance, which was genuinely happy helped Haley to relax a little. She had to admit being with her mother made her happy too, and she thought, 'Maybe I was wrong about my mother. She just wants a relationship with me.'

Haley sighed, "I think I'm beginning to understand." Haley looked her mother in the eyes with sincerity. "Sorry I've acted like such a brat. All of this just came so suddenly, and I wasn't prepared. And, I really miss Jess. We've never been away from each other more than a couple of days. But, may I call you 'Mother' instead of Madame? That's what your staff calls you. And, as you said, I am your daughter."

Jade smiled, "I'd like that. And, yes, I'm sorry, too. I know how overbearing I can be when I want something. You'll learn that, too. Never take 'no' for an answer. Sweetheart, I'm so sorry for the slap. I'll try never to do that again. Now, let's check out the kitchen."

Like everything else in the castle, the kitchen was over-the-top. It was industrial-sized with white marble floors featuring black diamond-shaped inlays. There were not one—but, four—restaurant—worthy refrigerators, stoves, and ovens. Haley gravitated to the most extensive fridge, her mouth practically watering when she opened it. Immediately, she reached for ice cream and a soda to make a float.

"I was hoping you might eat actual food first, before the treats."

"But, you said I could have anything I wanted in here, didn't you?" Haley countered.

The pointy-tooth, crazy-tall butler in the formal, black and white uniform walked into the kitchen, "Madame, sorry to interrupt. But, the staff is waiting in the library to meet Mademoiselle."

"Thank you. We'll be there momentarily." Jade then cocked an eyebrow, grimacing as she watched her daughter practically inhale the ice cream soda. Chuckling at Haley's white ice-cream mustache, "I think you've had quite enough, Haley. Come along. Besides, I have so much to tell you, and we must get to it if I am to get it all in before your bedtime. However, it's important that you know in this house, we adhere to a schedule—everyday."

Haley followed her mother through what seemed like miles of hallways—walls field with unusual paintings which spooked Haley out a bit. She took a deep breath and told herself, 'I'm with my mother—nothing to be afraid of.' The enormous, circular library was a marvel. Books filled shelves from wall-to-wall and floor-to-ceiling. Haley had never seen this many books. She began wondering about how much money and power her mother had. The staff of two women and three men formed a receiving line, at attention, in the middle of the room—these were personally introduced. Lesser staff members stood in the back of them.

'Man, they're a sour-looking bunch,' Haley observed—to herself.

One of the women, the only one who seemed even remotely welcoming, introduced herself first. She appeared to be mid-30ish with bright blue eye and a single, blond braid that nearly touched the floor.

"Bonjour, Mademoiselle... I'm Ms. Abarim, your in-home tutor, and governess. I look forward to providing you with the finest education a young woman your age could have. We begin first thing tomorrow morning."

Haley whipped around to Jade to object, "Mother, really? A tutor? I thought I was finishing my senior year at an actual high school, with other kids my age! And, why would I need a governess? I'll be 18 on my next birthday!"

Jade slipped an arm around Haley's shoulder, "An ordinary, pedestrian high school for my daughter? You will be provided with knowledge that no school could ever teach. And, as I've told you, 'My house—My child—My rules.'"

Haley had learned that disagreeing with her mother on anything was a losing battle. She sighed with exasperation, "Fine."

The next staff member to step forward was a gorgeous young man with glossy, black hair and reddish, bronzed skin, Jack.

"Welcome, Mademoiselle." He bowed. "I'm Jack. I run the stables and will be your riding instructor."

"Riding? As in horses?" Haley choked placing one hand on her throat. "Why do I have to ride a horse? What's wrong with me driving my truck?"

"Of course, Darling," her mother responded, curtly. "Every well-bred young woman is a skilled equestrian. Riding builds character and strength—qualities you must possess."

Haley eyeballed the handsome instructor and mused that learning to ride might even turn out to be fun. "OK, but, when do we go and pick up my truck?"

Jade laughed out loud, "Baby, that poor excuse of a vehicle has already been hauled off to a scrap yard to be sold for parts. You're with Mother now. And, my daughter is going to ride around in only the best! Of course, if you must drive, it would be for fun. Now, please, without another fight, can we get through this?"

Haley looked again at Jack. His long black hair, red skin and built was pleasant to her eyes. 'Yes, this Native is gorgeous and strong.' She thought to self and secretly couldn't wait for riding lessons. Haley once again nodded in agreement and said, "Yes, Mother."

The creepy butler stepped forward, "We haven't yet formally been introduced, Mademoiselle. I am Chance Zeus, at your service. You need never to open any doors that lead outside the castle. I insist—that's my job."

Chills ran down Haley's spine when Chance spoke—looking at those sharp teeth again with such a wicked smile. Haley quickly turned her attention to the next inductee.

A stocky, unattractive woman with large, rough hands stepped forward, "I am Enyo. But, everyone calls me Ms. Cook, because the kitchen is my domain. I can whip up whatever is your pleasure, Mademoiselle."

Haley thought of her love for food and thought, yes, she will be useful. "A pleasure to meet you."

Then it was the hairy chauffeur's turn, "I'm Chris Norm." He took a bow. "I'm your faithful driver. I am honored to take you wherever you need to go, with Madame's permission, of course."

More casual introductions of cooks, housekeepers, groundskeepers, dance teachers, music instructors and personal assistants followed.

On their way to Haley's quarters, it occurred to her that she hadn't seen her mother's husband. "So, Mother, where is Husband? Haven't seen him all day. Is he still pissed that I missed the ceremony?"

Jade's eyes darkened and narrowed, "Two more important lessons, young Lady. Language and respect. 'Pissed' is an unacceptable term.

And, my husband is currently overseeing development of our overseas interests. You likely may not see him at all."

Haley's new bedroom was a suite. Everything in the sitting area was cream-colored. Both the sitting area and her spacious bedroom featured ornate, and marble fireplaces with mantles that had carved designs in its wood. The king-sized bed was canopied in a dark, smoky, mauve tulle. Everything was beautiful. The expensive designer clothes and accessories in her walk-in closet and drawers were much too formal for Haley's taste; but, they were pretty.

After a gourmet meal with just her and her mother at the extravagant, massive mahogany table that seated 24, Haley settled into the impossibly comfortable bed. She was reluctantly getting acclimated to her new life. But, when she finally fell asleep, she dreamed of Jess.

21

Understanding It All

At Grandmau-ma's house waking up alone ripped away the protective scab that was forming over Jess' pain. This morning, there was none of her grandmother's sweet humming, no aroma of freshly brewed coffee wafting from the kitchen or bacon frying on the stove. The quiet was almost unbearable.

Thoughts of her loss and loneliness were blessedly pushed into a smaller compartment of her mind when she remembered her destiny and the mission at hand.

Re-charged, Jess hopped out of bed, slid her booties onto her feet, and ran into the bathroom, zipping through her morning routine. Cold cereal and juice were as much as Jess could handle this morning.

'First things first...' she thought. 'The honor of safeguarding the second globe was given to her distant cousin, Judas, by her Uncle Andrew hundreds of earth years ago. If the past few days had taught her anything—she now knew that everything was possible, that the separation of time doesn't necessarily exist and that nothing is as it seems. But, where to begin?' She pondered. 'At the beginning, Grandmau-ma had me to go into her most sacred and secret place.' Jess answered herself, heading immediately for the attic. 'I must listen to my instincts.' She said aloud.

At least it was daytime now, with a little light coming through the attic window. With the help of the naked overhead bulb, she spotted items she hadn't seen before. Her eyes landed on a box with old pictures and a crate of old books. Jess knelt in front of them, coughing from all the dust flying around. Not knowing what she was looking for, she unhooked and clutched the mini-book charm hanging around her neck, "Okay, so what do I do now?" The book resumed its original size and glowed. The message searing onto the new page read:

> *Jessica, there are three layers of protection covering your cousin's whereabouts. All of the layers start with the first and the last, the beginning and the end, the Alpha and the Omega. Layer one is your bloodline. Layer two is this book when teamed with the Codex Bible. The third layer is the penetration into the gates of hell. There are two keys to those gates. Both are required to gain entry.*

After reading the instructions, Jess continued to dig through the old boxes. She found the massive Codex Bible. Throughout its pages were handwritten notes from Grandmau-ma. She read the first:

> *'My Darling Jess, if you are reading this now, you are on your sacred mission to save Christmas. The highlighted bible passages and my notes will guide you along the way. Study and remember the words. Safeguard this old bible, as it is the only link to God's chosen people; and, is critical for their return and awakening.'*

Jess carried the large Codex Bible down the ladder with her and gingerly placed it on a table in the sitting room. The Book-of-Knowledge charm around her neck began to glow again. Jess opened it again and read as its writings appeared before her:

*Remember, Jess, the physical world's measurements of time and space do
not exist elsewhere. Do not be caught-up in times and places. There are
many worlds and many lands; none are the same. Time is not what you
have known it to be in other worlds. In fact, there is no way to measure
time, and in most worlds, it doesn't exist. In the physical world, you must
pay attention to time. Managing time will become apparent to you later,
but for now, ponder quickly—all will be clear with the knowledge of the
Codex.*

Jess opened the Codex's ancient, yellowed pages carefully and with one
hand, she held onto the globe and asked for clarity, understanding,
and memory. Suddenly she could read its ancient, Greek text magically
translated into words she could understand. Jess, understood although
the bible read the same way—Christ would reveal to each one its meaning for them particularly. The holy book would hold different, specific
messages for her and in her heart, she knew it was from God Himself.
Her heart jumped at the thought, 'A message from the Creator of all,
just for me.' It Read:

*In the midst of the candlesticks, one like the Son of man, clothed in a robe
reaching to the feet and girded about the breasts with a golden girdle; but his
head and his hair were white as white wool, like snow. And, his eyes were as
a flame of fire and his feet were like burnished brass, as if they burned in a
furnace, and his voice as the sound of many waters. And, when I had seen
him, I fell at his feet as dead; and he laid his right hand upon me, saying,
'Fear not. I am the First and the Last.'*

Jess sank into Grandmau-ma's chair, pondering and processing the
scripture she had just read. She remembered how she had walked to
Christ first, rather than Santa, in her vision. The message couldn't have
been transparent. Keeping Him first, before anyone and anything, is
the only way to win the day, to succeed in her mission. Jess was hungry
for more so she continued to read:

And that lives, and I was dead, and behold, I am living from age to age, and have the Keys-of-Death and Hades.

Jess stopped and started thinking aloud and said, "Christ is the first, the last from age to age. He also must be the way to the third place I must go. The book said that I must travel through the gates of death and Christ holds the keys to that place; one Key-of-Death and the other Key-of-Hades."

Jess, continues to ponder and read more:

To the angel of the church in Ephesus write: 'These things says he that holds the seven stars in his right hand that walks in the midst of the seven golden candlesticks. I know thy works, and thy labor, and thy patience, and that thou canst not endure evil men, and hast tried those that say that they are apostles and are not, and hast found them liars, and thou hast patience and hast endured because of my name, and hast not fainted. But I have against thee that thou hast left thy first love.'

The last passage was troubling. Jess thought, 'Who is it that loved Christ first, but turned evil? Am I to encounter a traitor?' And, yes, Jess fully understood Christ to be speaking of her saying she has to endure because of his name—forcing her to be determined and steadfast with whatever lay before her in the name of Christ. Jess read more for she was in need for more insight:

Therefore take up the whole Armor-of-God that you may be able to withstand in the evil day, and having done all, to stand. Stand therefore, having Girded your waist with Truth, having put on the Breastplate-of-Righteousness, and having Shod your Feet with the preparation of the gospel of Peace; above all, taking the Shield-of-faith with which you will be able to quench all the fiery darts of the wicked one. And take the Helmet-of-Salvation, and the Sword-of-the-Spirit, which is the word of God; with all prayer and supplication in the spirit, being watchful to this end with all perseverance and supplication for all the saints.

Jess wanted more, but the words mystically reverted to ancient Greek script. A loud crack of thunder startled Jess out of her chair and her thoughts.

She had been warned about time in the physical world and knew that was a sign to move alone. Jess picked up the old picture album. Carefully flipping through its fragile pages, recognizing no one, Jess finally landed on a shot of Uncle Andrew with a handsome 20-something man. The globe charm around the young man's neck was glowing—the same as hers. 'This must be my cousin, Judas!' She'd thought excitedly. The next page brought even more questions. Judas was standing in an old-timey, apostle-like robe.

Jess wondered out loud. "Hmm, so if Grandmau-ma and Uncle Andrew met every Christmas by touching their respective globes... I'm her apprentice, and Judas was Uncle Andrew's..., and why didn't I run into him instead of Jose when I touched the globe?" Then it hit her with crystal clear clarity, "Oh my God! My cousin Judas somehow betrayed Christ and turned evil. He was sent to Hades and took the globe with him! His betrayal must be why I have to go through the gates of Death and Hades to retrieve the second globe!"

The Book-of-Knowledge immediately emanated with light. She read:

> *Jess, there exist seven candlesticks in six Holy Places throughout your physical world. The seventh Holy Place has special instructions that you will receive later. Your quest begins with the largest of the Holy Places. Look to the skies for seven blessed stars that will illuminate to reassure that you are on track and guiding you to the remaining Seven Wonders of the World. Each Star is activated and brightens due to each candle's positioning. You will collect one candle per location, except the final Holy Place. There, you will find two. Each candle represents a battle you must win, and you must collect all seven. In all worlds, physical, spiritual, mystical and magical and within every realms—even those without time and space—seven is the number of completion, perfection and all things Holy to the Creator.*
>
> *Understanding the different worlds are essential for you to be free of errors. You must know which worlds best benefit you throughout your journey. Because time only exists in the physical world, the battles must commence on the physical plane, then, through Holy waves—doors open*

from the physical world, allowing your fight to continue to the Sacred Holy Places. Once on Scared Holy grounds—these doors are to connect you to seven different realms in different worlds.

The most significant evil in this battle is Nefari. She stole and continued to hold on to the Key-of-Death. It gives her power to cheat death, as she has through the ages. That key is necessary for the completion of your holy mission, and you must retrieve that key. Don't forget her weakness lies in the magical world and the ability to lose immortality lies on entering through the physical to the magical world. Immortality only exists in the physical realm because time exists in that world alone. As long as the evil ones can stay in the physical world, they can live without end. Always remember that it is in the physical world where evil is most potent and immortal. Nefari and her kind are weakened in the magical and spiritual realms—this is where you will defeat them.

With every individual victory, you will use the candle to gain the Armor of God. There are six pieces of this Armor, and it is vital for you to battle Nefari. With the seventh candle at the seventh Holy Place, (not in the physical world) your engagement with Nefari will begin. Once you defeat her and take possession of the Key-of-Death, Christ's final gift to you will be bestowed to ensure victory, the Key-of-Hades.

Your trusted friend, Rufus, will lead you to the entrance of the very gate of Hades. Use both keys to gain entry. Hades is where your final battle will present itself. And, Hades is where many other unrepentant "lump-of-coal" children, who grew into heinous adults, await Nefari to join them in eternal torment.

Each gift is given to you as a vital tool for victory, Jess. As has commenced, all knowledge and power of each will continue to be revealed. Know them by heart: the complete Suit of Armor, the Globe, the Book-of-Knowledge, the Codex, the Keys-of-Death and Hades, the seven Candle Sticks and the seven stars. Hades is where you will find the second globe. Keep in mind—the power of having one globe can only take you to the physical world and the magical world. It cannot cross specific worlds, realms, and lands such as the North Pole. However, with both globes, you can freely travel between all worlds, lands, and realms, except the spiritual worlds.

God alone holds the key to those. Remember, you are the Apprentice, and
only, an Apprentice can take the second globe from the other Apprentice.
Upon possession of the second globe, the two keys will be returned to
the Christ. Do not give in to distraction. Stay the course and go with God.

Jess was infused with and empowered by the knowledge, information, and power from the Book-of-Knowledge and the Codex Bible. Thankful for the globe; she'd retain it all. She reduced them to their tiny state to wear as inconspicuous charms on her necklace.

Out of nowhere, she remembered how much she missed Haley, wondering how her best friend was doing. Jess shook her head as if to dismiss such thoughts and feelings, knowing that absolute obedience was the only option in this journey.

22

A Plan

The phone in Grandmau-ma's house rang. Jess so hoped it was, Haley. It wasn't—instead, it was Haley's loving Uncle Bob. Jess heard the tension in his voice immediately.

"What's going on, Uncle Bob? Is it Haley? Is something wrong?"

Bob sighed deeply, then stuttered, "It's... It's more than Haley. You had better come over. You need to see for yourself."

"I'm on my way." Jess slammed the phone onto its hook, ran out the door, gazed at her grandmau-ma old beat-up truck and thought of the time consumed just to get it started. She remembered what Jose said about personal gain; but, this sounded like an emergency. She held the globe charm, with faith, thinking of Uncle Bob. In the blink of an eye, she was on his front porch, which had already been repaired from that hellish storm, and rang the bell, marveling that it worked.

Bob opened the door with a grim expression on his face, and startled that Jess was there so quickly,

"Jess? How did you get here so fast? We literally—just hung up a minute ago." Bob rubbed his forehead, "Come on in."

His panic alarmed Jess, "Omigod, Uncle Bob. What's going on?"

Bob shook his head, "Jess, it's some really weird stuff going on, and my spirit said to ask you about some of these things. I am at a loss for words."

Jess sat on the sofa next to Uncle Bob, "I hope I can help. First, tell me what's wrong."

Bob nervously stood facing Jess, "It's Renee. She's missing."

Jess jumped up, "What do you mean—missing?"

"She's been gone for days. There's no way she would leave the house without letting me know. And, sure as hell for not this long."

They both sat back down, with heavy hearts and minds racing about possibilities. Jess listened intensely, knowing something of had happened.

"I know something terrible happened to her because I get the same recurring nightmares every night in the few moment of rest. I can't eat, I can't sleep from these dreams. The agony has me hearing and seeing things, not just in my dreams, but while I am awake! All day, I suffer from this."

"Uncle Bob tell me about these dreams." Jess listened carefully.

"Renee is being tortured and tormented somewhere dark and horrible. And, God forgive me, but somehow Haley is playing a part in Renee's suffering. I know that's not possible; Right? But, that's not all... As I continue to pray—the Lord whispers loud and clear, 'Call Jess.' Can you tell me why? Am I going mad or do you know more than you let on? Or maybe I should call the authorities? But for a missing wife? Folks would ask what did I do for her to leave. Jess, I love my wife. I miss her."

Seeing Uncle Bob cry caused Jess heart to moan in sympathy. She had to be careful not to give him the information he apparently couldn't handle. Jess, undressed this and knew that this had something to do with her mission and wanted answers. But first, she had to take care of poor Uncle Bob.

Jess held his hand and said, "Uncle Bob, I'm we must keep praying for Renee safety, but you must rest. We need you strong when she returns."

"But, I'm worried sick. How can I rest? I pray to God that she's alive and unharmed." Bob held his head low. He was exhausted.

"You need some sleep; I'll stay with you until you sleep. Then, I'll start a search."

Jess, grabbed his arm and aided him to his bedroom, asked her uncle to lay down, and covered him with a cozy blanket.

Jess sat in the chair across from him and said, "You rest, while I pray for us all."

When Bob fitfully closed his eyes, Jess clasped her globe charm and asked for restful, peaceful sleep with beautiful dreams. Uncle Bob was out like a light under the Creators protection.

Jess thanked God and left the bedroom, shutting the door carefully behind her. She sat out on the front porch, took off the Book-of-Knowledge charm, and asked for insight into what she had just been told.

The book resumed its form and glowed. Jess could hear the magical, invisible quill scratching its words onto the page. She opened and read:

> Jess, there are more than Judas who turn their backs on God to serve instead, the Creator's enemy. These monstrous individuals may take on different personas in different worlds; however, they still hold on to some aspects of the original form that God created. Your Uncle Bob's visions are revelations to what will happen. God has given him the insights to allow you to know who and what Jade and Haley's precise form is. In this physical world, you know them as Jade and Haley, but Jade is Nefari and Haley is her offspring. Nefari uses her empire of toy stores throughout the physical world to poison children's minds and hearts against Christ, Christmas, and Santa. How? The tale of these stores are to make the children believe that parents are the ones who buy the gifts so, there is no Santa Claus. If parents are acting like Santa Claus, why call on the real Santa? Worst, why be good? No more Naughty or Nice book. The children have believed, no matter what, good or bad, they will get gifts for Christmas from their parents. Jade/Nefari owns every store in this physical world. In your journey, you must find a way to bring back the children's faith in Santa Claus.
>
> Come Haley's eighteenth birthday; she will no longer exist as the girl you knew. As is her mother's reality, no shred of good can reside in her heart, only evil.

You must defeat both to come out victoriously. Do not succumb to distractions or veiled deceptions. Bob will sleep until that time when he becomes an essential part of your mission.

Jess was crushed by the book's message; but, she knew she had to stay strong and focused. She waved her hand to reduce it to a charm. She held the globe charm, thought home, and was back in Grandmau-ma's front room. She sat with a heavy heart as the amulet from the Book-of-Knowledge glowed. When Jess touched it—a complete reminder of all gained information flooded her brainwaves, and she was empowered.

Jess placed her quilt and papers from Grandmau-ma into her back-pack, then slipped on the sweater. It was time to sing for Rufus.

As he'd promised, Rufus was knocking at her front door, his nose still shining red, "Hey there, Jess." Rufus' nose lit up as he continued. "Where would you like to go?"

Jess hugged her friend, laughing, "That nose of yours always makes me feel so happy. How about the North Pole?"

Rufus raised an eyebrow, "The North Pole? Why would you want to go there?"

Jess anxiously explained, "Rufus, I have a plan to start the process of braking Nefari's evil spell on the children in this physical world."

"Woe, Jess, help me get caught up. 'A spell on the children?' How? Why?"

Jess saw Rufus as a partner in her mission. She somehow knew it was important to tell him the details of what she'd learned. "I learned that Nefari is using her toy stores to cause the children stop believing in Santa Claus. She's able to make them think that their parents buy the gift and so if the parents are buying the gift, why be good? Why need Santa? I need Santa to grant me a wish that involves the globe."

Rufus' nose shined brighter, as he said, "Tell me more on the way. I see that you have the sweater and blanket your Grandmau-ma made for you."

"Yes, I do. Isn't the craft wonderful!" Jess smiled thinking of her dear grandma.

"It looks great, but more, it should keep you warm because travels through worlds are very cold."

Jess replied, resolute. "I can hardly wait to talk with Santa." She wrapped her blanket around her. "He and I need to have a heart-to-heart."

"You got it! Sing the song." Rufus smirked.

Before she knew it, the man became the reindeer, and they were off! But, this trip was magical, not physical, flying through a crystalline mist. Rudolph's hooves landed with a thump on the whitest, and most glistening snow Jess had ever seen. The reindeer looked into Jess' eyes and nodded in the direction of a single Christmas tree not too far away. Jess understood. Touching the tree opened a whole new world—a small world. Jess, shrank just as the charms on her necklace. Although small, everything appeared huge at Santa's place. Everything that was unseen was now clear and glorious. The North Pole and Santa's Village with stables for the reindeer, tiny candy houses, Santa's house and workshop.

Ralph, whom Jess had met during that horrific storm, was immediately at Jess' side, winking, "Hey there, Kiddo. Remember me? Right, this way. Santa has been expecting you."

Jess smiled at Ralph, her face lighting up like a Christmas tree, practically bursting with joy and wonder. It was just as she had imagined and read about, maybe better! Everything around her further strengthened Jess' resolve, confidence, and determination for victory.

"HO, HO, HO! Welcome, dear Jessica," Santa laughed as he opened the door to his home, pulling Jess into a loving bear hug. He was just as she expected—round, jolly, larger-than-life and exuding love, kindness, and joy.

"It is so wonderful to meet you, Santa finally. But, I'm here because I need your help."

Santa smiled knowingly. "And, I thank God and Christ for sending you here, my dear. We have all been increasingly concerned about the waning belief in all things Christmas. Tell me exactly what you need."

Jess' said, "My idea is for your elves to make millions of child-size snow globes, infuse each with a bit of Christmas magic and power from my globe, then distribute the globes to all of Nefari's toy stores by the next Christmas Eve. When the children shake, look inside the globe and believe—they will see you in the North Pole. The magic inside each globe would break Nefari's spell and children would believe again."

"Splendid plan, Jessica. You are showing why you are the Apprentice. Let's see your snow globe. I'll take it to the workshop, mix its power with Christmas magic and give it right back to you; because you are going to need it. We will have the toy globes ready when you need them," Santa chuckled. "I have every confidence in you."

While Santa worked with the globe, Ralph happily took Jess on a tour of the entire workshop—unbelievable in its endlessness. Everyone was done at the same time. Jess hugged both Santa and Ralph, reduced her globe to charm and called for Rudolph.

"Home?" he asked?

"Yes, back to the physical world," Jess answered solemnly, fully appreciating, now more than ever, how imperative it was that her destiny and mission be fulfilled.

Jess assured Rudolph. "I must fill you in on everything and await my next sign."

Rudolph agreed with a nod and off they were.

— —

Once back in the physical world's atmosphere, an evil presence was taking over the sky. Jess knew filling Rufus in on her knowledge was imperative for his survival if he was going to take her to these dangerous places.

They landed and entered Grandmau-ma's home again. Rufus was helping himself to some hot cocoa when Jess Book charm lit up. She opened, and it wrote:

> *Jess, Rufus knows which Holy places that have the candlesticks you are to look for because he and Santa visited these holy places every year. It's vital that you watch for each star. Remember, just as the North Star that was used to glow over Christ when he was born in the physical world—It will*

shine for you now. Fear not, of any beast or man that comes against you.
For when thy Lord be with you—Who can be against you and survive?
Have Rufus to touch your globe. It will impart all needed knowledge to
him. Time is limited. You have none to explain these things to him. Hurry!

Jess called Rufus into the front room with urgency. "Rufus touch my Globe charm."

He did, and a rush of information caused his body to freeze for a few moments.

"I think we need to go." Rufus acted a bit in a daze. The storm outside howled louder, and it was clear that evil was behind it. "Sing the song, Jess. It's time to get to the first Holy Place."

Jess, sang and again—they were off.

23

The Test

All-the-while, Jess prepared and searched for the largest Holy Place; Haley was falling deeper under her mother's spell, seduced by the wealth and the power that Nefari flaunted and dangled in her face.

Jade took pride in the increasing evidence of her influence over Haley as yet another accomplishment, another rung on her ladder to eternal and universal power. Genuine mother's love for her child was never part of the equation. In Jade/Nefari's estimation, love only made humans weak.

While Haley—still but a mere human for the time being—slept; Jade spent her nights hidden away in the castle's lowest levels. Conjure up spirits, strengthening her dark magic and feeding her evil became a must for the war she was preparing to wage against that insipid, so-called Apprentice, to destroy Christ, Christmas, and Santa once and for all.

Late one morning, Jade decided to put the awakening level of evil she was so carefully cultivating inside of Haley to a test.

Haley strode into the castle from her riding lesson, whip in hand, looking particularly satisfied with herself as she entered through the side door, into the mudroom of the castle.

Her mother noticed the imperious attitude immediately, "Do tell."

"I've finally conquered the beast, mother. I think my instructor would concur that not only have I quickly developed into a superior equestrian; I ride without attachment and sentiment. The horse is actually afraid of me," Haley laughed cruelly.

Jade smiled devilish. Thinking how her plan was working faster than she'd thought it would. The lessons weren't to build a positive character, but on the contrary, it was to create a burier that uncovered Haley's feel of a supreme being. By dominating the animal, kicking and pulling at every turn, it became easier for Haley to think of the animal as inferior and not a pet.

Jade circled her daughter in measured admiration, "I see. Walk with me." Jade placed her arm around Haley. "Your tutor informs me that you are surpassing all expectations of excellence in your studies. Congratulations, my dear... It would seem you are truly your mother's child. This kind of progress deserves a reward."

"What kind of reward," Haley's eyes grew big in anticipation.

"I'm thinking a mother-daughter trip. Six days! Your bags are being packed as we speak."

"A vacation! A change of scenery would be awesome! Thanks, Mother. I'm just going to take a quick shower and change."

Haley uncharacteristically kissed her mother on the cheek and ran toward the staircase to her suite. She called over her shoulder, "Thanks again, Mother! Love you."

Jade feigned clearing her throat, "Yes, love you too, dear. Please remember to walk, not run. You are a proper young woman now. The world will wait for you."

Jade turned to pour herself a brandy from the cut crystal decanter, murmuring, "And, the world will bow to your will and serve you." She swallowed the entirety of the burning liquid without a single flinch.

Jade's ever-faithful, hairy, lapdog chauffeur, pulled the black, stretch limo through a mile-long driveway to the front of a sprawling, luxury hotel. Uniformed staff members nearly stumbled over themselves to get to the limo first. Nearly, but not quite, because Madame loathed clumsiness. Several bellhops unloaded the luggage from the trunk. Jade's werewolf-looking chauffeur opened the vehicle doors for Jade and Haley.

The vehicles drove them to a building that Jade owned. It was large, and unlike any place, Haley had ever seen, and her mouth was open wide again.

Jade chuckled and said, "Haley, you mouth dear." She then placed her arm around her daughter, and they walked towards the welcoming counter.

Before their feet hit the pavement, they were met by an eager-but-impeccably capable, uniformed woman with her hair pulled into a tight bun, white gloves, and puppy-dog brown eyes. "Good Afternoon! Welcome to the Spinous Hotel and Resort. How may I be of service?"

"I'm Madame Spinous, the owner, and your employer," Jade responded curtly. "You can begin by taking our bags to the Empress suite."

"Yes, of course... Madame. Right away." The servant kept her eyes on the ground, and her head tucked in fear.

Even though it was the middle of a bleak winter, somehow the Spinous Hotel and its grounds were enclosed in a tropically warm enclave with no visible boundaries, except for the dramatic shift from stark to lush vegetation. It was filled with obviously wealthy guests—checking in, checking out, playing golf or tennis, lounging in one of the several elaborate pools with floating bar service or laughing, eating and drinking at one of the establishment's choices of best restaurants, boasting world-class chefs.

After Jade and Haley freshened up in their opulent suite, Jade chose the hotel's most expensive restaurant for dinner. Only the best for her spawn.

There was so much deliciousness to choose from, Haley didn't know where to begin, sitting with her elbows propped atop the elaborate, formally set table; opposite her mother.

"You will remove your elbows now," Jade ordered.

Haley compiled. Even though all of this almost felt as intimidating as her mother, Haley couldn't help but think; I could get used to this.

"Indeed," Jade responded, as though she could read Haley's mind. "This hotel and resort are but one in a chain of dozens around the world. Like it?"

"What's not to like, Mother? This place is like any in the world and ahead of time!"

Jade intertwined all fingers together and peered into Haley's eyes, "This is all yours as well, Haley. Just like the toy stores. I need for you to understand the power you hold fully."

Haley pondered that as an army of servers catered to hers and her mother's every need or want. She liked the way it felt. Power. Haley realized, for the first time, that there was much more to enjoy in life than partying, hanging out, a best friend or playing. She told herself she had no more time for such foolish, childish ways. She was an heiress; and, was beginning to feel the part.

Haley, gave a sinister smile and said, "Yes, Mother. I'll be ready to learn whatever you desire to teach me and completely at your disposal."

Charmed, Jade's mouth curved into a satisfied smirk. She and her daughter enjoyed a sumptuous meal, savoring the servitude and attention more than the food.

Back in their lavish suite of rooms, Haley still had no idea that her mother didn't sleep. She did not need to rest at all—ever.

24

Evil Lurking Within

When Haley awoke the next morning, her clothes and accessories had been carefully laid out on the chaise next to her dressing table. After a luxurious bubble bath in a tub so large Haley could swim in it; two different people dressed and styled her. When they were done handling her like a live Barbie, Haley stared at her image in the full-length mirror. "Is that me?"

There was a brief tap on her bedroom door before Jade merely let herself in, without waiting for a response. She nodded approvingly at Haley, "You're absolutely stunning, darling."

Haley was draped in a blood-red, body-con designer dress with matching trendy cape, dripping with ropes of pearls, matching earrings, paper-thin, three-quarter length lambskin gloves and stilettos that she had only seen in fashion magazines. Her hair cascaded in perfect waves, not a strand out of place.

Jade air-kissed her daughter on each cheek, "Now, the chef has prepared something special for breakfast. Then, we drive into town so that I can introduce you to the family's primary business."

— ⁓

Finally, they arrived! Jade gestured with her finger for the driver, "Ah! Here we are—Spinous Toy Store. Does this excite you to see your last name in such an awesome place?"

Thoroughly excited Haley nodded, 'Yes.' After exiting the vehicle, they stopped, looked around in awe. The Spinous Hotel and Resort's neighboring town was bustling with activity. Directly across the middle of the town's area was Spinous Toy Store. Giant, colorful toy soldiers flanked the heavy glass double doors. Dolls, stuffed animals, toy cars, games, trains and every toy a child could imagine were impressively displayed in the windows. Inside, aisles of shelves were stocked with toys of every category. Adults and children alike laughed and shopped in the bright and happy space.

That is until Jade entered. With Haley in tow, Jade appeared even taller with her long neck, frighteningly regal stride and icy glare. Store personnel scattered. Children hid behind their parents, who backed out of the way. Jade turned to Haley, who marveled at how people cowered in her mother's presence, "Behold, Sweetheart. A Spinous Toy Store, the lynchpin of our little family business... How do you like it? Tell you what. Why don't you look around while I handle a little bit of business?"

The short, plump store manager approached Jade, scared to death, "Good day, Madame Spinous. How may I be of assistance?"

Haley pretended to browse, making sure she was within earshot of her mother's private conversation. Jade didn't have to see Haley for her to know that she was there; she could sense and smell her, taking pride in her daughter's impulse to be sneaky.

"You can show me my books," Jade spat at the terrified manager. "And, don't bother bringing me any of that electronic nonsense, I like to see my numbers the old-fashioned way. Hand-written on paper in actual ledgers. Any other way is just lazy!"

The manager hurried as fast as her short legs would carry her. She nervously returned with three large books, placing them on an individual, intricately carved, gleaming wooden desk in the corner of the store that was reserved for Jade's spontaneous—and dreaded—visits. The woman made the mistake of wetting the tip of her index finger with her tongue to better turn the pages.

That collective action sent Jade on a rampage, "You worthless, disgusting pig. Do you expect me to touch these pages? After you've slobbered all over them?" She so enjoyed terrifying everyone around her. "Wash your hands and rewrite every book! I refuse to touch them. So you'll be turning the pages today. Later, I will expect every page re-written without the slobber. Where's the assistant manager?" Jade continued to rant. "Have you ever known me to conduct my business in front of my customers?"

The assistant manager came running—nervous. "My deepest apologies, Madame, you asked for the books and—"

Jade tilted her head and sighed.

The assistant continued. "Your peculiar business hub is awaiting you. I just thought you'd want to keep an eye on your offspring."

Jade cut the manager off. "You thought? I don't pay you to think for me. I pay you to be efficient! Bring the books."

"Yes, of course, Madame... Please follow me."

The manager gathered up the ledgers that were almost as big as she was and headed to the back of the store and heavy, old-fashioned, velvet curtains.

Jade glided behind the manager and through the curtains. Haley followed to hear what was going on; just as her mother knew she would.

After a few moments of barely scanning the ledgers, Jade growled, "The inventory and profit don't add up. What, are you and the rest of you mopes stealing my merchandise? Toys are missing that are not accounted for! How do you explain that?"

The poor store manager was sweating and stammering, trying to explain, "You see, Madame, we have to account for a small percentage of inventory loss. There are always a few bad apples, and some kids steal. It happens in every retail business."

"Not in mine, it doesn't!" Jade hissed. "You allow my merchandise to be stolen and expect me to take the loss? You do whatever you have to do to make sure those toys are accounted for to the very penny—or else!"

The storekeeper began to sweating and doubling her talk as she tried to explain, "Madame, I have taken from my pay to offset some of the stolen toys, but not even my pay is enough to pay for the stolen toys."

Jade eyebrows raised high and her voice shook, "Let me repeat so as to be clear—even you small nugget can comprehend. Never will I take a loss! Never! You will sell your personal merchandise to pay me for my toys! I want what is mine in a week, or you and your pathetic family will pay. Do—I—Make—Myself—Clear? Clear!"

Tears flowed down the woman's chubby cheeks, "Yes, Madame. I'll make sure of it personally."

"You'd better—if you want to keep your job! Or whatever family heirlooms you possess."

"Please, Madam. I have a family. I need this job—"

Again, Jade cut her off, "Do you think I care about you or your family? You have one week to balance the books. And, I'd better not hear of one more item leaving this store unpaid for."

Once Jade stormed back through the curtains, she spotted a particularly adorable little girl walking through the store holding her father's hand. They looked as though they didn't have much money; so, Jade decided to have some fun.

Sporting two curly pigtails, the little girl picked up a stuffed bear to admire. Jade used her magic to force the child to hide the bear inside her threadbare sweater. Haley was watching; just as her mother knew she was.

As though possessed by a wave of evil, Haley snapped. She ran to the little girl, snatched the bear away from her and pushed the child onto the floor. Frightened, the little girl started crying. Her father tried to intervene; but, Haley was channeling her inner Jade, "Get some control over your brat! It's losers like you who are robbing my mother blind. Apparently, your town is full of thieves! Get out of our store. Now!"

Jade couldn't have been prouder. Haley passed Jade's test with flying colors, coming into her own evil. She stood next to her daughter. "You heard my daughter. Get out. And, I'd better not see you—or your kid—in my store or any other of my properties ever again. Do you understand what I'm saying?"

The father was stun; his ordinarily good child was stealing? It didn't make sense, but he knew Jade was no ordinary female and didn't dare question anything said. He picked up his still tearful little girl, nodded his head, 'Yes,' and carried the child out of the store.

Jade beamed at Haley. "That's my girl! Lunch?"

Haley, in front of her mother, gazed at the scenery as they entered another fancy restaurant, owned by Jade. A brief silence fell over the place as the two walked in. Shortly after the noise resumed, an older host approached. "Good afternoon, Madame Jade... Seating for you and your beautiful Mademoiselle?"

"She sure is beautiful." Adoring her creation in Haley, "Now, please show us to our private table."

The host showed them to their booth which was offish from other people. The booth seats with plush fillings and soft leather surrounded by sizable heavy velvet curtains for privacy. On top of the marble table were several candles the scene with radiance and opulence.

The host signaled the new waitress to serve Mrs. Jade. After all, they all had their fair share of insults from the 'Dark One' (a nickname costumed for Jade), and it was time to break in the new help.

Candice, a young 5 feet 7 inches, curvy, curly hair brunette, with saucer round eyes and upbeat spirit approach the private booth—only know little bits about her pending customer. With a dashing smile, "The regular for you, Madame?"

Jade nodded ever so slightly, her thin, cruel lips pursed.

"And, for you, Mademoiselle," the server continued, "a burger and fries? We make the best in town!"

Haley exploded, "Do I look like the average, super-basic teenager to you? Don't you have eyes?"

The young woman began to tremble. Oddly, Haley took great pleasure in the girls on fear and discomfort. It felt powerful. A sentiment her mother had been talking about all along. Although, Haley wasn't used to such mean-spirited feelings; but, she liked them.

Jade took over, "I've got this, dear." To the terrified waitress, she demanded, "A platter of caviar on toast points and a bottle of the coldest, most expensive champagne we stock."

The waitress forced a nervous smile and scurried away.

"Mother, I'm not 21. I can't drink."

Jade threw her head back and laughed as though this was the most hilarious thing she'd ever heard, "Don't be ridiculous, darling. I own the restaurant, everything and everyone in it—for all intents and purposes. You and I can have and do whatever we want."

Settled in the private booth, Jade noticed that Haley's eyes were turning darker, a sure-fire sign of evil taking root. Now, all she had to do was feed and water it for full growth.

After gaining the full scoop of whom she was serving, Candice was back with the champagne, crystal flutes and champagne bucket on its own golden stand. As she nervously poured two glasses, a waiter delivered the caviar.

Jade dismissed them with a wave of her hand. She took Haley's hands, "I think it's time to tell you about your family bloodline. You've earned it."

Haley smiled, thrilled that she'd managed to please her mother. The two clinked glasses and each took a satisfying congratulatory sip. Haley studied the bubbling liquid in her flute, "Wow, this is amazing. I've never tasted anything like it."

"Of course you haven't. But, you're with me now. See? I've been saying it all along, haven't I? Only the very best for my daughter. By the way, how did it feel?"

Haley tilted her head, "How did what—feel, Mother?"

"That sniveling little waitress... You had her shaking in her boots. And, the brat back at the store. You had no problem reprimanding her, pushing her or making her bawl her stupid little head off."

Haley took another sip of the champagne, "Hmmm, frankly, it made me feel powerful, like an amazing high."

Haley polished off her champagne. A waiter was immediately at her side to refill her flute. "Kinda like these bubbles."

"Don't guzzle, dear, sip," Jade instructed.

"Sorry, Mother... It's just delicious. Anyway, that waitress got on my last nerve."

"How so?"

"Well, she was so chirpy and friendly, she reminded me of my old life with Jess. Jess was like that. Goody-two-shoes happy all the time. She tried to make me the same way."

"Did she?" Jade asked, absent-mindedly nibbling a caviar-topped toast point.

"Maybe sometimes... But, she was—is—such a-well, she never wanted to have any real fun. Always helping her grandmother took president over. Good riddance..."

"You mean that?" Jade asked hopefully.

"Yes, Mother, I do. That waitress was automatically sizing me up as a pedestrian burger, and fries teenager was the icing on the cake. I belong to you. I want to be with you."

"And you don't miss Bob or Renee?"

"Well, I did. At first... Then, the memory of them just seemed to fade away. Like a bad memory."

"I've meant to ask you, Haley. What about the holidays with Bob and Renee? All those lies about the Christ, Christmas and a Santa Claus? Did you ever fall for any of that nonsense?"

"When I was little, maybe... They always made such a big deal out of it. Lots of decorations, caroling, baking, and gifts."

"Let me stop you right there," Jade slapped the palm of her hand on the table. "Christmas and everything associated with it is a load of crap! I vowed to kill all that generated Christmas ever since I was young. All that hooey about a Creator who loves all unconditionally, becoming man and dying for the sins of mankind because he loved us all. What a crock! He didn't love your family! Our forefathers are inflamed literally because of Him and his so-called traditions including that Santa Claus. Crap! Just a bunch of crap! All of it means nothing."

Haley's darkening eyes grew large. She knew better than to contradict her mother. The life as she had known it quickly faded.

Jade was on a tear, "Good kids get toys, while the naughty ones are stuck with coal in their stockings. Generations of children were tormented as they tried to be good for a damn toy! Good isn't in most humans, so it was unfair front the jump! Now, I sell the toys that parents buy for their brats—good or bad alike. My family has been selling toys for generations to parents allowing the children to forget there ever was a Santa. I will accomplish this because most humans are silly. They'll fall for anything. And, soon, the entire world is going to know our toy stores! Through this passage, they will lose faith in Christ. No, Christ! No, Christ Day! No, Christmas! No, Santa Claus! I am going to eliminate the world of good and replace it with evil—once and for all. Do you understand what I am saying?"

"Yes, Mother," Haley answered, as though in a trance. Jade's poison darkness had successfully pierced Haley's soul. She offered no more resistance.

Jade was pleased and confident in continuing the indoctrination of her once-innocent daughter. "Drink up, darling. I need to know that you're fully ready to receive the family background that I'm going to share."

"I'd love to know more about our family, mother. All I know now is that Uncle Bob is your brother."

"Let's not bring up Bob again. He's a naïve fool that I'd rather forget even exists. Hundreds of years ago, our ancestors happened to the most powerful force in the world, magic. Black magic. We vowed to destroy the stupid notion of Christ, Christmas, and Santa Claus. At last, my powers have reached their peak, so that our noble mission of destruction will be finally be completed through me."

Haley was intrigued.

"Would you like a little sample?" Jade teased, knowing that Haley was ready. Her eyes glued to her mother, Haley nodded, 'Yes.'

Jade signal the waitress to come; she requested the curtains closed and to be left alone. The waitress did as instructed—afraid and hurried out of sight. She was of good spirit and good spirits know when evil is present.

Jade closed her eyes, open them back to reveal the dense darkness of them.

Haley looked into them and said, "Mother I am ready."

Jade took Haley's hand from across the table into her own, "Yes, the reveal of our family begins."

In a moments touch, Jade transformed into Haley all her knowledge about their family line, all her transitions, past and present lives, and the unmeasurable hate for all things good. After releasing Haley's hand—Jade closed her eyes again, outstretched her arms and reiterated a black magic mantra. An insignificant amount of time passed, Jade opened her eyes allowing Haley to see her completely black eyes with no sclera. Jade stood, Haley, followed. Jade waved her arm. Everything, everyone and every motion in the restaurant had abruptly stopped. Dishes falling off a busboy's tray, hair swinging, people's open mouths, waiters serving food, steam in the kitchen, and bubbling, boiling water on the stove all froze in place, silenced. With a blink, Jade transformed into her true self with black eyes—not a sliver of white showing—blistering red skin and black nails which grew into long, pointy claws. Haley watched with excitement as her mother became taller, shoulders widened, and she witnessed the evil incarnate, she'd only had a glimpse to encounter. Hideous... yet, terrifyingly beautiful, nonetheless... Haley was not afraid as she girls her mother's powerful existence, shadow the current universe.

"Behold," Jade swept an arm through the impossible scene.

Haley smiled, impressed. Power. "You are a god, Mother. I am your seed forever! I wish to be as you are."

Jade's evil filling up, "This is immortality as well as power. Are you certain, it's what you want?"

"It's what I want." Haley drooled for power.

"Then, of course. I've simply been waiting for you to ask, my child, shall be in my likeness."

What Jade neglected to reveal is that it would cost Haley, her soul.

In another blink of an eye, all was back to where it was, including Jade's human persona. No one even knew what happened.

— ⁓

Haley's rigorous training and emergence into the dark arts began as soon as she and her mother returned from their "vacation."

It lasted for months, through the remaining winter, spring and summer into fall. Jade was pleased that Haley proved to be such a quick learner. Evil began to come naturally to the girl. But, absolute indoctrination and saturation of evil took time. Soon, Haley's hunger for power and mastery over dark magic consumed every fiber of her being, eliminating any lingering thoughts or memories of Uncle Bob, Aunt Renee or a best friend named Jess.

Just in time for her eighteenth birthday.

"Someone has a big day tomorrow," Jade cooed.

"Yes, I'll be 18 at last."

"Indeed... And, the staff is out right now picking up your in gift. You're going to love it."

"Thank you, Mother. I know I will."

"Yes, well, off to bed for you. We have a full schedule tomorrow, Birthday Girl."

Haley smiled in anticipation, admiring her mother's evil. "Goodnight, Mother... I love your evil."

Jade was confident Haley was ready. She knew Haley understood without being told—an evil love can only exist to ones genuinely evil. No more would she hear Haley speak those irritating words, 'Mother, I love you' and couldn't be more pleased.

25

A Birthday To Remember

The morning of her eighteenth birthday, Haley woke with a sense of anticipation and excitement. She was a September baby and was accustomed to bright, sunny Indian summer on her birthday. But, today when she opened her drapes and blinds, dark, threatening clouds hung in the sky.

For the first time in her short life, she didn't care what her birthday skies looked like—it didn't matter anymore. "No matter," Haley shrugged off the gloomy day. She was beginning to prefer dreary to sunny. Haley felt as though it suited her new, sophisticated self.

Jade swept into the room, "There—she is! My beautiful creation, eighteen-years-old, and all grown-up! I thought this day would never come. Happy 18th!"

"Good Morning, Mother... And thank you. What do you mean by thinking this day would never come? My birthday has always been September, 23rd."

"I'll explain in a bit, dear. But, first, you get dressed and meet me in front of the elevator in the West wing hallway on the ground floor. Then, you'll get your big birthday surprise."

Jade took her daughter's hand when Haley met her at the elevator, "You're going to love your present."

"I bet—I know what it is—a fabulous, new, top-of-the-line sports car that I've been wanting."

They stepped into the elevator. "Darling, your gift is so much more than some mundane automobile. Everlasting, in fact—you'll see."

The elevator plunged downward so profoundly and so quickly, Haley felt that her stomach was left on the castle's first floor. When the doors opened, Jade's motley crew of five closest staff, were there to greet them.

The area was vast, dark and dank. "What is this place?" Haley asked, her curiosity growing at the moment.

"Well, this is a castle. And, as with all castles, we have a dungeon," Jade replied cryptically.

Having nothing with which to compare it to, Haley felt as though she was in the middle of a carnival's house of horrors or a weird video game. Creepy, giant monuments, unusual looking animals were scattered throughout. The chauffeur: Chris Norm, horse trainer: Jack Drag, the butler: Chance Zeus, Haley's tutor: Abarim Wales and the cook: Enyo all held lanterns and led the way through twisty tunnels.

They walked to what looked like an ancient amphitheater, complete with spectator tiers. But, on the top tier—separated by six rectangular shaped stone steps, there were only two seats that looked more like thrones than chairs. They were heavy and black with gold trim. On the floor of the amphitheater was a stone altar, surrounded by kindling wood. Jade motioned for her to take one seat, while she settled into the other.

"This is a pretty elaborate game, Mother."

"It's no game, my dear. It is your rite of passage, the greatest gift I could bestow upon the fruit of my womb."

Haley looked puzzled.

Jade continued in an even more formal tone than usual, "You must have wondered, at some point, why I left you in the care of my weak brother and his even weaker wife. It was because—like it or not, and, I loathe it because I loathe Him—a child's innocence is protected by the Creator until he or she comes of age. You should know that our great lineage spans far beyond this physical world to many unseen worlds and realms. My descendants, our descendants, are from the royal bloodline of the devil himself. You see, God had thrown out angels from the spiritual realms and they come into the physical realms—taking wives and creating children—wicked children. Most of our family were giants—must larger than the average man and we ruled everything on earth. We were called Nephilims. The Creator didn't like us ruling the earth and causing all things to be wicked, so most of our lineage was killed by the flood. But we found a way to survive and for this reason—wickedness has passed unto me and now, unto you. You should know that our great lineage spans far beyond this physical world to many unseen worlds and realms. I am an immortal, as are my most devoted staff and confidantes, who have served me for eons."

The corneas of Jade's eyes had turned to flames. Haley watched, unshaken, as though this was an everyday occurrence.

"Before I could take you out of the fragile human conditions that you were forced to grow up in, you first had to be exposed to both good and evil. The thought of you with Bob made my flesh crawl, but I had no choice. You had to know both, so you would fully understand both before making a choice. My gift to you, daughter, is immortality, eternal life, the power to rule all worlds as my equal ultimately, forever. That is what my side, which idiots call evil, offers. Then, of course, you're still free to choose the ordinary world of goodness that you of in, the one that worships a God and a Christ who couldn't care less, the celebration of Christ's birth, Christmas, and worst of all, belief in an overweight elf called Santa Claus. We have no power over the Creator; but together, we do have absolute power to manipulate all that He created. Your choice, my dear..."

Haley was no longer any semblance of her innocent self. Without any hesitation, she answered, "It's a no-brainer, Mother. I choose you and immortality."

"Excellent!" Jade tapped her long nails together. "Now, since we are celebrating your birthday, how about a party trick before your gift?" Jade gave the slightest nod.

The staff stepped forward one by one. "Ah, Chris, our faithful chauffeur... We go back long ways. Like me, he was one of Santa's so-called "lump-of-coal kids." That's because we thought for ourselves and followed our own rules and our desires. Chris had a special desire for animals. Not to play with, you see, but to devour. He loved hunting animals, but occasionally his taste evolved to include humans when the moon was full—a symbol to dominate animals for hunting. In this world and others, he is a werewolf. You look surprised, dear. Did you think werewolves were just a story? I assure you, werewolves are more than a story. People learned of Chris's need to hunt humans along with animals. They gathered some witches power and cursed him to another realm of silver—in this realm he had no control and was a mere human, but if he were to return to the physical—the cursed would cause him to turned into a wolf every full moon. The transformation would be very painful, and he never remembered what happened. He found magic in that realm and returned to the physical world but not without those consequences of turning into a beast. I encountered him in the woods one day—all beat up, bloody and, naked. I offered him a home with me and a cure from turning unless he willed it. Chris, display who you are."

As Madame commanded, the hairy chauffeur stood near the center of the circular lower stage and morphed into an enormous beast with four legs, razor-sharp claws, and teeth. With the head of an ugly man-wolf combo, Chris stood on his hind legs and howled. Then his animal-muscled body shook out two large black wings.

"Whoa, that's pretty cool," Haley observed, thrilled and not at all afraid.

"Thank you, Chris. Now, as you were. Your turn, Chance Zeus," Jade pointed to her butler. "Show us what you've got. Now, Chance here is known for his bloodlust in all worlds. Human blood—once, I granted him immortality, his thirst for human blood increased, and he gained power from each soul he drank from because the Creator placed the soul in the blood everyone. He became known as a vampire. See how it all fits together?"

Jade chirped, as though she were teaching a history lesson.

To illustrate Jade's point, Chance turned into a bat, flew around the room, returned and shape-shifted into a giant man-beast with red wings, long sharp teeth, spell stricken eyes, a staff in one hand and a rock in the other. Suddenly the stick was a bolt of lightning. Chance stabbed the ground with it, invoking the howls of a killer storm. Jade chuckled wickedly. Now, she understood where that seemingly bizarre storm came from last winter that battered her uncle and aunt's home.

Jade smiled at her daughter approvingly, "Perfect, darling. You're putting it all together."

Jade clapped her hands once, "You're dismissed, Chance, thank you."

Jack was always in dark places when he was young. He was enticed into a distinctive cave with an unusual animal in it. This animal once lived in a mystical world and although the animal's world was destroyed it managed to follow its captive into a unique land and became trapped there. The animal survived on fish of that land and lived in dark caves to stay hidden. One day, the local inhabitants that lived in that enchanted land spotted this animal, and upon seeing this creature with fear, they battled him, and he was wounded severely. Jack was a collector of precious stones and shiny jewels in that, land, but he could fight better than any in the land. Jack was looking for more polished rocks in a cave when he found the creature weak and injured. This creature was shiny and beautiful like the stones he seeks. The animal was in pain, but Jack could see he also had unchangeable anger. Jack touched the creature's claw and was able to feel his pain, to see his life, to know the source of his hopelessness. The creature's hatred for the Creator grew when he felt abandoned and lost his entire world and family. He also saw his power to grant wishes. Jack wanted to help the creature and himself. Jack helped the beast by uniting his life with the creature's life. He felt he now collected the most precious jewel by being a part of this mystical creature. Jack became united with the animal and to possess its power. I came to learn of this creature, and in exchange for loyalty and servants, I gave the creature immortality here. Jack, you're up..."

The riding instructor that Haley had once thought was so darkly handsome, now writhed and twisted into a giant creature right out of mythology. His winged body shimmered with the kaleidoscope sparkle of every known jewel. He grew six heads, each breathing fire through their long-snouted mouths. This monster almost took Haley's breath away because it was so oddly beautiful. She still felt attracted to Jack, even as his true self.

"Very impressive, Jack... And thank you. As you were." Haley was having the time of her life.

"Now, Abarim's story is particularly intriguing," Jade continued. "She's a bit different from the rest of us, as she was first a favored child of the Creator. True to form, that fickle, thin-skinned Creator, God, turned His back on her the minute she failed to complete one silly, little assignment. Abarim and her brother, Jonah were charged with delivering an allegedly important message to humankind from the Creator. To accomplish this in the physical world, Jonah was swallowed by a whale and Abarim by a shark.

As the story goes, Jonah remained faithful after being swallowed whole and was vomited on earth by the whale. Well, Abarim was not a happy camper inside the belly of that stinky shark. She resented the Creator for the assignment and cursed it. God didn't like that; so she was stuck in there for a while. For years in physical time, Abarim sat there eating small fish that the shark gulped down without digesting.

Eventually, the shark swam into the waters of another world, a magical underwater world. By then, Abarim's skin had been replaced by fish scales, and her hair grew long, reflecting the blues and greens of the seas. One day, she escaped the shark's belly. Instead of hating the beast, she learned the art of darkness in the magical sea world and made a pact with the beast to combine their strengths as one. Her long, seaweed silky hair game Abarim power. But, poor Abarim grew lonely and longed to be with God's people, even though she hated Him. The Chosen People of God were the Nation of Israelites, Jews.

Somehow, clever Abarim found her way to the surface world and the humans she craved. She met and fell in love with a king. Sadly, he broke her heart and abandoned her. But, by then, Abarim was already impregnated. As you might imagine, my darling daughter, a genetic angelic-beast fusion like Abarim getting knocked up by a human was a no-no. She ended up giving birth to an entire litter of babies by this king, not just one. She called them mermaids.

But, God stuck His nose in once again where it wasn't wanted and blessed those little mermaids, making them unfailingly good.

When I ran across poor Abarim centuries later, she had no king, no babies, and no family whatsoever. I offered to be her family and to grant her the gift of immortality if she would serve me. The rest, as they say, is history. Enough talking— Abarim, show my daughter who you really are."

With a whip of Jade's hand, an unwalled pool of water appeared. Abarim shared what passed for a smile, quietly walked through and grew to thirty feet in length. Her upper body remained human-looking, except her now ruby-red eyes, wings that sprouted from her back and hair that was alive, multi-colored and responded to her commands. The lower portion of Abarim's body was a blue-scaled fish body and tail. A strand of Abarim's magical hair wrapped itself around a harmless pole and hurled it across the amphitheater.

Jade applauded, "Excellent, display, Abarim. That will be all." Abarim smile was showing off her shark whites.

Jade smiled at Enyo. "Last but not least, my very first ally and the best cook in this world or any other, Enyo." Enyo stepped forward, and Jade continued. "Enyo is also of royal pedigree, one of the Graeae coven. In ancient times, these three deliciously malevolent sisters were the most powerful witches ever to exist. Their one weakness was that they were blind and shared one eye between them. After many centuries of wreaking their havoc, humans began trying to rid the world of evil, targeting witches. Countless witches were captured and burned at the stake. Enyo's youngest sister, Deino was caught off-guard and slaughtered by witch hunters.

I had discovered and was practicing dark magic for many lifetimes when I met Enyo. Each of us sensed the other's powers immediately. We made a pact. Enyo and her remaining sister, Pemphredo, opened my eyes to who I was, the granddaughter of Satan, the Master of All Evil. I, of course, became an expert at spells that were previously unbeknownst to me. With this new magic, I stole the Key-of-Death, the worldly sphere, and the universal map. With the key, I was able to grant the gift of immortality to others, if they agreed to follow me. I also gave the sisters eyesight without the need of the all-seeing eye. The best part is that Enyo older sister is someone close to you. We'll get to that later. And, she's part of the family I've created for myself. Enyo, reveal yourself true form to Haley."

Enyo took the stage, quadrupling in size and height, her skin turned a deep green. Enyo's eyes and lips blazed fiery red; her arms reached as though made of rubber and her hair acquired a smoky purple hue. Unlike the others, Enyo had no wings. But, she had a broom to fly on whenever she wanted. Enyo also possessed knowledge of black magic, spells and dark secrets that existed before time in the physical world. That made her invaluable to Jade.

The staff circled the altar on the floor of the amphitheater. Jade rose from her throne, kissed Haley on the forehead and joined the others. "Now, my daughter, BEHOLD... Your Mother!" Jade's voice had changed to a deep growl.

Then, it was as though Jade's chalk-white skin burst at the seams, oozing a thirty-foot tall creature with smoke-colored skin, giant black wings, opaque black eyes, talons for fingernails and split hooves for feet.

She was now in the physical world as Nefari. Rather than being afraid of Nefari, Haley was drawn to her. One of the dragon heads lit the kindling around the altar with its breath. Two of Nefari's lesser beasts dragged out the sacrifice.

Haley's breath caught for a millisecond when she saw that the sacrificial lamb was her Aunt Renee.

Nefari hissed with a snake tongue. "Happy birthday, my daughter... Another lesson; as with everything, the gift of immortality comes with many costs. You will sever the head of this frail mortal, also known as your pathetic Aunt Renee, and drink the spilled blood from this magnificent goblet, a family heirloom straight from Hades. You must then die in the physical world for a total of five earthly days. During that time, your spirit will learn at the feet of the Master-of-Hell—your ancestor, the devil.

It will feel as though you are physically there; but, your mind alone will temporarily reside in Hades. That will put a bit of a temporary damper on your abilities. Find one known as the first apprentice. He betrayed the Creator and burned in hell with a magical globe in his possession. You can't bring it back physically, but you can pinpoint its location while soaking in the juices of immortality. On this end, I will dispatch my slaves to capture the second apprentice and globe, along with the Book-of-Knowledge. We must pair the Key-of-Hades with the Key-of-Death to access home physically. The Christ will never relinquish the Key-of-Hades; but, I can work around that.

Haley's entire being was filled with insatiable longing for it all.

Satisfied, Nefari spewed, "Then let the battle begin. With my daughter at my side, we will collect and destroy all symbols of good. Faith, belief, Christ, Christmas and Santa Claus will be decimated in this and all worlds. No longer will we have to witness the sickening weakness of happiness anywhere!"

Renee relinquishes her fear and goes into a deep meditation to find Christ. Christ does not disappoint her. He shows her a vision of a future, and she knew her love for him was not in vain. Although, she was physically weakened from continuous torture; but she heard every word, tapped deeply into her faith in God and declared in a firm voice, "Let Christ, now—command thy servants, which are before thee, to seek only righteousness; and wait for His justice. It shall come to pass, when the spirit of God is upon thee, that He shall play with His hand and thou shalt be well. If, when evil cometh upon us, as the sword, judgment, pestilence or famine, we stand before this house, and in Thy presence—for Thy name is in this house—and cry unto Thee in my affliction, then Thou wilt hear and help. For man also knoweth not his time. As the fishes that are taken in an evil net and as the birds that are caught in the snare, so are the sons of men snared in an evil time, but only for a time. Your will, be my will, Christ..."

Nefari glances toward Renee, cackling with disgust, "Are you done yet? No! Christ won't be saving you." She hands a saber and the goblet to Haley.

Renee searches for any trace of good that might be left in Haley, "Don't do this terrible thing, baby. I don't care about me. But, I fear for your immortal soul. There's no coming back from such evil. Please, baby. Save yourself. I raised you to love Christ."

Emotionless, Haley makes her way around the altar holding a helpless Renee, a red-tipped nail tracing along her aunt's bare skin, her heels clicking on the cold, damp, stone floor, "Blah, blah, blah. God this— Christ that— See, now you're just embarrassing yourself. Auntie— Where is He? I don't see any God. He wasn't there for you when you worried and prayed about every damn thing. And, He isn't here now! What kind of God is that? I chose my mother, my true nature. Get over it. You lose. Wait, no. Allow me to introduce you to your precious God."

Without blinking an eye, Haley deftly slit her Aunt Renee's throat open with one hand and collected the draining blood in the goblet with the other. She eagerly guzzled the blood without flinching and instantly went limp. The rest of the creatures untied their powers lifting Haley's body in midair as they chant. With all the dark magic in the dungeon, Haley's body never hit the ground. The gates of death opened and Haley's mind separated from her body. Her body was released from their enchantment. It hovered in the air until it could rest in her mother's outstretched arms.

— ⁓

Haley's body lay in state in a pitch black bedroom with no windows, no light, inky charcoal bedding and lifeless, black roses. The death chamber represented the life of evil Haley chose and the absolute void of goodness.

— ⁓

Neither the moaning nor the cries of tortured souls in Hades moved Haley's wandering mind one bit. She marveled that her consciousness was sharper than ever without the cumbersome heaviness of her human form. Haley was in her element, her kingdom where she was royalty and felt right at home.

Soaking up evil's knowledge like a sponge—Haley learned that her mother's power was most active in the physical world. She discovered, time only existed in the physical world due to it being the last and only re-maining world that hasn't shown true faith in Christ. After Christ (man God) emptied himself for the sins of mankind—most rejected him—the only world left to be transformed for God purpose. This knowledge gave hope of their ability to take over and turn things evil. 'That's why time allows for immortality.' She smiled as she took mental notes of all being revealed. She learned that the Creator was not only real but has had His Godly hand in their family pool forever. 'This was no new battle—this battle has existed since the beginning.' Haley felt determined to win. She saw it all—the entire stories and the current situation. Haley jumped with awareness. "Jess! The Apprentice! It all makes sense now. No-one is that damn good! That damn happy! I will crush her and her dreams!" Also, she learned what was needed for her mother to gain power. Finally, Haley won the same information her mother had, as well as knowledge of specifics that her mother neglected to reveal. Jade/Nefari had sacrificed her firstborn, a son, to gain immortality. Haley was shown visions of the first spiritual battle for Christ, Christmas, and Santa between Nefari and the first apprentice, Judas. Judas' faith in God weakened, ultimately betraying the Creator and allowing Nefari to gain the Key-of-Death. The apprentice lost his mortal soul and was removed from God. Haley's spirit roamed all of Hades in search of the turncoat.

In the physical world, Jade was mobilizing her monstrous troops for the ensuing battle between good and evil. She had already encountered Haley's puny, gullible former friend, Jess, in the magical world. Because evil could not touch the globe which Jess now possessed as the appren-tice, Jade's goons were instructed to find the girl and bring her back with both the globe and the Book-of-Knowledge.

While her followers searched for Jess, beginning by following the same guiding, heavenly star—Jade kept vigil at Haley's side. Once they located Jess, they all would return to meditate together until Haley's transfer was sealed.

26

Battle Of The Wolf Beast

Rudolph, in his wisdom, has been a magical reindeer for centuries, advised Jess to first learn as much about each Holy Place as she could, before they flew off to kick evil's butt. "Knowledge is power," he reminded her, half-jokingly and half-serious, as they left the North Pole.

All of a sudden, the atmosphere palpably shifted. In mid-flight, both Jess and Rudolph were engulfed with a heaviness, sucking the Christmas joy right out of their spirits. Evil's subtle insidiousness was stirring its head, picking up strength along the way for the battle that was to come.

An emergency landing seemed like the best option. Jess held on tight as Rudolph began his rapid descent to protect them both. Thump, thud. It was a crash landing in the middle of a dessert. He and Jess plopped, drained, onto the sand.

Rudolph switched back to his human form. "You can feel it, can't you?" Rufus swallowed.

"Yeah, I had no idea that it would affect me like this. I can barely breathe through this evil fog." Jess complained.

"That's how evil works. I'm afraid the battle has begun, Jess. It started the moment you touched that snow globe and accepted your destiny as The Apprentice. As Jose said, Nefari's radar honed in on you at that very moment."

The reality was sinking in even further. Jess was well-aware of her mission and was committed to it with all her heart. For a moment, though, Jess looked like the innocent teenaged girl that she was.

Rufus took her hands in his. "You know you're not alone with this, right? The Creator has given you all the spiritual insight, magical tools, and resources you'll need to win. And, in that—you have your personal army of humankind and magical beings with you every step of the way, beginning with me. Santa said it himself. I know my way around mystical stars and Holy Places. I will take you to each one and back home again."

"Thanks, Rufus. You're such a good friend. Know what?" Jess' eyes twinkled. "How about I make us a little more comfortable while we talk this plan through?"

Jess held on tightly to her globe charm, closed her eyes and made a wish. A fully furnished tent manifested right there in the middle of the desert. There was plenty of food, water, and soft drinks.

"Cool," Rufus observed approvingly. "Yeah, I'd say you've got this, girl." He reached gratefully for a bottle of icy cold water. "How'd you know I was thirsty?"

Jess laughed, "Because your nose wasn't glowing quite as much as usual!"

She opened her water bottle. Jess and Rufus tapped bottles in a toast to Jess' victory.

Jess tilted her head in thought, "The hardest thing for me to get used to, I think—is the whole time thing."

Rufus nodded, "Yup, that can be tricky. What feels like mere hours here in the magical lands can translate into months in the physical world. Ready to talk about the Seven Holy Places and the Seven Wonders of the World."

"Ready as I'll ever be. I had lessons about the Seven Wonders of this physical world from grandmau-ma." Jess smiled at the thoughts. "She was my history tutor. They're breathtaking."

"Ah, but did those lessons explain why the Seven Wonders and Holy Places exist in the physical world? God, is the Creator of all. You remember the first of the Ten Commandments?"

"Sure, 'I am the Lord, your God. You shall have no other gods before me.'"

"Right, but, as we know, all of us were given the gift of 'free will.' Entire civilizations of ancient humans in the physical world used that free will to ignore God's commandments. They built magnificent monuments and structures to honor their earthly rulers, kings, false gods and golden idols. Even though the Creator was angry, He is also a merciful God and permitted these wonders to stand, throughout this world to cause wonderment of the Creator's worshipers. It is written that He will only allow these Wonders to exist until His concluding judgment in the physical world, in the final days of humankind."

The Book-of-Knowledge proceeded to glow. Jess touched her charm, and it resumed its original size. Jess opened it to a new message:

> *Jess, use the Codex Bible. Your Grandmother's notes will continue to guide you through the Creator's Words. The Bible is His letter to all.*

Jess immediately returned the Book-of-Knowledge charm, exchange it for the Codex Bible. She saw another tab that wasn't there before. She opened it and read aloud:

> *"And I will destroy your high places, and cut down your images."*

Rufus chimed in, "Yes, only seven would remain, others He said he would destroy. The Creator allowed seven which is a Holy number to stand as a reminder of what He wants for them and from them."

Jess, nodded with complete comprehension.

Rufus continued, "Santa and I visit the Seven Wonders of the World and Seven of the largest Holy Places every Christmas cycle to give God all the glory. We never wanted to forget. Without Him, we would not be able to serve with our magical gifts." Rufus took a sip of water, then continued again. "There are seven Holy Places, seven Candlesticks, and seven sacred stars. God's perfect number of completion in all things, as well as ridding the world of Nefari's evil."

Again, Rufus took Jess' hands to reassure her. "I am truly blessed to be your guide on this sacred journey."

"Blessed yes we are—but," Jess chuckled. "I just hope you still feel that way after it's over. My prayer is that I do not fail."

"With God on your side, you can't fail." Rufus took a deep breath and exhaled slowly. "The skies are swelling with Nefari's wickedness. Are you ready?"

"To the first Holy Place..." Jess popped up like a weed.

"Okay, grab ahold and sing the song. Grant me the ability to talk as we fly."

"Done—" Jess started the song and they were off.

While airborne, Rufus shared more detailed instructions. "The Holy Place and The Wonder of the World are together, but later you will find it more challenging because they are apart. We're headed to the Karnak Temple in Egypt, where the first Candlestick is. I've seen it; but, never would I touch something so sacred. Inside the temple, you will enter the land of Giza. It houses the Great Pyramids, the oldest of the Seven Wonders of the ancient world. That place is like a giant maze. You must find the dark room of the gods. This room was a discard to god for this is where they worshiped idol gods. Remember, use your tools to find your way to the first candle."

Rudolph skidded to a stop on the ground in Egypt, creating a mini-sandstorm. For a moment, it was very thick, and Jess didn't see the temple right in front of her. It was changed! As soon as she stepped onto its path—it evinced to antecedent glory. An even more colorful fantastic sight; however, a more disdainful sight to all lovers of the Creator of all, God.

She kissed Rudolph on the nose and clutched the sacred charms around her neck. "I'll be back."

"And, I'll be waiting," he nodded.

Inside the temple were enormous statues, many with animal heads and human bodies. The walls were covered with ancient drawings. Jess stepped so carefully as if she were stepping on soft pillows—arriving in the center of the temple. Keeping her fingers wrapped around the miniature globe, Book-of-Knowledge and Codex Bible to guide her, Jess saw a tunnel that she knew led to an underground city. At the end of the tunnel and down some steps was a door that wouldn't budge when Jess tried to open it.

The Book-of-Knowledge charm began to glow. It resumed its original size. Jess opened it to a new message:

> *Jess, remember, you are imbued with extraordinary power from the Creator. You must proceed quickly. Use the gift of the globe.*

The book instantly shrunk to its charm size. Jess held the globe charm which expanded to its original form. "I'm not alone; God is with me. Show me the way."

When she tried the door again, it opened smoothly. She moved through the dark rooms, the grace of God giving her the ability to be strengthened in faith. Using the globe allowed her to envision each trap that had been set for intruders. At last, she spotted the first candlestick. Its holder was solid gold, encrusted with every precious jewel of the earth. Jess touched the candle and declared, "And, the Lord said, 'Let there be light.'"

The candle's flames gyrated around the entire room—aluminizing the place with a heavenly glow. A door that wasn't there before appeared. Again, the Book-of-Knowledge glowed for Jess' benefit:

> *Enter and wait for your enemy. The first battle is nigh. It is time. God has linked the Seven Wonders of the physical world to six mystical worlds and a magical world—a prevision made just for these days. It is in the non-physical realms where the immortal beasts can be destroyed and returned to Hades forever. Of this, they are aware. But, the Creator is your strength. Lure the monsters to these realms for their defeat.*
>
> *On this battle, the first mystical realms are rich with blessed silver which are the essential elements to defeat the beasts'. You will require the*

knowledge of this book less and less during your journey. For additional
strength before each battle, merely meditate on the Creator.

The Book-of-Knowledge resumed its charm form. Jess ran her hands
along the ancient script and read with understanding, and spoke aloud,
'Pyramid of Giza.' The new door opened. Upon entry through the door,
Jess approached a great pyramid, "Okay, I am in a pyramid's pyramid,
in a mystical realm. Sheesh, this is complicated." Jess, sat on the ground
going into intense prayer and meditation. Suddenly, a strong gust of
wind sucked Jess inside the mighty structure. The globe provided light
as she carefully made her way.

She slid behind a wall for cover, hearing roaring and what sounded
like a giant animal, galloping on all fours. Jess grasped the globe charm,
asking for a magical rope and flex-rod.

Then, she saw it, huge and hideous, drooling and snarling like a
mad dog. But, Jess was not afraid, looking directly into its menacing
eyes. The opponents ran toward each other. Upon reaching the mon-
strosity, Jess used her rod to leap onto the back of the best. It flapped its
wings and tried to shake her off, hitting against and activating one of the
pyramid's traps. The ground opened. Both the beast and Jess tumbled
into it. Instantly the walls began to close to crush them both. Jess hung
onto the beast's back as it rattled its monstrous wings flying upward—
managing to escape, inadvertently saving Jess, too.

The brute continued to resist, kicking and snarling. Jess was fed up,
touched the globe charm and said, "Show me the blessing."

She saw the silver, jumped from the brute's back, ran in a circle collecting silver off the walls onto her flex-rod. After, spinning the rod
around, above her head; she jumped back onto the beast's back—declaring, "In the name of Christ, Christmas and Santa Claus."

With that, she plunged her rod into the monster's back. Its roar of
agony shook the walls of the pyramid before it landed on the ground
with a thud. Jess jumped off.

Before she could catch her breath, hundreds of more beasts were
heading her way. Jess clasped the globe, "Give me two." There were two

Jess'. One flicked off the army of creatures with the mighty rod. The other Jess grabbed the large candle with both hands, releasing it from its holder.

A tornado force gust sent them all swirling through a tunnel of winds further into the mystical world.

Before Jess were mounds of the magical silver—not just small amounts on the walls. Jess quickly thought, 'This is what the book spoke of—blessed in abundance of silver.' With the power of the globe, the silver transformed into a magical blade. One by one, Jess destroyed each beast. Some were stabbed in the heart. Some were reduced to tiny, vicious cubs. Jess herded the small animals into a waiting silver box, lined with walls of thorns.

Once all through, she closed the box, squashing it until there was no more sound. Jess stepped back into herself and became one again and clasped her globe charm. "Send this package of evil to Hades!"

Instantly, the four winds from the four corners of that world carried the carnage of beasts straight to Hades. This battle was over. She reached for the sacred candle. Another door appeared. Next to it was a candleholder. Jess prayerfully placed the candle in it.

The door opened. Jess took a deep breath. Her eyes glistened in awe and gratitude for the Almighty God. There, on a golden pedestal stood a shining girdle to shield her core. She snapped it in place and remembered the words in the Codex bible, 'Stand, therefore, having girded your waist with truth.'

Chris Norm, her first beast nemesis, had been returned to Hades for all eternity. The globe sealed him there.

Brimming with bolstered confidence, Jess clasped the globe to be reunited with Rudolph.

Rudolph's nose glowed even brighter when he saw Jess' beaming strength. She happily kissed the tip of it and climbed on, "Oh, yeah, we got this. Next, Holy Place!"

Inside the castle's dark death chamber, Haley's body began to shake violently. Jade was at her side. The body levitated. Its eyes opened, opaque, milky white. Haley spoke in a low, deliberate, foreign voice, "Chris Norm failed. He and his army of beasts are all in Hades with a fierce curse from the Creator." Haley's body returned to the bed.

Furious, Jade stormed out of the room, screaming, "Abarim, go and do the job Chris couldn't. Crush that little bitch and bring her to me! Do—Not—Fail."

27

Divine My Love

Jess and Rudolph were flying through the skies, and no stars were shining. Jess sensed her friend's uneasiness. Landing on top of a mountain, Rufus emerged.

Jess gently held his face in her hands, "Something's bothering you. What is it that you're not telling me?"

Rufus lifted his head so gently, gazing at Jess, "Since time is measured here on earth, we're running out of it, and there's almost none between battles. I was just thinking, you've got the first part of the Armor of God now and the seven stars to show you the way. The globe can take you to these places. Maybe you don't need me anymore? If you want me to return to the North Pole, I will." Rufus then turned away.

Jess realized that for the first time, Rufus was uncertain of the role he played. She, too, noticed that there was no light from the moon or stars, so physical time was running out. "Rufus, look at me... There's no way I can do this without you. You are the one with intimate knowledge of each Holy Place. It is written in the book and, you said yourself that

I need you with me in these battles. Come on, Rufus! For the sake of Christ, Christmas and Santa Claus, you know that you are exactly where you need to be. Nothing is by accident or coincidence. Each of us was given different gifts, the perfect gifts, from the Creator."

Rufus looked at Jess with a new glimmer in his eye, "You're right. I know... We're in this together. I almost forgot that I feel more and more hopeful after every one of our chats and adventures. Being so low on the Christmas magical spirit and roaming these wicked skies got me feeling some kind-a-way. Guess I was a scary deer for a moment."

Jess giggled, "Scary deer? That's a good one... And, you are the bravest guy and reindeer—I know."

Rufus laughed, "I'm the only guy—reindeer, you know—you know?"

Jess giggled, "I guess you're right. I think you need a special something to build you up."

She asked the globe for a special reindeer-blend drink for Rufus.

"Thanks," Rufus chugged gratefully, "I don't know what's in this stuff. But, it's delicious and just what I needed. My spirit will lighten up along, and my nose is going to light up that wicked, darkening sky like crazy!"

"Exactly... Santa needed that nose to light shies for Christmas travels. Now, I need that nose even brighter because the skies had never been so dark—filled with hopelessness, gloom, and pure wickedness. So Drink up... That drink is like vitamins for your nose and will allow your nose to shine brighter like never before. It will also allow you to change along with the Christmas magic. Although, magic is very low and I will need you to be able to change whenever needed."

The Book-of-Knowledge charm glowed and a rush of a cool mist in the nightly airbrushed across them. But, Jess didn't have to remove it to read it. For the first time, a warm, nurturing, female voice emanated from it—as when God's Holy Spirit speaks—clearly without a doubt:

"Jessica, I must share the actual history of the second Holy Place, so that you'll entirely armed for defeating the next beast. You are familiar with the

story of Jonah and the whale. Jonah, one of God's chosen people, had a sister, Abarim, who was also directed to a spiritual mission by God.

Abarim, however, refused and cursed God's name. She was thrown into the belly of a shark and imprisoned there in the waters by God. However, Abarim was clever. Eventually, she escaped. For many years, Abarim dwelled alone under the two main merging rivers near her people, the Euphrates and the Tigris—between these two rivers exist mystical waters. While in these mystical waters—she learned the art of black magic— becoming part fish—a dark mystical creature. For many years, Abarim dwelled alone but remained keenly aware of all things involving her inherent family. She was well aware that the people of God had displeased Him and knew that the Almighty would deal a punishment.

When the waters vigorously rushed to and fro with the wind, the Israelites knew it was a sign that Babylonian King Nebuchadnezzar would over-throw their kingdom. Abarim observed the slaughter of her people but felt nothing. Many Israelites were killed. Many others were taken as Babylonian prisoners and slaves. The king ordered that the waters be searched. A faithful guard and adviser to the king spotted Abarim. She quickly dipped back into the river to shield herself from their sight. Abarim no longer felt safe in that part of the river, so she settled closer to the Euphrates River, which happened to be near the palace of King Nebuchadnezzar. One lovely night, Abarim dared to leave the river to get a better look around.

To her astonishment, Abarim's fishtail dried and split into two legs. Her long hair, which floated like seaweed in the waters, now blew like silk in the gentle evening winds. Her human form was magnificent. The king's guard was determined to capture her as a prize for the king to improve his status with the monarch. Abarim was lonely and gave him no fight. The guard covered her nakedness with his cloak and took her to the palace.

Upon seeing Abarim's beauty, King Nebuchadnezzar welcomed the guard's intrusion and quickly, rid himself of his battle plans.

The king was enchanted—an Israelite beauty. He was in awe—as was Abarim upon laying eyes on each other. After years of loneliness, Abarim did that which was forbidden—fell in love and mated with the human king. King Nebuchadnezzar didn't care that she was an Israelite or that she was a mystical sea creature. Abarim loved the sea gardens, so the king built a hanging garden over the waters to express his love for her. They both shared a sworn hatred for God.

All was well as long as the king's Median wife, Queen Amytis, was kept in the dark about the illicit affair. Abarim became pregnant with a litter. The king's divine love grew cold, and he abandoned her. Abarim accepted love's defeat and never attempted to see the king again. However, the king had many nights wishing he could see Abarim again but his relentless status wasn't going to allow it—therefore he had a temporary moment of insanity. Abarim babies—little mermaids were protected by God's Grace, made good and separated from Abarim.

Broken-hearted, at a loss from everything—she retreated to the rivers. Angrily cursing the gardens only to live when she's near. The hanging garden withered and died, like the forbidden affair. After centuries of human time, the gardens and the gated grounds around them were never seen. However, it was said, in the presence of pure love for Christ, Christmas or Santa Claus; the gardens would come to life and cause Abarim come out of hiding—retracting the curse, posed by the Creator.

Rudolph has accompanied Santa near the garden's grounds. They ever stepped onto the actual ground, or they too would have seen a reverse of Abarim curse—they two have a genuine love for Christ, Christmas, and Santa Claus. Rudolph knows this location well. He has feasted on its sweet grasses near the gates. The solution to defeating Abarim is this; love has become Abarim's hate. Use it to beat her.

And yes, you can hear me now because you wear a piece of God's armor, and that Girdle-of-Truth is what you'll need in the next battle. You no longer need to access my assistance by reading messages in The Book-of-Knowledge. Nor do you need to touch the globe to activate its power. The Girdle-of-Truth allows you to see all that is true. I now—can speak directly to your mind whenever you need my counsel. Just listen to me with your heart. My name is Bride, the bride of the Holy Spirit. Call me, and I will answer. The Book-of-Knowledge, the Codex, and the Globe must remain safe with you. Hide them within the Girdle-of-Truth. The translation of Abarim's name is 'passage.' Make sure she does not escape. Make haste,

Dear Jessica. All events must unfold in order. Inform Rufus that his role in the third battle is critical. He will know what it is when the time comes."

Jess shook her head as though waking from a deep sleep. Rufus was staring at her, suspiciously.

"What?" Jess yipped.

"You were talking to yourself, Lady. Should I be worried?" Rufus raised one brow inquisitively.

Jess playfully popped her friend on the shoulder. "No, but I do have a message for you from the Book-of-Knowledge. Well, actually—it's the voice behind the book."

Rufus' eyes widened.

Jess laughed, "Don't look at me like that. I'm not crazy. She's the bride of the Holy Spirit. In fact, her name is Bride. She said you would know how important your role is in the third battle. Meanwhile, we've got to fly up out of here."

Jess hugged Rufus and began to sing his transformation song. When he became Rudolph, she hopped on his back and grabbed the straps.

They saw the star at the same time.

"Look!" Rudolph yelled. "The star shines on two locations, Babylon and Jerusalem."

Jess closed her eyes to be still and listen to Bride:

"Jess, your battle with Abarim begins at Babylon's Hanging Gardens. Then, lure her to the next Holy Place, Beit HaMikdash in Jerusalem. Lead her to the temple. You'll know exactly what to do. Each of God's gifts provides you with special abilities. Use the Girdle-of—Truth to shapeshift."

Rudolph had never stopped talking, not realizing Jess was in a trance. But, she hadn't missed a word he said.

"The Beit HaMikdash is near. The Sanctified Temple, where they performed all the sacrificial rituals is there. So, that's probably where you'll find your next candlestick," he explained.

Jess leaned close to his ear, "I'm so happy to have you to guide me, Rudolph. And, happy that you're my friend."

Rudolph smiled the best a reindeer could, "Me, too. You're growing on me, kid. Hey, there it is. The gates to the entrance of the gardens are there. I can smell the sweet grass from up here."

Thump! They were down. Rudolph morphed into Rufus again.

"Smooth landing," Jess teased. She reached into her backpack, pulling out a string of bells.

"Jingle bells? At a time like this," Rufus questioned.

"What better time than now? The sound of Christmas bells has always made me happy. These will serve as a constant reminder of how important it is that I win every battle. Here—how about we tie them around your neck? That way we can both enjoy the joyful noise and keep our Christmas Spirit revved up."

As instructed by the Bride, Jess hid all of her charms inside the Girdle-of-Truth. Then something truly miraculous happened. The Girdle shined brighter as each precious charm was absorbed. The light and love of God poured gloriously through Jess' eyes, mouth, and fingertips. Rufus praised the Creator and kissed Jess' hand.

Jess lovingly placed her hand on Rufus' cheek, "Thank you. Now, stay safe. You must shift back into Rudolph so we can make a quick getaway. Oh, by-the-way, you're going to need to drink this before I get back."

Rufus knew it was another portion to help him develop another something. He took the cup, sipped it, "Yuk! All that power and you couldn't have made this taste better."

Jess, laughed again at Rufus, "Enjoy."

"Sure thing..." Rufus downed the drink. Feeling more vibrant, he shifted to Rudolph—without a song from Jess. He shook as a dog does. "Now, this is cool!" Rudolph circled Jess. "What other tricky drinks you got on you?"

Jess laughed, "Eat the sweet grass it should take the edge off that drink."

"Edge! Woe, there... girl. What do you mean, edge?" Although Rudolph loved Jess courage and spunk; she makes him wonder.

Jess shook her head. "Gotta go! Rest."

"Rest! Be alert! I'm confused. Which one—girl!" Rufus was nervous.

"I'll be back." Jess smiled walking away but looking back at her funny friend. Climbing up the mountain until she disappeared into the bushes from his sight altogether.

Fortified with faith, strength, and courage, Jess found herself in front of the gates to the gardens. She slowly walked past the gates and sat for preparation through meditation and prayer, "Not my will, Creator of all, but Thy will into."

With each battle, God revealed more details on the full matter in all worlds and lands. Through this information, she becomes surer and more eager to know more about God's plans.

Soon, Jess felt the presence of another being. The ground began to shake violently. Touching the girdle, which now housed the globe,

Jess cast a protective force field of Grace around her. God unfailingly revealed to Jess what she needed—exactly when she needs it.

When the ground calmed, Jess walked, running her fingers along the gorgeous greenery of the beautiful Hanging Gardens of Babylon. As they continually changed from weeds to the healthiest of colorful gardens, Jess began speaking aloud to force Abarim to show herself—using Truth.

"This garden is breathtakingly beautiful. How lovely and special the person who received it as a gift must be. I know you're here, Abarim. And, I know about all your losses—your lover, your children, and worst of all—your loss of God. But, that was your own doing."

As she'd hoped, Jess pushed just the right button. The plants and vines in the garden begun to move—vibrational sounds of sharp snapping branches, waves of running vines crackled all around her. Jess look up as they grew, twisted and intertwined until they had formed a giant plant woman. She stood ninety feet tall with shimmering ruby red eyes. Abarim's height made the Gardens appear very small. Abarim shot vines from her fingertips to wrap around Jess' body, seemingly restraining her, lifting her into the air.

Jess continued to scream Abarim's painful truths, "Your hatred for all that is good springs from your weakness. Abarim's branches tightened their grip on the girl. She used thorny limbs to attempt to silence Jess. The Girdle-of-Truth shone. Jess was imbued with new, physical powers. She marveled at her hands as they transformed into machetes, chopping away at Abarim's wines and branches. Abarim shrieked in agony, filling with rage. Disarmed, she shrank into her human form, Haley's mousy tutor. Abarim took off toward the water. Jess ran in the opposite direction, knowing Abarim would follow. The re-birthed Abarim as a sea beast with blue scales, wings, sharp teeth and long seaweed hair. It drooled, thinking the teenager was helpless and weak. The Abarim beast tried to trap Jess feet in its moving tangle of roots; so, Jess ran faster. She whistled to a waiting Rudolph and hopped on his back when he swooped closer to scoop her up.

Feeling encouraged, invigorated and blessed with the power of God as she and Rudolph soared through the skies, Jess yelled, "To Jerusalem's Holy Temple, Beit HaMikdash, my friend!"

The beast flapped her enormous scaly wings to follow Rudolph. She was gaining on them.

Suddenly, Rudolph noticed a change in his body—more power. "The drink is taking a different effect than earlier!"

"Let it happen!" Jess demanded.

He felt a change in his body. Powerful, new muscles formed and he begun to sparkle through the dense dark skies. Uplifted by another miraculous Divine Intervention, Rudolph sprouted not two wings—but four! He and Jess took off like a rocket. The beast could barely keep up.

Jess leaned towards Rudolph's ear and spoke loud enough for him to hear, "Make sure she follows! We must keep her at a perfect distance."

Taunting the beast with truths was Jess way to be sure she didn't give up the chase. It worked because the creature was infuriated.

"Abarim your children must have been smarter. They followed God. No need for a mother when you've got God, right?" Jess yelled.

Abarim stayed on their tail—wanting more than anything to kill this girl. Close enough to wack Rudolph on the behind cause them to fall from the sky. Rudolph and Jess landed in front of Temple Beit HaMikdash, with Abarim right behind them. Jess ordered Rudolph to fly away as she Ran into the Temple, knowing Abarim would follow her.

Jess backed slowly toward the Temple's inner chambers. Abarim mistook Jess' action as fear and thinking the landing wasn't a plane location. "Such a weak little girl," she drooled. "Why would the Creator send a stupid, fragile, human child to save the destiny of all worlds? I can't wait to take you to my mistress and watch her eat you alive."

By the time the beast realized it was a trap; it was too late. Jess reached her target, spotted the second candle and yanked it from its holder. A deluge of water whooshed over both of them, along with powerful winds which whipped into a tunnel to transport Jess and the beast to another realm. It was a world composed solely of water.

Jess instantly shape-shifted into a silver, mermaid-like creature with reptilian eyes framed by long, black lashes. Her upper body was human-shaped and snugly fit with the golden Girdle-of-Truth. Just below it was a single, fuchsia-scaled fishtail. Jess marveled that her red hair was the same vibrant color as her tail. She was also gifted with a bow and arrows. In her transformation, she lost track of Abarim.

Jess flowed through the waters, searching throughout the worlds waters with bow and arrow erected. Many life forms knew why she was there. They communicated differently in that world with grunts, chirps, and pops and told their stories—telepathically. Truly afraid of Abarim—she had been there before attempting to spread her evilness. Jess communicated to them to go into hiding.

However, Jess was blessed by the Creator with resources and knowledge of exactly what to do. She taunted Abarim telepathically, "Do you ever think about your children? What kind of mother leaves her babies without a fight? The Creator was good to you, and you betrayed and

cursed Him. You have no loyalty. You are an abomination, having rela-
tions with a married human. You are a failure who is failing right now,
Abarim! Your demented mistress will be as disappointed with you as
God was. And, still is."

The tactic worked. Abarim and Jess were tangling in the water.
Abarim with her razor-sharp shark teeth took a bite out of Jess' tail. Jess
was injured and lost her bow and arrows during the battle. The Bride
spoke to her heart, spirit, and mind:

> *"Jess, the Creator will grant one blessing to Abarim. That blessing will
> weaken her. Use the opportunity to finish her."*

Jess touched the girdle and prayed, "Thy will be done, not mine."

Ten half-human, half-fish creatures that strongly resembled the
non-beast version of Abarim, circled her in the water—allowing Jess to
find her Bow and arrow. Seeing her children took Abarim off-guard. If
they were on land; there would have been tears running down her face.
However, Jess did not forget; nor, did she allow her heart to feel pity for
Abarim. Jess retrieved her bow and arrows, shooting one directly into
Abarim's heart.

A hole opened in the floor of the watery environment. Its darkness
sucked the beast right into it, carrying her straight to Hades. Then, it
closed as if never there.

Jess turned to the God-blessed mer-children, communicating with
them through her mind, "You guys are lovely. I'm sorry about your
mother."

The eldest answered telepathically, "The Creator is both our mother
and our father. We lack nothing. Thank you, Jess. We invite you to come
back and visit us when you can. Godspeed..."

Jess smiled and waved good-bye. She wished upon the globe and was
back in front of the Temple in a heartbeat. She placed the candlestick
back into its holder. As before, a door opened with light radiating from
within. Perched atop of another golden pedestal was her next sacred gift

from God, the Breastplate-of-Righteousness. She placed it over her head and shoulders, then dropped to her knees to praise and thank God.

Within moments, Jess wished her way back to Rudolph, who was taking a nap, probably after filling his tummy with sweet grass and the side effect of the potion drink, Jess mused. The reindeer was startled awake when Jess kissed him on the nose.

"Hey, there... Sleepyhead." Jess laughed. "Time to saddle up for our next battle."

"No rest for the weary, huh?" Rudolph joked. "But could I get another drink and one more taste of sweet grass?"

"You mean this drink?" Jess winked as the bottle appeared in her hand.

"I'll never get tired of that, but the other. YUK!" Rudolph exclaimed.

"You know, you were correct. I can make all your drinks so that they taste wonderful." Jess nodded.

"Taste is all I care about." Rudolph chewed on as much of the grass as he could, then washed it down with the distinctive drink.

━ ～

Although she'd received no official word, Jade sensed that Abarim, too, had failed in her mission and cursed God. He wasn't going to make this easy.

Haley's dead body, which should have been cold, was instead burning with a fever. It was an unnatural-but-typical physical reaction to Haley's hellish mental visit to become immortal. Jade telepathically summoned another of her evil disciples, Chance, the vampire butler, to go and get it done. It was critical to Haley's complete immortality process that Jade keep her physical body cool.

Even as she played the part of a doting mother, Jade warned Chance Dickson to dare not fail her.

Chance assumed his form as a bat and flew away to defeat this annoyingly relentless Apprentice.

28

Secrets In The Blood

E
ven though he enjoyed them, Rudolph realized his new wings took some getting used to, but they were cool. While Jess was silent in one of her now-familiar trances, he decided to practice.

The Bride's reassuring voice through the Book-of-Knowledge again prepared Jess for the next battle:

> *"Jess, sheer mental strength is critical for the next fight. The Breastplate-of-Righteousness will give you valuable insight into the past of your enemy. Use it to defeat him. His skills enable him to travel across time zones in the physical world freely. The enemy and his kind have wreaked havoc, death, and destruction in the physical world for eons. Know that there are three secrets in the blood.*
>
> *"First, through a single bite of the monster's fangs, he can sap the remaining life expectancy of his victim. He must feed to remain immortal. The beast is 'undead' but will cease to exist in any form if it does not feed and the younger the victim—the better.*

"Second, there is a caveat to that. The Creator has provided protection for children under 18 years of age. If a blood-sucking beast bites a child, it will have created its own worst enemy; a child vamp that would hunt them all and feed on them and they will die off—ultimately exterminating the breed.

"Third, the souls of a vampire's victims are trapped in exile inside the creature, unable to move on to either heaven or hell. This blood secret develops the vampire's ability to mind control. The enemy can also manipulate the elements of the physical world—lightening, winds, and water—and bend them to his will—a gift from the evil Nefari. Protect yourself."

Jess came out of her trance to the treat of Rudolph merrily singing Christmas Carols and having fun testing the limits of his new wings. The bells around his neck jingled in perfect harmony with the songs. She loved it but knew they had to be about the mission.

As a compromise, Rudolph delighted Jess by playfully flying up and down like a roller coaster as they searched the skies for the next guiding star. Again, they spotted the star at the same time.

Rudolph's nose grew brighter than usual. "It's leading us to Turkey, hold on!"

Arriving at the Mausoleum at Halicarnassus, old anxious feelings gripped Rudolph. He never liked it when he and Santa visited this desolate place and implored Jess to be extra careful. With a nod, she dismissed Rudolph.

As soon as Jess stepped foot onto the ancient ground, it shook violently with the presence of her goodness. The earth's dangerous unsteadiness did not affect Jess' determined stride to the Mausoleum. All of the quaking eventually revealed the Mausoleum's original construction. Jess being girded with truth—the spirit revealed that unspeakable things were done on these grounds to dishonor the Creator.

Before entering, Jess paused to listen within for God's instruction and additional knowledge through the Bride. After sitting in meditation and prayer; she praised Him for the newest clues and released her red curls from their ponytail. She touches the girdle, used the power of the globe, and Miraculously, Jess' hair transforms into a brass shield that encircled her neck to protect it.

Walking up the building's steps slowly at first, Jess was well-aware of the six stone, winged lions that protectively flanked each side. As she climbed, the eyes of each beast glowed, bringing them to life, pulling away from the cement foundation that held each in place.

Jess used the power of the globe for a spear and an impenetrable net.

Jess ran up the stairs now, the roaring beasts now free, galloping after her, as their wings became free to move. Reaching the top, Jess yelled, "Not my will, but Yours." She twirled the giant net and flung it toward the beasts, entrapping them. Jess pierced the heart of every winged lion. One by one, they turned to dust.

Before Jess could catch her breath, an army of gigantic, black

Bats swarmed toward her, circling to envelop her. Jess ran to a near-by door, touched her girdle and screamed, "Open." Because it was pitch black inside the room she entered, Jess implored the globe, "Let there be a light of fire!" A ball of fire materialized in her open palms. Jess hurled it toward the ceiling. The cavernous space was illuminated.

Two enormous statues—one male, one female—dominated the room. The bats had followed her inside, now noisily intertwining with each other to create what resembled a man. The stone statues opened. Out stepped the decayed remains of a man and a woman who uttered in unison, "Son." The bat beast bowed.

With her ever-growing reservoir of knowledge, Jess realized this was the tomb of the ancient Persian King and his Queen. The beast was their son. The three embraced, becoming one enormous and dangerous creature.

Remembering that Rudolph was crucial in this third battle, Jess quickly devised a plan. She implored the power of the globe to give Rudolph everything he needed to ensure victory in this battle.

Outside the Mausoleum, Rudolph was changing both mentally and physically. His mental clarity sharpened. He tripled in size with bulging muscles and new long, pointy spikes on his four wings. A helmet encased his head, leaving his antlers free.

The globe gifted Jess with the most durable possible holy rod, made of silver and magical stones. With it, Jess easily eluded the frustrated grasp of the triple beast. Mistakenly staring it down for the briefest moment, the creature was able to awaken a memory in Jess' mind while looking into her eyes. In it, she, Haley and Grandmau-ma were sitting in Grandmau-ma's kitchen, laughing and talking. Tears stung the back of Jess' eyes. But, she refused to give into the beast's attempt to weaken her, instead; using the power from the Breastplate-of-Righteousness— she turned the memories right back to the beast.

All was revealed for each of them to see and experience at the same time through a series of visions, with Jess at the helm. Jess became the beast trio's "Ghost of Christmas Past, Present, and Future." However, it was with an edge.

The present was revealed first. The three-in-one witnessed the pain and suffering they caused by ruining Christmases in the physical world over many lifetimes to the present. Chance watched and heard Jade/Nefari ranting about his many weaknesses, what an embarrassment he was to her elite army of followers. Jade cackled that he was expendable and fantasized about what might be the most amusing ways to torture him through eternity since he was also an immortal. The part of Chance that cared was seething.

The past next brought more agony to the beasts—vicious family secrets.

The vision of the future also held the stench of sulfur and the cries of eternal, agonizing torture and this was the evil trio's fate, as written in the Creator's book; and, there was no escaping it.

It was torture for the beast; but, it couldn't separate, even as it bucked and tried to bore its triple set of fiery eyes into Jess. The struggle was too much for the ancient walls. They caught on fire, tumbling and crashing down. Jess' mental spell on the triple-beast was broken. She quickly whistled for her flying buddy.

A newly empowered Rudolph flew right through the fiery walls. Jess leaped on his back and took off for the skies. The beast trio was on them immediately, just as Jess hoped they'd be. They needed to get to the next Holy Place and magical realm.

Because they were a wickedly intertwined family unit, the beast had a slight advantage. The bats annoyingly nipped at Rudolph while he was in flight. The mother beast dropped the temperature in an attempt to freeze his wings. Grandmau-ma's sweater was prophetically meant to keep Jess warm for this very battle. But, even though Rudolph was used to the cold of the North Pole, this was different, and his wings were stiffening. Jess used the power of the globe to give Rudolph another head with fire-breathing ability. One head continued to fly in the direction of the Holy Place, and the other head looked backward and used its fire-breath to warm his wings. The father part of the beast reached for Rudolph's wings, but its spikes drove into the beast's flesh. The monstrous enemy became discombobulated and tumbled through the air to the grounds of Gobekli Tepe that Rudolph had led them.

The beast was wounded physically and mentally—busy trying to rid themselves of the thorns and the mental invasion. Jess pulled out her silver rod and leaped from Rudolph's back to the ground. The ground began to quake. Twelve, ten-foot tall stone columns circled her with a bluish bubble of protection around her. As the beast approached, Jess summoned chains which bubbled from the sacred ground, binding the legs of two of the beast trio. The third escaped as hundreds of bats. With a wave of her hand, the bats hurled to the ground in a death-like sleep.

As soon as the beast was contained, Jess saw another door between two of her protective pillars. A candlestick hovered at its entrance in mid-air. Jess closed her eyes in meditation for continued guidance. When she opened her eyes, Jess grabbed the candle. The door opened. Angry bolts of lightning appeared, accompanied by hurricane-force winds.

Even Chance's power over weather did not affect stopping this. He and his parents were sucked into a magical world of lost beasts, filled with wandering zombies with no thoughts and monsters who were tortured with mental anguish—this was one stop before Hades. Furious, Chance lunged at Jess to sink his vampire fangs into Jess' flesh and rip her apart. He could not remove the armor of God and thought to go for her wrist. Jess skin hardened and left him toothless. Jess taunted, "A toothless Vamp—now, that's impressive."

Jess touched her Breastplate-of-Righteousness to defeat the three with their evil pasts.

The Persian King and Queen relived the birth of their second son, feeling the love as he grew to six-years-old. Twelve-year-old Chance had overheard an argument between the two when the baby was born. The King insisted that the youngest son be the one to take the throne as his wife had disgraced him by laying with a servant and giving birth to Chance.

Now, his father's harsh treatment and constant criticism all made sense to Chance. He wasn't his father's son at all. Chance was angry and resentful and ran away from home. He soon stumbled upon and practiced black magic with angry Greek gods.

As a grown man, he was beautiful in his physical appearance but hideous in his heart. Chance fell in with a nest of vampires, allowing them to turn him into one of them—an immortal, un-dead, blood-sucker.

Chance returned home to his grieving adulterous mother and resentful stepfather. Feeling all-powerful, with a full muscular appearance of his birth father. His green eyes, golden skin, masculine facial structure and his dark hair that drifted through the air as he walked into the quarters had every female longing to bow before him and every male envious of him. His half father wasn't impressed; in fact, he resembled his biological father so, it boiled his step father's blood that he would even come back. Ignoring the hatred in her husband's eyes, the queen commanded preparation of a celebratory feast, whispering threateningly to the King, "If you wish to maintain your dignity among our people, you will make a public show of rejoicing with me on our son's return."

The King swallowed his feelings and ordered the servants to prepare the feast. As he did, a little boy ran to the King and wrapped his arms around his legs. Knowing full-well who the child was, Chance played the part of the doting big brother, excited to meet his half-sibling.

The night of the feast, the little boy was settled into his sleeping chambers by his servants. His mother kissed him goodnight and joined the party. Chance pretended to say goodnight to his little brother. Instead, he turned into the monster he was and sank his fangs into the child's neck, draining him, leaving his lifeless body as though he were sleeping peacefully.

Chance returned to the celebration to eat, drink and be merry as though nothing had happened. Afterwards, he retrieved his little brother's body and gave it to his evil friend, Nefari. Nefari was well-schooled in the laws of the blood and whisked the child's body to a magical world where there were no vampires for him to kill.

The King and Queen were devastated by their loss. Chance maintained the charade of spearheading the search for his brother, taking masterful command of the King's army. Witnessing—and believing—Chance's faux compassion for his brother and his leadership skills, the king left his kingdom to the treacherous vampire. And with a drink from the same cup—death took both parents. Left to remain in concrete tombs.

Jess tore the trance to let the visions sink in. The rage between the three broke them apart. A tiny, vicious zombie with black eyes descended on Chance, clamped onto his big brother and began to devour him gleefully. While Chance screamed and the mummified king watched, and the Queen cried to see the truth through proof of her young son's black evil eyes. Jess waved her hands, commanding the winds to seal them in mid-air. With the globe's power, she was armed with four silver stakes. Her mind skillfully directed the stakes into the heart of each beast, including the child.

She threw back her head, arms open to receive the gifts of the Creator and exclaimed, "Let there again be light in this world!"

And, so it was. Countless innocent souls escaped the evil purgatory of Chance's un-dead body and ascended into heaven. She praised God for His mercy and blessed them all as they returned to Him. Jess was moved, witnessing the mercy of the Creator; she understood why he would empty himself as Christ to save them and so many others who become trapped.

As for the fallen beast, Jess merely waited for the rays of the sun to burn each to ashes. The ground opened, and the ashes were swept to Hades.

Jess sighed with relief and gratitude, touched her girdle with all its precious cargo and whispered, "Gobekli Tepe."

$$\sim$$

Instantly, she stood before the Holy Place in the physical world. She reached into her backpack to grab the candlestick and place it back in its holder. As before, a door appeared and opened to reveal its glorious light. There, atop another golden pedestal, was the Helmet-of-Salvation. She donned it, gave thanks to the Creator and left to find Rudolph.

Jess could only giggle watching her buddy struggle with the extra head and the protective gear. The Bride from the Book-of-Knowledge chimed in:

> *"Some things and situations are being lived now through your experience with Rudolph would be embedded in parts of history throughout this physical world. You see, Rudolph has two heads. One is looking forward, and one is looking backward—this is a symbol of why the beginning begins with January. The beginning, but never an ending... Help him, Jess, to calm down."*

Rudolph was mostly frustrated because he couldn't coordinate his forward and backward heads to eat.

"Jess," he sighed with relief, "please, get this thing off of me. I'm starving and practically dying of thirst after all that fire-breathing. I singed my own tail."

"As it was," Jess ordered, touching her girdle.

Rudolph shook his reindeer head with relief, "Whew, thank you. Whoever said, two heads are better than one couldn't have possibly tried it. But they did come in handy when we needed them. I hope we don't have to do that again."

Jess grabbed Rudolph around the neck in a grateful hug, "No, thank you!"

$$\sim$$

One of Jade's snitch birds spilled the tea about Chance's colossal failure.

Jade shrieked in a fury, "Who does this manipulating little brat think she is? No one is ruining my plan for the total elimination of Christ and His ridiculous Christmas and Santa Claus! Look for a sign in mid-heaven. He always gives a sign. Follow it! When you find that little manipulator who's interfering with my evil plans, bring me her head! Jack, put an end to this!"

Jack quickly changed his form into the dragon and flew out for revenge.

29

Into The Fire

Nightmares robbed Rufus of peaceful dreams, so he got no sleep. "It's time to go," he blurted out, sitting straight up, disoriented. Jess had also fallen asleep, waking up now, confused. "What? Why? What's wrong? I haven't even heard from the book yet with further direction. You were sleeping kinda fitfully, dude. You okay?"

Rufus took a deep breath, "No, I don't think I am. These next battles aren't just about you, Jess. They're about me, too. It's about me choosing to be faithful... Even through—all the fear. Fear is a powerful, paralyzing force, Jess. An absolute absence of faith that's ultimately seeded in evil. There's something you should know about me."

Jess wrapped her arms around her knees, all ears. Rufus almost never got this deep.

Rufus touched his nose, "And, you'll understand why I've got this red honker. I haven't always been me. I mean, I've been me; but in three different forms during my existence. Perpetually in a mystical or magical world... First, I was a dog, then and man and now, a reindeer. Ours was a mystical world of dogs, and I was more intuitive than most—and, as it turns out, more vulnerable. One day, my world came under attack from evil with a vengeance. You know the darkness as Satan or the devil. The attack was so invasive; it tested the faith of every one of the Creator's heavenly creatures. Even though I knew better, I let doubt—which is caused by fear rooted in evil to seep into my consciousness.

This doubt and fear distanced me from the love and protection of the Creator. Because of my weakness, doubt and distance from God, I assisted in the birth of one of Satan's descendants into the physical world. I dug up the three sacred bones of faith that protected my world and gave them to Satan, the father of the lie.

Through my dreams, I've learned that this is how the devil's spawn, Nefari, was able to access the Key-of-Death. But, our Creator is a merciful God. I was forgiven for the atrocity I had committed. My red nose is a constant reminder of how close I was to the fire and that I will never again allow fear to affect my faith in the Creator and my devotion to Him. Whatever form I take, I will have my nose for all eternity."

"Wow!" Jess' mouth was hanging wide open. "Well, I am grateful for God's mercy, too. There's no way I could fight these battles without your amazing strength and courage, Rufus. Your sense of humor is a bonus! Don't worry. You got this. No stinkin' fear is ever going to sneak up on you again."

"Thanks, Jess. I needed that. We got this. Sit tight. I'm gonna go and find some more firewood."

"Cool. But, hurry back, ok? It's getting dark now. Hopefully, we'll see another guiding star in a little while."

As Rufus rustled through the forest for wood, the Bride spoke to Jess:

"Jess, Rufus' concern is not unfounded. The coming battles will mightily test each of you. The Creator has given you the Helmet-of-Salvation—allowing you to see the fate of your enemies and with that, you'll see other things. This gift along with the gift of the Breastplate-of-Righteousness which allows you to visually see the past of the lives of the enemy will serve difficult sentiments. Use your divine gifts of God's Armor to defuse your enemies.

Choose your words carefully. And, remember, things are not always as they appear. Deception lies in your path. Rufus will serve his role. Do not be distracted by it. Stay focused on your mission."

Rufus returned with wood to build a friendly fire and berries for them to eat. Jess had stopped using the globe to conjure creature comforts—making sure Nefari did zero in on her location.

The two snuggled together for extra warmth. It was terrific for both Jess and Rufus to have a moment to rest and enjoy each other's company. The bond between them felt even stronger after Rufus shared his story with Jess.

Next, it was Jess' turn to open up. Everything had moved so quickly after Grandmau-ma left her, Jess hadn't had any real time to grieve. Sharing details of her life with Grandmau-ma was cathartic. Rufus was an empathetic listener and comforter. As though a dam broke, all of Jess' pent-up grief poured out in sobbing and painful but necessary—wailing.

Once Jess calmed down, the Bride spoke with her usual nurturing voice, this time tinkling with the nuance of loving mirth. To both Jess and Rufus this time:

"Tis true that love and bonding proliferate when it's right."

Rufus was taken aback, "What?" Rufus jumped up looking around. "Who's that? Did you hear that, Jess? Am I dead? Hearing things—Jess? Or am I nuts?"

Jess giggled, "Seriously, dude? Calm down. You live in the North Pole with Santa Claus, sprout spiky wings for battling monsters... then, you nearly jump out of your skin over a voice? That's the Bride of the Holy Spirit that I told you about, speaking through the Book-of-Knowledge. But, since you're able to hear her, too, that must mean something super-special."

Rufus' face turned almost as red as his nose. The Bride spoke again:

"It was not my intention to startle you, Rufus. And, I understand. Jess, you see, it was a demonic voice ages ago that tricked Rufus into choosing fear over faith, resulting in the loss of the Key-of-Death to Nefari. But there is no need to be wary of me, my red-nosed child. I bring to you a message and instructions from the Creator, Himself. He has endowed you with extraordinary strength and gifts to right the wrongs of the past.

Christ's message is from the Codex Bible, 'Trust Him with all your heart. Do not lean on your own understanding. In all ways take notice of Him, and He will make your path straight.' Together, you and the Apprentice, Jess, form a perfect storm against evil.

The next beast is already on its way. Its primary weapon is deception. While in the physical world, use the Helmet-of-Salvation to freeze time, when the moment is right, Jess. May God be with you."

The voice silenced. Jess and Rufus hugged each other with affection and mutual support... and an absolute wonder to what was next.

— ~

The two stayed that way, staring at the inky sky, waiting for the star that would guide their way to the next Holy Place. When it appeared, Jess touched her girdle, "We're on. Time to transform and battle."

"Just no more extra heads, please," Rufus pleaded.

Jess chuckled, "You got it. No more heads. But, get ready to be super-sized Rudolph again!"

Down on his arms and legs, Rufus morphed into Rudolph, gaining girth, muscle, ten extra feet in height, the mighty, thorny wings and giant hooves. Rudolph knelt as gentlemen's gesture of respect and Jess could climb on his back; with another hug, they were off.

Airborne, Rudolph realized the star was guiding them back to Turkey. "Santa would always sprinkle magical sleeping dust over the land so that no one ever noticed us. Sometimes people are afraid of the unknown. With the sleeping dust, their innocence is protected."

Jess understood, closed her eyes asking for such magic now and a bag of the dust appeared in her hands. She sprinkled it to protect the humans below from the ensuing battle.

A beast with six fire-breathing heads was on their tail.

"I complained about the two heads. This beast has six! He must be mad about that."

The beast continued to gain and now, spitting fireballs at them. "Fire! I hate fire! Jess, do something!" Rudolph screamed.

Jess always saw the beauty in everything, "He has six head and fire, but he's beautiful."

Feeling the heat from the beast, "Girl! Get with the program. There is nothing beautiful about fire spitballs! It's hot! He's just as fast as I am."

By then, the beast was neck-and-neck with Rudolph, speaking in a threatening, growling voice, "I know you." His eyebrows raised, "You're the reason why my mystical world was destroyed. My entire family perished. What do you think you're going to save now, reindeer-dog? You can't get past me. And, the so-called warrior on your back is but a weak human child."

With her powers, Jess shielded Rudolph from the flames and sent him into warp speed. Incensed, the beast unsuccessfully tried to knock Rudolph off course. Instead, Rudolph streaked toward the Temple of Artemis.

Jess realized this monster's ire was with Rudolph. Upon landing, she leaped off his back and commanded, "Santa's shield, be upon Rudolph!" As the beast and Rudolph menacingly circled each other, the reindeer over with knowledge, greater size and strength, clawed hooves, razor-sharp teeth and the ability to roar and with fire laser eyes. The six-headed beast was now the smaller one.

As the two beasts fought in an earth-shaking battle, Jess backed away to step onto the grounds of the Temple of Artemis. Her heart almost sank when she saw it in ruins. But, upon Jess' arrival, the Creator restored the temple to its original glory.

Jess gave silent praise and spent precious moments in meditation. The beast's rapid approach broke the peace. Jess used the power of the globe to freeze time, allowing the Breastplate-of-Righteousness to reveal the creature's past.

In a trance, she peered into several separate lives. A boy named Demetrius who grew up in the physical world, his brother; who originated in a mystical world but transformed from an egg (Infancy) in the physical world, a mother, of two as Diana—later to become a mother to many as the Ephesus goddess, Artemis.

In a village in a mystical land, Diana had two young sons, Demetrius and Jombus. An epic battle between good and evil was brewing. Opening wormholes took unique jewels and were forbidden because one wormhole allows entrees from different worlds to visit without the Creators approval. However, Diana was desperate to save her family. Diana placed her sons in a wormhole. Before Diana could do the same for herself; she was captured. Demetrius cried for his mother as he dissolved through the life-saving tunnel—knowing his world was destroyed. Its enemies destroyed the entire mystical world but Diana's beauty was as many jewels, and this factor changed her fate. Instead, of death—she was captured for sacrifice and taken through a different wormhole to the physical world.

Diana's son, Jombus didn't form into a human species on the travel as his brother did. Being an egg in a protected shell prevented it—left to in his original form. Jombus would later, form into the mystical creature in the physical world. Also, the protective egg and Demetrius were separated as they were sent through the magical wormhole to safety.

Its enemies destroyed the entire village but Diana's beauty was as many jewels, and this factor changed her fate. Instead, of death—she was captured for sacrifice and taken through a different wormhole to the physical world.

Demetrius landed in a world and body form unknown to him. He studied the ways of physical creatures and tried to fit in. Most could see that he was without parents, but none of the surviving villagers in the physical world were able to take in another mouth to feed, so a lonely young Demetrius was forced to raise himself. Because he had to survive on his own, the boy taught himself to hunt, to fight, to be cunning, ultimately becoming a collector of precious stones—jewels.

His brother, Jompus stayed as an unhatched mythological egg and took time to crack, grow and find its way.

As for Diane, shortly after arriving in the physical world brut wicked winds blew and out from the dust storm were thousands of bulls. Diane didn't know where they came from but knew the wormhole could be the reason. As the beasts charge Diane and her captors, to her surprise, she was able to use her ability as a mythological being to control their minds, and they all turned around—running in the opposite direction. She quickly thought to try mind control with her abductors—it didn't work on the human species. Her abductors saw this and hurry to take her to their king. "Surely, she is a god. Her dark skin, silky hair is another symbol of her godliness!"

They rush her off the King. After witnessing her beauty and the story told about her power over the animals—the King agreed that she was a goddess. Her "abductors" stealthily replaced Diana with an animal that was slaughter on the altar in her place. Jess was shown that this was how the mother of Demetrius and Jombus had become the Ephesus goddess, Artemis. Jess, understood this was why the Temple of Artemis was the chosen battleground.

She was never sacrificed as young Demetrius had been led to believe. Artemis was seated on a thrown as a mighty one—declared a goddess and worshipped for her great beauty and ability to bring forth other gods in her likeness. She became the mother of many influential leaders in different fields. However, she still longed for her two lost children, and she set out the word to be on the watch for them. After many moons—she got a hit! A guard reported one location—Demetrius'.

Artemis was pleased; she straddled up and had to see him for herself. After viewing him cutting wood—she had not the courage to fight for him. He thought she was dead—she turned away and never saw either one again.

She later died of what might have been "Mother's heartache." Massive jeweled, golden statues were erected in Ephesus of the beautiful goddess' Artemis in honor. Designed to signify her meaning as a god; under its neckline were the many breasts symbolic as to feed the small gods—born to her and in her garment—creatures represented the power of the many gods she birthed.

Jess was so unsettled and weak to what appeared to be unfair circumstances with the Mother Diane and her two sons. She wanted to know what happened to Jompus. Using the Breastplate-of-Righteousness; she peered for more insight. Jess saw a beautiful jeweled creature small surviving on fish in a dense dark cave. It was lonely and furious—longing for a mother, it never saw. The creature hared grew for the Creator who abandoned him, his world, and his family. Jess, knew this was Jompus. It became large—flying through the enchanted land for fish until a local inhabitant spotted him. Fear of this creature and a thrill to hunt the unknown cause these inhabitants to seek Jompus and destroy him. In the battle, Jompus was heavily injured. He licked his lesions but was slowly dying. Demetrius 'Jack' followed shiny stones that had fallen from Jompus into the dark cave where the injured animal lie desperately for help. He was shining just as the stones he sought all his life. Demetrius touched the creature's claw and instantly saw his pain, his life, and the source of his hopelessness. Demetrius also saw his ability to grant wishes. More than anything—he found his brother! Who was last seen as a mere egg! Demetrius had to act quickly. He asked for a wish... to be reunited as one with his brother and fused into one being for optimum power. The creature agreed—granting the request. The exchange strengthened the beast and flew to the known Nefari to exchange—loyalty for immortality.

Jess yearn to know their fate, so she used the Helmet-of-Salvation to look into their future. In the next vision, Jess observed both brothers—tortured in Hades. But, then she had to blink. She couldn't believe what she was seeing! Next to them was Rufus, hanging his head in tormented tears.

The visions broke. Jess' head nearly exploded with questions, her heart racing. She shot past the still-frozen beast to find Rudolph. The reindeer had returned to the man—bloodied and lifeless.

"No-oo-oo-o! This can't be!" Jess screamed, kneeling next to her friend. "Why, God, Why? He was a faithful and discreet servant. Why would you allow this to happen to him? Why would you send him to Hades?"

Dead silence... There were no words of comfort from the Bride... And no insights from the Creator. Jess was devastated. Then, she remembered that her faith was merely a test in this battle and that she must go on.

With bolstered strength, courage and resolve, Jess picked herself up off the ground and declared aloud, "Trust in the Creator with all your heart! Do not lean on my own understanding! In all ways, I will take note from Him that guides me, Him that leads me, Him that watches over me, Him that loves me! The Creator of all is good. Nothing will deter me from His love! He makes the path straight; even when it seems meandering."

That new strength and a sense of purpose transformed Jess into a warrior—tall, muscled and ever more powerful. Magnificent white wings sprung from her back; her red hair grew longer and lit up like beautiful fire. The Armor-of-God grew with her, gleaming.

Jess flew to the beast and unfroze it. With a spiritual whip from the globe, she struck the monster mercilessly, fueled by rage over the death of her friend. Each strike, struct the beast spiritually as it did physically—causing ultimate pain. Knowing she had to lead it into the Holy Place, Hagia Sophia, Jess sped through the temple causing complete destruction of its rooms. Hot with anger—the beast followed, spitting fire from all six of its heads. Jess doused the flames with holy water as she alternately ran and flew.

Reaching Hagia Sophia, a little distracted by its beauty—fireball singed one of her wings, and she began tumbling downward. Jess touched her girdle, and two new wings popped out her back. After regaining traction, she landed at the entrance of Hagia Sophia. Jess used her Helmet again to freeze the beast in time, allowing him to witness his fate. She ran through a tunnel to retrieve the next candle and unfroze the creature. It mistakenly thought it had cornered Jess when she grabbed the candle out of its holder. They both were sucked through the magical wind tunnel into the mystical world—his original world.

Taken off guard, an expression of loss seemed to fall over the beast's heads. The dragon's tears fell to the ground like acid. One of the heads spoke, "There is life in this world. How could this be? Nefari said a world destroyed would never again see life."

Jess remembered the Bride's words that this monster's greatest weapon would be deception. "You are from the devil, father of the lie! Your mother made a deal with the devil's spawn, Nefari, to save you in a protected egg. Nefari manipulated the meeting between you and your brother, Demetrius, knowing that you would combine your darkness to satisfy your hunger for power. More power is what you crave, beast! But Hades is what you'll gain."

All of the creature's heads spit fire at Jess. With the wave of her hand, a heaven-sent deluge extinguished the flames. The beast tried to fire up again, but only puffs of smoke came from his mouths. Jess taunted, "A fireless dragon. What are the worlds coming to? Haven't you heard he that gives it, can take it away?"

Willing a giant net, Jess captured the beast. Jess knew the key to killing a dragon was his heart. She used the power of the globe to gain a robust long arm and a cutting claw that would go through dragon skin. She ran fast and slid under his body. She reached upward and snatched out the dragon's heart. The massive beast fell forward and melted into Hades, leaving not a trace.

"To Hagia Sophia," Jess commanded, exhausted and heart-broken. Back at the Holy Place, Jess placed the candlestick back in its holder and collapsed. The pain of losing Rufus was overwhelming. She needed to sit with the Creator and meditate to regain her strength. In physical time, the meditation lasted for days. Jess required no food, water or other human needs while in the spiritual state. The sacred communion with God was nourishment and strength enough. Afterwards, she received another divine gift, the Sword-of-the-Spirit. It would allow Jess to cut through any life force.

She gave thanks and praise and returned home to Grandmau-ma's house where she could grieve her friend. Jess knew there was a reason for everything; but, that did not stop her from missing Rufus.

Nefari nearly exploded with rage upon learning of the latest defeat. Even though it was almost time for Haley to awaken with immortality, she was not yet prepared to go to battle. Only Enyo remained. Nefari didn't even have to give the order. Enyo had manifested her broom and was on her way, determined to win where the others had failed miserably.

.

30

Wicked Family Ties

When she returned to Grandmau-ma's home, When she returned to Grandmau-ma's home, Jess had removed and carefully placed all of the pieces of her Armor-of-God in the most special place she could think of, around her neck as charms.

For a few precious moments, after she'd showered for the first time in—forever and dressed in the teenaged uniform of jeans, an old hoodie and sneakers, Jess was almost able to convince herself that everything was normal. But, it wasn't. Her entire life turned upside down from the moment Grandmau-ma died nearly a year ago in physical time, last Christmas. Haley was taken away. And, now, she'd cruelly lost her new best friend, Rufus, in a violent battle—something she'd never thought would happen.

'Listen to your instincts...' She thought to herself. With no new direction from the Bride, Jess headed back to the attic for additional answers. She was drawn to a dusty old box. Jess wiped at it with the sleeve of her sweatshirt and opened it. The box was filled with old letters to Grandmau-ma in her mother's distinctive handwriting. Jess tucked the box under her arm and headed down the ladder to comfortably spread out in front of the fireplace with a mug of cocoa and read at her leisure.

Instead of relaxing in the hopes of feeling closer to her mother, Jess was horrified and sick to her stomach as she read about witches, black magic, and relentless witch hunters. She could barely breathe, and her heart felt as though it would leap out of her chest. Her mother, with whom she had romanticized all these years, was a witch. And, not just any witch. Pemphredo was one of the heinous Graeae sisters Grandmau-ma had told her about, who shared one eye among them. They had surreptitiously gained individual vision and teeth. Grandmau-ma had referred to Jess' mother and her aunts as part of the "lump-of-coal" gang, but she'd never shared this. Jess wondered, "Did that mean I am a witch, too? How was it even possible that my sweet, loving Grandmau-ma was the mother of such evil?"

The pieces were beginning to fall into place for Jess as she mentally pounder through each piece of information—past and present. Remembering days when her mom would be frightened by something but shortly after the extreme fear, Jess noticed her mother's actions became more frantic. Thinking back to the day—she'd been taken to her Grandmau-ma's house—never to see her mother again. It made sense to her that her mother dropped her off with Grandmau-ma when Jess was just a little girl. "In her own way, she must have been trying to protect me." Jess thought as she tried to hold on to some good in her mother. She read how, the youngest sister, Deino, was apparently killed by a witch hunter centuries ago. But, the most evil of them all, Enyo, was still on the loose and hunting for the all-seeing eye and the powers it possessed. "Ah ha!" Jess spoke out loud. "This is why there was no trace of my mother's body after that terrible, fiery car crash. At the very least, charred human bones would have remained. But, an ancient witch would have incinerated, leaving nothing behind. Woe! How old was my mother, anyway?"

As Jess' head was spinning, the spiritual gifts that comprised the Armor-of-God lit up—this was Jess' cue to 'lock and load.' Possessions of The Globe, access to needs; The Codex Bible, a personal letter from

God as guidance; The Book-of-Knowledge, Bride of the holy spirit to guide her; Four Candlesticks, the key to Gods gifts in light; The Girdle, allowing her to transform into different beings—a shape-shifter; The Breastplate-of-Righteousness, allowing her to visually see the past of the lives of the enemy; The Helmet-of-Salvation, letting her know the fate of her enemies; The Sword-of-the-Spirit, allowing her to cut through any life form. Jess became one with each treasure given her for the battle. Although, Her armor was not complete—it all gave her the power she needed to defeat the next beast.

Jess walked in the woods, growing in height as she exited the house—transforming again into the Amazonian-sized warrior. Her body snatched her five feet into the air—releasing the powerful angel's wings, green eyes able to pierce through solid objects and flowing hair that possessed its own fiery strength.

Jess turned in circles trying to see her wings. She gave a short snicker; thinking of what Rufus would say if he saw her. She then observed her favorite tree, leaned on it, and went into meditation. Jess' mind, heart and spirit absorbed all the information she needed for the next battle, seeing the past, present, and future with crystal-clear clarity.

A powerful warlock, Phorcys, was the head of Europe's largest witch's coven before the 4th century BC, from Rome to the Greek Isles. His kind was dwindling in numbers, being hunted, slaughtered and torched by villagers. It was Phorcys' job to keep their kind alive. He learned that running in packs was the very reason they were trackable which allowed the witch hunters to kill them off in groups of families. Using all the forces of his dark magic, Phorcys devised a plan to stop their demise and manipulated an entire people and culture—affecting almost every Greek city-state.

History would record that the 27 year-long Peloponnesian War was a scorch-the-earth conflict between democratic Athens and oligarchic Sparta, the two most powerful city-states in Greece. Both city-states were nearly demolished, subdued through conquest and diplomacy by the smaller kingdom of Macedonia under the reign of King Phillip II, the son of Alexander the Great, Perdiccas ll—this introduced Greece's Hellenistic period, led by the now all-powerful Macedonian Empire.

The Helmet-of-Truth and Breastplate-of-Righteousness revealed to Jess that Phorcys was the instigator behind the hard-fought shift in power. Phorcys, using the most potent witchcraft—he infiltrated the mind and body of Alexander's son, Perdiccas ll. In a form as Perdiccas, he instigated the 27-year long battle—planning to ultimately claim Macedonia as his own and expand his witches throughout Europe. When the spell wore off, no one was more surprised than King Phillip to witness the power and riches his Kingdom had amassed. When praising of Perdiccas began, Phorcys cast yet another spell. This time, Perdiccas introduced Phorcys to King Phillip as a God who blessed them to win and all praises went to Phorcys, as planned.

One day—as Phorcys planned—the king happened upon the warlock, also known as an ancient sea god, perched on a rock in all his glory. The way the sun shone on him, King Phillip immediately was confident this golden being to be the reason for Macedonia's rise in power. Word spread quickly. The warlock was dubbed and worshipped as the Greek Titan god of the sun, Helios. Worshippers of Helios constructed a giant statue of the sun god in the city of Rhodes. It became known as the Colossus of Rhodes.

Everything was working according to Phorcys' devious plan. As a warlock, he re-populated the world with witches by mating with those human women he deemed most powerful. Deceit was one of Phorcys' most excellent gifts. All of Europe thought he was a sun god, but he was indeed a male witch out for revenge against the very people responsible for killing thousands of witches. Under this deceit, the female witches intertwined with the Macedonian people and they were instructed not to practice magic until authorized by the male witch, Phorcys. They lived as regular people for years, and their actual identity was unknown.

On the mission to produce the most powerful witches, Phorcys was charged with procreating with a holy creature of the Creator who possessed strong white magic. That lovely woman of goodness and light was

Liz, Grandmau-ma. She was tricked into marrying Phorcys and gave birth to three powerful female witches by deceit called the Graeae. The Graeae were three malevolent sisters—kin to the Gorgons. The Graeae were not the friendliest bunch, and they shared an eye, which they passed between themselves because they were cursed with blindness. This curse was because of the male witch's deceit to have children by a holy one (Liz or Grandmau-ma) of the Creator.

After many years, the King discovered the source of the growth of his empire and witch hunts resumed, picking them off one-by-one. Phorcys used the magic of the all-seeing eye of his children to shield himself. His spirit became one with the wondrous Colossus of Rhodes. But, the spell also trapped Phorcys inside the statue until that time when one of his own released him.

— ⁓

Jess broke from her trance. This next battle was personal. She would fight the last of the Graeae, Enyo, to avenge the sin of deceit committed against Grandmau-ma; as well as battling to save Christ, Christmas, and Santa Claus.

The next holy star led Jess to Greece and the fifth wonder of the world, the Colossus of Rhodes.

Jess tucked her wings in and planted her feet on the ground. Now in ruins, destroyed by an earthquake in 226 BC, the Breastplate-of-Righteousness gave Jess the power to see the city-state of Rhodes as it once was. There it was; the Colossus of Rhodes, the statue of the Greek Titan-god of the sun Helios, erected in the city of Rhodes, on the Greek this Island. The structure itself was enormous; it's giant legs straddling the harbor of the Greek Island, allowing boats to pass beneath its limbs. The area was alive with fishing boats and open-air stalls where both men and women exchanged food, goods, and services. The statue had a bow and arrow on its back and torch in its right hand, a sword in its left, a sun crown on its head, a muscular built and a piece of fabric around its waste looking like a child's diaper.

Although, knowing that Phorcys—the powerful male witch was trapped inside the statue, Jess could not control that inner child of hers and started laughing. "What would possess them... What it must have meant for them to put a baby diaper on the powerful sun-god statue?" Jess, held her stomach. "Whoa, that was called a sun god? Doesn't look like any kind of god to me with that dipper to cover that little pickle of a penie. If this statue resembles any kind of truth—grandma wasn't happy." Bent over in laughter over her own joke, sensing that she wasn't alone.

"My—my—my—a mere human child playing a superhero is absurd. I really don't much care for killing children."

"Hello, Auntie," Jess responded calmly. "I've been waiting for you. What took you so long? Losing your touch?" Jess turned to face the witch, Enyo. "Wow, where's the family resemblance? My mother was beautiful. You are—how can I say this politely? Well, you didn't win the lottery in the looks department. Kinda the opposite—actually..."

Enyo circled Jess, menacingly, half-amused. "And, you, niece, look exactly like your mother. A lot of good all that beauty will do ya. Well, we were all undesirable, so we stayed in a smelly cave. We had to continue to hide because our appearance told everyone that we were witches and we would have been killed. I was the courageous one and ventured into the outside world. You know, your smart mouth is going to make it even easier to kill you than it was with your mother!"

Jess' shocked silence urged Enyo on, "Oh, didn't know? Oops... Well, allow Auntie Enyo to fill in the blanks before I destroy you, you insipid little trouble-maker. Of the three of us, your stupid mother was the weakest link. And, so ungrateful! I assume you know the part about the all-seeing-eye that we all shared for hundreds of years, forced to hide in a disgusting, dark, dank cave from witch hunters. I made a friend, a deliciously wicked girl who wanted to learn everything she could about black magic. That ignited her own innate powers. In turn, she granted my sisters and me the gift of sight. My two weaker sisters wished to be beautiful. I didn't care about anything as useless as beauty. I opted for power... to be the most powerful of the three Graeae witches. My youngest sister was caught and tortured by hunters. Your mother wanted nothing more to do with us. She wanted to abandon her birthright for a 'normal' life. So, I let her go; but only on the condition that she safeguards the all-seeing-eye, lest my 'friend' discovered its real powers.

After centuries of pining about, your weak mother fell in love with a mortal, breaking every witches' code. Worse, she allowed herself to get knocked up and delivered a human child, you. Of course, there are consequences for such forbidden behavior.

"Ever met your daddy, dear?" Enyo taunted, waiting for some reaction that would reveal a crack in Jess' resolve. "No? I didn't think so. That's because I cursed him. He vomited his own blood until he was drained dry. That cowardly Pemphredo went into hiding with you for years. When I found her, she was alone. She left you with our holier-than-thou birth vessel, Elizabeth. I recovered the all-seeing-eye, and well, your mother received the punishment she'd long deserved. Poof! Up in smoke. Literally... I'm not sure if my father knew how powerful the all-seeing eye is."

Jess remained stoic, a warrior, "Bathe much, Aunt Enyo? Or is it true what they say about witches and water? You reek. Smell like— awful breath, from head to toe."

Enyo snorted, scooped the all-seeing-eye from within her and repeated an incantation, floating around Jess:

> *"Powerful me... powerful you...*
> *Witches curse, not like voodoo.*
> *Nor here, nor there, but everywhere,*
> *Awaken the witches, if you dare.*
> *No spring, nor fall past the summer.*
> *Awaken the witches from their slumber."*

Jess drew her sword and aimed it toward the heavens, mocking the witch with poetry:

> *"Power given and power taken away. Lord, help in my battle today."*

And although mocking the witch—a brilliant, spiritual beam streaked like lightning from the skies into the sword. Jess and her armor grew exponentially.

Her incantation complete, Enyo cackled, "So, you think your size gives you power, half-human daughter-of-Pemphredo?"

She turned away from Jess, raising both arms into the air. "Rise and take your revenge against a Creator who cursed and trapped you in this iron and stone crypt. Rise, mighty father of witches. The time is now!"

The ground beneath Jess shook violently. Long-dead, empty-eyed witches rose from the earth, the water, all around her. Then, like an eggshell bursting with a new chick, the Colossus of Rhodes cracked wide open. The hideous, emerging warlock exuded evil fury.

Jess readied her sword, "Seriously? OK, Grandpa, whatcha got? Besides that diaper... Come on! Come get me. No witch will defeat me!"

"Stupid little girl," Enyo growled, "at one point, witches may have been lesser than demons. But, no more... With the power of the all-seeing-eye, we've made a pact with balsam the goat, the devil himself that makes us untouchable. Behold!"

The winds howled viciously and the sky blackened. The zombie-like, witches slowly but methodically prepared for the attack.

Jess laughed out loud, hovering in the skies with her majestic angel wings, "The devil is nothing but a reject from Heaven. Don't you know that I can move mountains with the faith of a mustard seed and the loving support of the Creator of All! Through me, you will feel His wrath!"

With her words, a mountain shifted, crushing the witches rising from the ground and the sea.

Enyo's wicked laughter roared through the atmosphere, "Whoo, child! Don't you get it? You are the offspring of a witch, which the Creator abhors. He's not coming to bail you out! Nor are His angels. You are an abomination! Perhaps we can't get to the Creator. But, you, my dear, are an untrained witch. Almost too easy to kill. With your death, we can assure the destruction of any thoughts of the Christ, Christmas or that ridiculous, over-sized elf, Santa Claus! And, that armor of yours... Well, you ain't seen nothing yet! Let's see if it can protect you from this!"

Hovering in mid-air, Enyo spun gleefully toward the giant, seething, red-eyed warlock. "Daddy, do your thing!"

The released Phorcys raised his mammoth arms, hands open, summoning thousands of demons to join his and Enyo's evil army against Jess.

For the tiniest instant that Jess felt a twinge of fear which allowed a hairline fracture in her faith, she began to shrink to standard size. The witch and the warlock started playing mind games with her. Jess sorrow over the losses of so many she loved—her mother, Haley, Grandmau-ma, and Rufus—tortured her to the point of rolling into a fetal ball on the ground, sobbing. Demons bound Jess in a cage of her own torment.

The Bride spoke to her encouragingly from the Book-of-Knowledge:

> *"Jess, remember, the Creator loves you so much. He selected you to be the Chosen One; you alone are the Apprentice! Remember all you have learned. Remember who you are. The Father has given you everything you need to defeat this evil. Remember that faith of a mustard seed of which you spoke. That faith is your power. Hold onto it with all your might, heart and spirit."*

Jess' strength returned. She unfurled and grew, breaking any power or spells the demons had over her.

Enyo clutched her sword to put an end to Jess once and for all. "Enough of the foreplay..."

But, Jess' sword was holy—bestowed upon her by the Creator Himself, along with every piece of her armor, and allowed Jess to slay demons and witches alike. Her eyes, blazing with the power of absolute faith activated as she layered through their wicked bodies. Twirling her hair, she burned many demons sending them back. Jess stopped Enyo's weapon in mid-air. With the power of the globe, Jess trapped a furious Enyo, Phorcys and their remaining undead army in a solid sphere. She flew the spiritual prison to the next holy place, the Temple of Apollo Epicurius.

Landing on the holy grounds, Jess was intrigued by the majestic pillars of the Temple. 'Listen to your instincts.' She told herself again.

Peering at them, "There is more to these pillars." Jess, tiled her head in awe and with the gift of the Breastplate-of-Righteousness, Jess saw the past and the hidden content of the pillars. Angels who had chosen the devil's path instead of the Creator's path were cast from Heaven, roaming the physical world and set for judgment in Hades. Missing closeness to God, the hearts and souls of these fallen angels, changed. Although, the Fallen Ones knew of their fate in Hades; they longed to serve the Creator anyhow. These Fallen Ones battled many battles in the physical world for the sake of good vs evil—until a loss in a fight where demons and witches united. The defeated Fallen Ones were trapped in the into these impenetrable stone pillars for millenniums.

Knowing better than to question anything the Creator allowed—her heart was moved with pity for these fallen ones. She begged the Creator for them to have a second chance. She touched her Girdle-of-Truth and knew His approval of her next move. Using the Power from the Globe, Jess commanded, "As you were. Come out. Be free in the name of our Creator! The Almighty God! I... AM... to battle for Christ, Christmas, Santa Claus, and yourselves!"

The angel's heavenly bodies flew through the pillars, knowing their new mission: battling at Jess' side. Fighting the demons and witches commenced when Jess released them from the spiritual sphere. With the angelic soldiers to cover her, Jess ran to the pillar that held the next candlestick, releasing it from its holder. With that swift movement, all were sucked through the powerful wind funnel into the mystical world, where they were fallible and perishable. Enyo and Phorcys used every trick and weapon in their wicked arsenal. Jess' sword was mightier and sent every one of the witches and demons to Hades, where they belonged.

Grateful for the opportunity to battle for their Creator, the fallen ones, led by Angel Rafael, asked Jess if she could use her sword to send them where they belonged—Hades.

Jess looked to the heavens, "I didn't get those instructions from the Creator. I remain obedient—only the Creator makes Judgments."

Jess liked Rafael a lot. She hugged and thanked the angels for their help. The decision of final redemption, however, was not hers to make.

As she was about to depart using her globe; An angel spoke, *"I send a message from 'I AM' to the Fallen Ones."* Several Trumpets went sounded before the Angel spoke again, *"You will be released soon to help humanity in the physical world where you must be victorious. For now, you are ordered to sleep in this designated mystical world until the Creator awakens you."*

Jess smiled at Rafael, nodded and in the blink of an eye, Jess was back at the Temple of Apollo Epicurius. Replacing the candle in its holder, she spotted the now-familiar, brilliantly lit door. Inside was another gift from the Creator: the Shield-of-Faith. Knowing that all she'd learned along the way—prepared her for this gift—for it required unmovable faith. It would shield her from any evil attack spun her way.

The girl inside the warrior was weary. Jess closed her eyes in prayer. When she opened them, she stood at the foot of her own bed in Grandmau-ma's. She exhaled—welcoming herself home. It was time to rest and recharge.

31

Matters Of The Heart

After removing each piece of her sacred armor, Jess was asleep before her head hit the pillow. Initially, her dreams filled with spiritual enlightenment and encouragement. There were sweet scenes with Grandmau-ma, Jose, Rufus, and children playing happily—some ice skating, some playing ball.

Then, her dreams took a dark turn. The happy images disappeared—suddenly, all the children ran as thought frighten of something—brightness replaced by dense darkness except a tunnel of light. A shadowy figure stood at the end of a long tunnel. It spoke, "So, out of sight, out of mind. I'm not even in your dreams. Some friend you were."

Jess' subconscious realized it was Haley, "What's happened to you? You've chosen the wrong side, Haley. And, that breaks my heart. I've always thought of you."

"Liar," Haley screamed.

Jess woke up in a sweat, panting. The dream felt very real. "What did it mean?" Jess thought as she got up to make hot coffee.

— —

Haley's body had awakened from its sojourn into death and hell for the achievement of immortality. Haley steeped in evilness. Since she'd died and come back to an unnatural, soulless existence, her body took on a new appearance. Haley's slender 18-year-old girl frame had transformed into something resembling a 'Jessica Rabbit' exaggerated, cartoon shapeliness but, with cascading black hair, instead of red. Staring at her hands, she marveled at her nails grew long, pointy and black—without an expensive manicure!

Nefari stepped back and smiled, admiring her handiwork.

Haley winked at Nefari, "This immortal thing is very cool! Thanks for the best birthday ever, Mother. But, you know, being dead for so long worked up an appetite. I hunger for food, but I'm thirsty to kill.

Nefari snickered, "Well, I see some things never change. Why don't you tell me all about your visit to Hades while we walk to the kitchen?" Nefari thought. "I'll bet my child thought of food in Hades. She has to be fat inside—somewhere."

"Of course, Mother. I even thought of food in Hades. By-the-way, in addition to these awesome curves, I can read your every thought."

Nefari looked askew at her daughter.

"You wanted to know what my gifts were, yes?"

"Yes," Nefari nodded, impressed. "Go on."

"I'm kick-ass with a bow and arrow, can sprout giant wings on a whim and can visit the dreams of anyone I want... whenever I want," Haley ticked off proudly. "As a matter of fact, I've already visited ole' Jess. I just shook her up a little. Since I've got the advantage of knowing what's up before she does, Jess will never know what hit her."

Nefari opened her mouth to object.

"Nope, it's a done deal, Mother. Jess is mine. I know exactly where the second globe is in Hades. Once I kill Jess, I'll have it. Easy peasy..."

"Remember, Daughter; only an Apprentice can take a globe from another Apprentice."

Haley rolled her eyes, "Yes, but once an Apprentice has both globes... In Hades... It can be taken, and I have that all figured out. In Jess dreams, she revealed two locations for battle. Mine and yours which is, the Lighthouse of Alexandria. It's been horrifyingly entertaining for people in many realms for many lifetimes. Humans call him a sea god or the Loch Ness monster. Some thought it to be a myth—but, they saw him all right. He easily travels between Hades and the physical world. Just fabulous, really... He's able to travel through hot, destructive fire while his insides stay cool as a cucumber. He travels through waters faster than light. The monster eyes give him the ability to see the light from the physical world—thus, allowing him to escape Hades many times over. Only thing, he's instinctive only—no real brain—the devil's pet. We will need the monster-pet to serve our needs." Haley smiled as her mother paid close attention to the plan.

"Now, Mother... The Lighthouse of Alexandria is where you must take your place. Before Jess arrives to battle you, she'd already think she has defeated me by returning me to Hades. But, I'm there on my own initiative. Once, I'm in Hades, and at the proper time, I will use the devil's-pet to scoop up legions of your faithful who are tormented in Hades, and he will bring them to the physical world to help you defeat Jess, but I will stay to await Jess arrival. While I wait for Jess; you and your servants shall start your battle—"

Nefari interjected, "You're returning to Hades! And staying... Wait!"

"Yes, Mother... It is a horrible place, and no one wants to be there— so retracted and crowded. How is it, you don't want me to return but seem to be okay with your faithful servant there? You can't forget the ones who have served you so easily, can you? Look, Mother, It will take all of us to complete the mission."

Nefari stood, arms folded in disbelief that she was taking orders from her daughter. Reluctantly...

"Really, Mother? Jealous? Not a good look on you—this is why you gave me immortality, right? To rule at your side? Well, I'm laying out the plan to do it."

Haley continued to explain the plan. "Your job is to get the sea monster to swallow Jess and carry her back to Hades. Once there, I'll force her to retrieve the second globe, then take it from her, of course, along with the one that she protects. We'll have both globes and all power. It's the only way to complete your vendetta against Christ, Christmas, and Santa Claus once and for all. When we succeed, the Creator has no choice but to hand over all realms. Then we will be the ones worshipped and adored."

Nefari felt her authority slipping away.

Haley intercepted Nefari's thoughts, polishing off a pound of raw ground beef which she greedily ate with her hands. "Don't be silly, Mother. You will always be our leader. You know how He works. There are only two more holy stars which will shine over the battle locations. Remember, while I am in Hades doing my part, you will be battling Jess in the physical world. As soon as Jess arrive with her globe, the lighthouse will once again become as it was in its past life. The lighthouse light and the reflection off the water from the Holy Star work in unity. You must direct the beam from the lighthouse light onto the water's reflection— it gives clarity to the eyes of the Loch-ness Monster, Devil's-pet, Sea Monster or whatever you want to call him—allowing him to make his way to the surface in the physical world. Your servants will exit the beast, but you must act quickly to make the beast eat Jess and return he to me in Hades. There is more, I've seen in Jess dreams, but I will tell you that later once we've defeated her."

Haley licked her fingers. "Ready?"

Outside the castle, Haley said, "I know I said that I would tell you later, but I see you want to know now. There was one more thing I need to share."

Nefari took both of Haley's hands in hers. "I'm listening."

"Just as good possesses the Holy Trinity; Evil has a trio also made up of the anti-Christ, Halloween, and Grampus."

Nefari smiled. "Yes, so many great things to expect when evil prevails."

The evil mother-daughter tag team embraced and went their separate ways.

— ~

Warmed by the second cup of hot cocoa at Grandmau-ma's house, Jess suited up in her Armor-of-God and walked into the woods to await the next holy star. God's gift through meditation and the armor allowed her to see exactly what Haley was up to and even though Jess knew what she had to do, part of her still mourned the loss of her best friend.

Seeing the star, Jess expanded to her warrior size with her mighty angel wings and followed it to Olympia, Greece, where the Statue of Zeus once stood. Upon landing, the ground shook to reveal the giant, seated gold and ivory statue of the god, Zeus.

As large as the once-wonder of the ancient world was, Jess, hovered over it, even larger.

At the base of the Statue of Zeus at Olympia stood Haley.

"Well, Haley. You've got the bomb body you've always wanted. I just hate that you lost your soul, God, your family and your best friend to get some boobs and butt."

Haley chuckled, "Best friend? That's a good one... You are a phony Ms-Goody-Two-Shoe. You never even tried to find me or change my mind."

A tear of loss slid down Jess' cheek, and she returned to normal size. Haley mistook this as a sign of weakness but Jess wasn't weak, she was reflecting Christ love. She also remembered when Christ cried although knowing he could resurrect his friend Lazarus he allowed his tears to flow. The momentary matters of the heart were brief. Haley immediately drew her sword. Jess was just as quick. The two fought all around the statue's base, each intent on destroying the other.

Haley used one of her new tricks to allow her spirit to jump into the statue, bringing it to life. "You will not win. Give up, and perhaps I will show you mercy."

Jess resumed her enormous warrior size and ensnared the entire statue in a holy net. "Sorry, Haley, can't do that. You're coming with me."

Jess took the net, with both, the statue and Haley trapped inside and threw it over her shoulder onto her back-like the sack that Santa carries full of toys. Jokingly she said, "Ho-Ho-Ho. We're taking the unclean thing to Holy grounds."

Her beautiful angelic wings flew her to the statue to the sixteen surviving columns of the once-colossal Temple of Olympian Zeus in Athens. She set it on the holy grounds, grabbed the blessed candlestick from its holder. All were sucked through the deafening winds into a purple mystical world.

In the eerie world, all was purple with all kinds of tunnels, and nothing appeared the same. Everything was unknown and uncertain here. Jess hoisted the statue into the air and slammed it to the mystical grounds, where it broke into hundreds of pieces—mere rocks with ivory plates details. Haley's spirit separated, furious and confused.

Jess snapped her fingers in Haley's face to get her attention. "You know nothing; you didn't receive any information the Creator didn't want you to have. Your invasion in my dreams only assured me that you really had chosen evil over good. I had to deal with matters in my own heart regarding you. In this world, you have no abilities and no immortality. You always knew your mother was a liar. I can't understand, why you would think she'd be truthful to you about anything. You chose the wrong side Haley, and I'm sorry. You are trapped! The only place from here is Hades."

Jess wielded her spiritual sword, praying aloud, "In the name of Christ, Christmas, Santa Claus and all that is holy, I remand you to eternal damnation in Hades!"

With that, Jess cut off Haley's head in one fell swoop. The doors of hell opened and dragged Haley and her head to its depths.

Jess was sad; but, she had done what she'd been charged to do. She touched the globe within her girdle to return to the Temple. She replaced the sacred candle and received the final gift from God, completing the holy armor—the Shod-of-Peace to cover her feet as she walks on the most discussing place, Hades. Jess gave praise and asked the Creator to show her the final star immediately; so that she might end the final battle, destroying Nefari in the magical world where she had first met Jose. God answered Jess' prayer. She was now the bait for Nefari's wrath.

32

The Questionable Escape

Haley, head in hands, landed in the middle of the misery of Hades. Because she possesses the protection of the devil, her bodiless head could still see and searched out her mother's followers. They were all on board, eager to escape their existence of torment. The plan to have them all swallowed by the sea monster and returned to the physical world sounded like a way out.

Headless Haley and her mother's disciples clumsily wandered through hell's endless tunnels of fire, brimstone, and suffering in search of the beast. There was an unexpected foe, though, planted in Hades to foil their plan. Rudolph—he had been sent there not as punishment, but to keep Haley and her army away from the sea monster and what they thought would be salvation. Rudolph was not alone. The Creator had sent the fallen angels—under the leadership of Rafael—to assist; their angelic powers restored.

Spotting a gargantuan, red-eyed reindeer, Haley and her motley crew stopped in their tracks, stunned.

"I see you've literally lost your mind," Rudolph quipped. "But, hey, at least you're ahead of the game. Sorry, pun totally intended," he laughed.

The fallen angels appreciated Rudolph's jokes. Haley, not so much...

She ordered her followers——"Charge!"

Rudolph, Rafael and the fallen angels quickly dismembered each and every one, entrapping them in holy chains.

It was Rafael's turn to give the commands, "Your mistake has been to underestimate your Creator! This place host the unrighteous, the wicked which are cut off from the lands and the worlds. And there are ones like you and these other misfits—the treacherous. You all are guilty of dealing treacherously—woe onto you! You are all reprimanded to the deepest crevasse of the abyss—worst than Hades!"

Rafael raised outstretched his arms and lifted his head, "Father, Creator of all, woe unto the treacherous ones who receive your judgment, with no salvation of Christ within their midst! Your will be done; for I serve only the Creator!"

The chains holding Haley and her mother's hapless followers were dragged into the lowest depths of hell.

Watching, the devil plotted his revenge for his family. The apprentice would pay.

——— ⌒

Afterwards, nothing was heard but Hades typical sounds of eternal anguish.

Rafael turned to Rudolph, "My friend, you have pleased the Creator with your bravery. It is time for you to reunite with Jess. This place was never meant for you. We belong here and will remain as the guardians of Hades to enforce God's judgment. We praise the Creator for His mercy and love."

Placing one wing on Rudolph he continued, "Please tell Jess I will always be grateful to her. As for you, time to be swallowed whole by the sea monster."

Rudolph peeped the monster, squeamishly, "Ok, I'm ready."

The monster opened its enormous mouth over the reindeer. Rudolph slid into the slimy lining of its belly. It flew through the walls of fire, breaking through all of Hades' barriers, waiting for the holy star to guide him to the physical world's surface.

All Rudolph could do was wait.

33

A True Defeat

Jess' eyes glowed with joy and gratitude when she saw the seventh and final Holy Star. Donning the complete Armor-of-God, she assumed her mighty warrior form. With the ultimate power to defeat any foe, Jess was fearless and ready to avenge all who had suffered from Nefari's evil.

The Creator dispatched an angel to imbue Jess with even more confidence. He spoke to her from the heavens:

> "God is well-pleased with you, Jess. The time has come for you to wrestle against the rulers of darkness in unheavenly places. Protected with the entire Armor-of-God, know that you do not stand alone. The Girdle-of-Truth allows you to shapeshift in whatever form best serves you. With the Breastplate-of-Righteousness, you possess the ability to see the past of your enemies; and, knowledge is power. With your feet Shod-in-Peace, you will both find the peace you need to sustain you and the physical ability to run like the wind. The Shield-of-Faith will make you invincible against any weapon the enemy hurls in your direction. With the Helmet-of-Salvation,

you will see all that is to come, another useful weapon against your enemies.
Lastly, you are blessed with the Sword-of-Spirit, which gives you the abil-
ity to slice through any evil life force. I am honored, dear Jess, to serve at
your side as your guardian angel through the completion of this holy quest
to save all that the Father has created."

Jess was fired up with spirit, faith, and gratitude. Staring into the skies with a full heart, she spotted the seventh holy star. She flapped her beautiful wings to follow the heavenly beacon to Egypt and the Lighthouse of Alexandria. As soon as her feet touched the grounds of the Gargantuan Lighthouse of Alexandria appeared as it did upon its original founding. Jess noticed its staggering height and on top the statue of Poseidon—god of the sea. A flaming fire and a brass deflector (mirror) were used to beam light onto the sea.

Nefari was already there, initiating her plan to release her followers. She was guiding the brass deflector to the sea, lining the light to the reflection from the Holy Star-invoking the sea god Poseidon to show her favor.

"It's not gonna happen," Jess announced, landing just feet from Nefari. "Yup, I know your plan. And—spoiler alert—it's not gonna work. By the way, Nefari, did you ever tell Haley about her father? Or, her brother? If not, no worries—they are all reunited right now, in Hades. One big, not-so-happy family..."

"Don't you dare speak my daughter's name," Nefari hissed. "My husband and my son were weak. They followed me at first, then lost their way. Haley is not like them."

A clap of thunder followed Jess' laughter, "When will evil learn? You and your kind will never win. You, Nefari, are the ancestor of unnatural relations between the devil and evil human women. I command you to bow down to the Creator of All! The almighty I Am, allowed you to escape the gates of hell once; but that will never happen again. It is written—the second existence of Hades has no escape, only eternal judgment. That is the fate you to which you doomed your family. What a wicked mother and wife you are."

Feeling like a cornered animal, Nefari spat, "Your visions and trickery couldn't be more wrong, dearie. Evil will be the victor, and we will be released and assisted by Santa's seven vicious brothers, Jólakötturinn, Frau perchta, Belsnickel, Hans Trapp, Pe`re Fouettard, Yule Lads, and the worst of them—Krampus. Each followed the deliciously wicked ways of their mother, Gry`la, except their stupid sibling, Santa Claus. Christ's evil accessory the Anti-Christ will join in the fun of manipulating the physical world from Christ, and your beloved Christmas's will be replaced with an evil celebration—Halloween. In fact, it would be celebrated during the time my father; Satan consummated himself with the humans bringing birth the Nephilims, A time when your pitiful Creator destroyed the wicked Giants in an attempt to rid the physical world from our evil—but—here I am! I can't wait to see the day that Halloween is the most revered of all holidays! I am the successor of my father the Devil and Haley is mine! Evil will have its way with the earthlings! Destroying all that nonsense, Christ, Christmas, and Santa Claus is just the cherry on top."

Jess growled with lightning and thunder in her voice, "You forgot, The Creator trusted in me, and I won't fail! The people in this physical world will have everything they need to understand why the Christmas magic must continue. They will put an end to this day you're so excited about and when I succeed you and your evil kind will never be allowed to be rereleased. Oh, I get it... The only ifs, is your driving force, right? If—the last physical world fail to acknowledge the Creator; if—every ounce of Christmas joy leaves; if—all the children stop believing in Santa; if—all human in the physical world stop believing in Christ message; if—Christmas didn't exist anymore, and if—I would fail this mission and others to keep the Good of Christ, Christmas and Santa Claus in all worlds. Sorry, Nefari! IT! WON'T! HAPPEN!"

Jess had enough of the debate. With her feet shod with peace, she whipped circles of sand around Nefari, covering the evil one with it. Nefari morphed as one with the sand. Jess countered by commanding waters to soak her, rendering Nefari immobile. Nefari, however, managed to free her arms, stretching them toward the Lighthouse. Jess grabbed the arms, only to have the fingers elongate with sharp claws at the tip of each. Jess chopped off each finger with her sword. And, each one directly grew back. Nefari went for Jess' throat with her poisonous claws. Jess shape-shifted into a snake to slither away.

In the split second that it took to shift back to her warrior body— Nefari had freed herself from the heavy sand. A sword fight and mighty battles of the wills—ensued. Every time Nefari attempted to turn the brass plated mirror—trying to line it with the reflection of the holy star, Jess stopped her, ultimately knocking the sword out of Nefari's hands. With the power of her globe, Jess called for sacred chains to bind Nefari from head to toe. With holy chains which evil cannot break free, Nefari cried for Poseidon help went unanswered.

Jess laughed. "It's just a statue. It has eyes but cannot see, ears but cannot hear, legs but cannot walk, mouth but cannot speak. It cannot help you."

At that moment, huge waves presented itself, and the statue that Jess thought was just stone became flesh, jumped into the water and grew to a monstrous size. Using his mighty fork towards the sea; he brought out monsters of the sea. "You dare mock me! You little god!"

Startling Nefari for the briefest instant, Jess raised her Sword-of-the-Spirit to the heavens and declared at the top of her lungs, "All power and glory be to the Creator of all things. For at all times, He is the Alpha and the Omega, the beginning and the end. Not my will but yours!"

Jess, secured Nefari chains around the lighthouse with no ability to escape or practice magic for her lips were sealed. Dashing her with holy water felt like a continuous burning. Jess then turned her attention to this so-called god.

Jess knew it was evil's best trick to use stone and fabric to appear as alive, but it was wicked demons behind these so-called gods. Jess called her Guardian Angel for assistance. Legions of angels came from the heavens and battled, in the sea. Slaying each demon possessing the creatures and stone-demon-gods until they were all depleted.

Jess gave her Angel a wink and gathered Nefari's chains. "Now, this, Nefari, is your end!"

Jess encased Nefari and flew her to the final holy place, the Twin Temple of Abu Simbel.

— ~

All of Nefari's evil reincarnations through the ages were revealed to Jess when she and her prisoner landed at the two massive rock temples, carved into a mountainside on the West Bank of the Nile. The Twin Temples of Abu Simbel were built by Pharaoh Rameses II in the 13th Century B.C., of himself and his queen Nefertari. Creating the massive statue was to serve as a celebration of the battle of Kadesh. Elevating Rameses to the status of a god, a false idol served its purpose.

Because of the gift of her armor, Jess was quickly able to interpret and comprehend the ancient writings etched into the monuments' sides. Nefari's immortality had afforded her lifetimes of 'reigns of terror' over the people she'd ruled over in the physical world. Ruling at the side of her husband Rameses II was his queen, Nefertari, one of Nefari's incarnations. The wicked immortal demanded worship and adoration from her people. Suffering and death were the consequences of noncompliance.

Nefari/Nefertiti, The Great Royal Wife of Akhenaten, would re-emerge years later as The chief Royal Wife of Ramses II's as Nefertari, instigating one catastrophic conflict after another, to influence self-worship as human gods; demanding followers serve their human gods. In the modern world, she'd made it her mission to destroy belief in the Christ who died for the sins of man, the blasphemous holiday celebrating His birth, Christmas, and the old fool who set the celebration in motion, Santa Claus.

As Jess examined the temples writings, she knew this was an astronomical situation. All of these world wonders were filled with false idolatry. Rameses' temple's inner sanctums were tangible demonstrations of his false sense of superiority over the Creator. She has to defeat Nefari, but she had to assist in the revival of faith in the physical world also. If she fails, the release of the treacherous ones will emerge onto the physical world during Judgement Day, and all good can end! Jess was ready to go further than expected in her mission to save Christ, Christmas, and Santa Claus but now, she must also influence the outcome in the physical world.

Now, Nefari fought and clawed futilely against the chains and netting of her holy prison, hissing and howling like the monster she was.

Jess minimized her size and the size of the chained Nefari. Deep within its walls of the Twin Temples of Abu Simbel was the last candlestick. Jess returned to Nefari, dragging her kicking and screaming into the inner chambers. She grabbed the candle from its holder, sending them both whirling through the powerful wind tunnel to the magical world where they first met.

The magical world's faithful guardian, Jose, watched their entry, poised to attack any new enemy. He didn't recognize the warrior Jessica emerging through the howling winds with what looked like a prisoner that was still putting up a fight or, trying to.

Jose, however, did recognize Jess' voice as soon as she screamed his name. "Jess, is that you?"

Jess ran into his waiting arms. After holding on tightly to each other for dear life, they reluctantly pulled apart.

"I've missed you so much, Jess."

"I've missed you, too. Sometimes I can't believe everything that's happened, everything I've seen and experienced, and how much I've grown up in the last year, literally." They laughed. "Well, nearly a year by physical measure."

Jose glanced at Jess' captive, who was foaming at the mouth with rage. "Is that—is that, Nefari?"

"Sure is."

"Does this mean it's almost over?"

"Almost... But, I'm now facing the biggest and scariest battle of all. First, let's get ole' Nefari somewhere more containable."

Together, Jess and Jose dragged Nefari to the Christmas town's most significant tree. Jess looked around, horrified, her eyes filling with tears. Before she spoke, Jess used the power of the globe to encapsulate Nefari inside a giant, transparent Christmas ornament. That way, she could neither see nor hear anything; on display like a caged animal in a zoo.

"Dear God, Jose, what happened?" Jess asked sadly, the tears now rolling freely down her cheeks. "I thought everything was returned to normal after we chased out Nefari the first time. There's no life, no joy, no laughter. It's so desolate and sad."

"Our people never recovered from Nefari's massacre. The physical beauty of our town depends on faith and belief. Most townspeople have remained heartbroken over the deaths of many loved ones. The worst part is their loss of faith and belief. The magic of this special world is slowly dying, Jess. I've tried everything to try to inspire faith, joy, and hope. But, they're broken. And, afraid…"

Jose hung his head in sorrow. Jess dried her tears and took Jose's face in her hands. "Jose, everyone has got to come back from the tragedy, even as horrific as it was. Faith in the Creator is the key! Loss of that faith is the greatest danger. Without it, Nefari will have won in her mission to destroy belief in Christ, Christmas, and Santa Claus. I am not going to let that happen. Her next stop is the lowest depths of Hades, where I plan to escort her personally."

Jose stared at the still beautiful and kind—but very different—young woman Jess had become. She looked and acted every bit the warrior that she was.

"Tell you what. How quickly do you think you can gather all of the townspeople together? I've got an idea. We're going to send Nefari away forever. And, we're going to do it together! Whaddaya say?"

Jose grinned from ear to ear. "Sounds like a plan!" He pecked Jess on the cheek and was off.

Jess used the globe's magic to restore sparkling Christmas beauty and magic to the entire town and surrounding area. The magic and spirit of Christmas allowed her to place wrapped gifts under the now-magnificently decorated tree for each man, woman, and child in the town. The largest and most important gift was the trapped Nefari in the ball.

A peppermint striped stage, just a few steps high, appeared in front of the festive tree. Jess reduced her size and stood there and waited.

Within less than a physical world's hour, Jose had managed to convince and coax the town's heartbroken residents out into the open. The joyous surroundings Jess recreated gave an automatic lift to broken spirits, as proved by the audible "oohs" and "aahs."

Jose joined Jess on the welcoming little stage, which helped to reassure the crowd. But, it was Jess who addressed them. "Hi everybody, thanks... Thank you so much for showing the courage to come out today. I know how hard that was for you. Your beautiful, magical world has been turned upside down. You lost loved ones under Nefari's vicious attack. And, my heart goes out to all of you. Some of you met me the first time I was here. For those who didn't, my name is Jess; the Chosen one—turned Apprentice that you have heard about and I am a friend of Jose's. I was given the honor to battle—and defeat—Nefari in her mission to destroy belief in Christ, Christmas, and Santa Claus. But, I can't win this alone. I need every one of you.

The wicked one; Nefari, is my captive. She is trapped in a representation of that which she hated the most, a Christmas ornament."

The crowd gasped in horror and began to back away.

Jess threw up her hands, "No please. You're safe. I promise. Holy chains and nets bind her. Nefari is on her way to where she belongs, eternal damnation. But first, my friends, this is where I need your help. I need for every one of you to dig deep into your hearts and remember your faith, your hope, your belief and your love. Without these positive characteristics, which we can't see, but must feel; there will be no more Christmas or any holiday celebration with meaning behind Christ. Nefari will have won by making the blessed season only about merchandise and money. Every time you say, 'Merry Christmas' Christ name, deeds and blessings are invoked. If we stop invoking the name Christ, Jesus—Nefari will win. She will win if we stop teaching our offsprings how wonderful it is to give than to receive—the very thing Santa display every Christ is sent day. Christmas is more than a celebration of a day or an hour! I've learned it has no time at all and it is present for all who love first Christ, Christmas, and Santa Claus. You must remember, this magic town has a direct link to the North Pole. The Christmas Spirit must not be lacking because every world and land depends on that magical spirit. I need your help! Will you help me? We all owe it to ourselves and the loved ones we've all lost. Please, remember your faith, your hope, your belief and, your love for one another."

Slowly but surely, it was working. Jess' words sunk in and everyone began to hug each other tentatively. Spirits were lifting. Hope restored each one. The name Christ was being invoked for they all were saying the magic words, 'Merry Christmas' which meant, 'Happy Christ is Sent Day.'

Jose hugged Jess and nodded. Jess asked everyone to step back just a bit from the stage and witness the greatness of the Creator of all people, creatures, worlds, and realms.

There were more gasps of awe as Jess grew into her taller, more muscular, warrior self. She grabbed the ball that was Nefari's prison. "Your time in this world and all of the creation is up, Nefari. In the name of the Creator of All, The Almighty God! I AM, the Alpha and the Omega, the beginning and the end, not our will, but Yours be done!"

Jess hurled the ball to the ground, where it shattered into a million pieces. Before the darkness of hell could rise through the into to snatch Nefari to its lowest depths, Jess deftly snatched the chain with the Key-of-Death, the witch-crafted atlas, and map from around the witch's neck. Within an instant, Nefari and any evidence of her presence were gone, sucked into hell forever.

The crowd cheered, and the magic town's Mayor took the stage! We thank you, Jess, for accepting your mission as Apprentice and more we thank Him that sent you. We will always remember the power of Merry Christmas; Happy Christ is sent day. Laughter, caroling, and merriment commenced. During the joyful noise, magical sounds of bells and chimes blew through the town. The best gift of all arrived—the children whom Nefari had destroyed, came running back into their parent's arms. Suddenly presents under the giant Christmas tree were discovered, distributed and opened. Food and drink flowed. Jess winked at Jose and slipped away without anyone even noticing.

— ~

Jess was magically back at the Seventh Wonder of the World, the Lighthouse of Alexandria, where the holy star still shone brightly. She knew the star had led her there for a divine purpose; although she was not yet privy to it. Jess Then turned the brass mirror hitting the fire just right towards the gleam in the water from the Holy Star, and she waited with faith. Suddenly, the star's, light broke into a prism of green, red and gold beams sparkling over the waters.

Just then, the giant sea monster broke through the water's surface, flopped its enormous body onto the shore, belched and regurgitated a deer. Jess screamed in excitement, knowing it was her beloved friend. She dearly loved Rudolph; but screeched to a halt when she saw that he was covered in thick, greenish, stinky, snot-like, inner-belly ooze.

"Ewww," Jess recoiled involuntarily. She touched her holy armor, "As you were." In the twinkling of an eye, Rudolph was clean, dry and conscious.

The reindeer grinned. Jess flew to his side, hugging Rudolph's neck that still held her bells, and kissing his black nose.

"Rudolph your nose... It is black..." Jess touched it to be sure.

"I know, right!" Rudolph did an extra shake. "I no longer need a reminder about my fear. Thanks to you—accepting the mission of the Apprentice has blessed me too. I am no longer the scary deer... I'm so thankful for the Creator."

"I was the scary deer after I thought I lost you. Dude, don't scare me like that again," Jess faux scolded, relieved more than words could express.

"You're telling me!" Rudolph laughed. "That was scary and so is that things stomach—just plain nasty! I'm happy and grateful to have done my part, but I hope the Creator never asks me to ride in that things stomach again in any of my lifetimes."

"Me, too, buddy. Let's get you somewhere safe and warm for a few minutes before you head back to the North Pole. I'm nearing the end of our mission."

Jess grew larger, as her magnificent wings unfurled.

"Wow, that is so cool," Rudolph remarked. "Boy, I've missed a lot, huh?."

Jess wrapped her arms around her friend and flew him into the woods. "Yup and I'll fill you in on everything later. Meanwhile, munch on some grass, regain your strength and head back to the North Pole. My mini-globes should be ready. Tell Santa I'll see him soon. I've got just a few more significant details to tie up. Then, we can have some fun."

The warrior girl kissed the top of her friend's head and flew back to the Twin Temples of Abu Simbel.

Jess sauntered, through the inner sanctums, stopping at another door radiating with light—she sat in prayer and meditation. Afterwards opening the door, sitting on a columned pedestal was the key to Hades, her final gift from God.

Before Jess could touch it, her guardian angel spoke with final instructions:

> "Jess, all of the terrible things you've seen, encountered and battled are nothing in comparison to the horror and agony that is Hades. Do not let the torment of the doomed souls in hell impact you or your heart. Get in and out fast, do not prolong your presence there. Staying in Hades for an extended time will alter your brain and deviate your faith. Remember that deception is the devil's most clever weapon. You must not look into the previous lives or choices of any soul in Hades. Stay focused. No matter what, do not allow yourself to be distracted from your purpose. His tricks are just that, tricks, lies.
>
> This key, when interlocked with the Key-of-Death, will carry you to Hades. But, they will not bring you back. You will locate the other apprentice with the second globe. The power of the two globes together will bring you home. You are loved and you into. Go with God, dear Jess."

34

The Abyss

ack in the woods, Jess did a once-over of her complete suit of the Armor-of-God, locked the two keys together and closed her eyes. When she opened them, she felt the heat under her feet, but no ground was under her. A burst of hot flaming wind blew throwing her hair into flames, but it didn't burn. She was in the midst of the terrible heat, tortured cries and all the fire and brimstone she had always heard of but nothing touched her.

There were many fiery paths and many forks in the blistering coal ground-strips, lined with flaming trees. With Jess' cascading fiery red curls fanning wildly from the force of the heat, Jess touched her girdle and breastplate. Stronger than ever, her globe guided her through the inferno.

The devil knew this one was protected; but decided to toy with her, nonetheless. He sent the voice of Jess' mother to her, pleading with Jess to abandon her quest and save her, instead. Jess cried out, "Get thee behind me, Satan!"

Jess took a different path with thick burning webs and large tarnish coal rocks that had many eyes watching as she passed. Jess noticed her feet were no longer above the surface of the ground but touching what appeared to be bones—piles of dead babies bones. Jess ached but was warned don't look into the soul and continued to walk until another demon stepped directly into her path, offering Jess all the riches of the physical world in exchange for her worship of the king of hell.

Jess shattered the demon with her sword, declaring, "It is our Creator who deserves all praise. I am a warrior of the Lord God. It is not lawful for you to offer what is not yours. I expect that you depend on all lovers of Christ to stop and for me to fail. We will remain, lovers of Christ, Christmas, and Santa Claus. There is none that could touch His hand! Again, get thee behind me, Satan!"

An angry Satan, called all in Hades to battle the Apprentice. After a few more steps, Jess slid down a fiery crevice to what appeared to be an even lower level of Hades. It was filled with every manner of witches, warlocks, vampires, zombies, monsters, and demons. All laughably weak against Jess' powers at first. But, no Nefari— And, no headless Haley— Still, they attacked. Jess abilities to fight them all was weakening.

Jess heard what sounded like a familiar voice. But, how could she be sure it wasn't another of Satan's tricks? Rafael appeared with the other fallen angels. They provided Jess' backup, slicing through and flipping the demon army into the deepest abyss of Hades.

When the battle was over, Jess hugged and thanked Rafael and each member of his legion of fallen angels, who were fulfilling their purpose of earning their way back into Heaven.

Jess turned and walked directly to the first apprentice, her deceptive, distant cousin, Judas. He sat in eternal agony on a searing bed of fiery coals, the globe chained to his chest. Judas lifted his head, spotted Jess and silently mouthed the words, "I'm sorry. Thank you."

Jess took the globe from Judas' arms, her eyes stinging with tears, knowing there was nothing she could do to save his soul. Judas had pridefully chosen the side of evil with his power of free will. He was sucked away by an even more evil level of darkness right before Jess' eyes.

Jess turned her head; soon his screams became imperceptible. It was time to get out of Hades. She manifested her globe, touching it with its twin, and was back home in the warm, re-assuring cocoon of Grandmauma's house.

35

Thankful & Renewed

Settled in the familiar, comforting surroundings, smells and sounds of Grandmau-ma's home, Jess was, at last, able to exhale. She carefully removed each piece of armor, reducing each part to the size of another lovely charm to add, along with her globes and her Book-of-Knowledge, to her pretty gold necklace.

She heated a frozen meal, then luxuriously soaked in a heavenly, hot bubble bath, singing "Jingle Bells." After patting herself dry and slipping into her comfiest flannel pajamas, Jess was fast asleep.

The next morning, everything in the physical world seemed so clean and bright and fresh to Jess. She sat in the rocker on the front porch, wrapped in Grandmau-ma's blanket which kept her nice and toasty against the briskness of the sunny day, sipping cocoa and quietly giving thanks and praise.

Jess was gently shaken from her private world of inner bliss by her guardian angel:

> *"It gives me great joy that you are restored physically, spiritually and emotionally, Jess. The battle, you see, is not yet won. You will need all of your strength*

to restore the faith of others. Nefari and her followers have been remanded to hell, thanks to you. But, the havoc they wreaked—the broken spirits, belief, faith, and hearts—remain in this physical world—the last of its kind.

Belief in Christ, Christmas, and Santa Claus are still in danger of disappearing forever. They must know there is no salvation without acceptance of Christ, and belief in Christ has had a constant enemy. The influence of the evil ones has been spreading like a dangerous virus for eons. So, it is a continuous challenge. If faith and belief are lost, evil will return from the depths of hell—worst than before. Our Creator is counting on you, Jess, and has armed you with everything you need to see this through but, all of God's creation was given the gift of free will. You can help to influence their choice; however, the decision belongs to each soul for salvation. Each world has proven which way they are going except the physical world in which you exist. Remember, this is why it's the only one to possess time—the only one yet to choose the real Creator, God. The other worlds belief can help with providing Christmas Spirit, but each soul must enact that spirit by using Christ first, Christmas Second and Third, Santa Claus. They all need you. Keep the armor, the Globes, the Atlas map. Return the Keys-of-Death and Hades to the Creator. Only he can protect it. Give them all you got or, all that is good in this world will perish."

As her guardian angel disappeared as quickly as he had materialized, Jess stood, steeling herself with both hands wrapped around her precious necklace of magical charms. "I will not let my Father down, nor each soul in this physical world. If evil had its influence; I surely can enact the influence of Christ, Christmas and Santa Claus for the good of all and more—for their individual salvation. I won't lose, and I will battle as long as it takes!"

～ ～

After dressing, Jess was back in the magical world, thrilled with the happiness that was everywhere she looked. It permeated the atmosphere. She and Jose spotted each other at the same time and flew into each other's arms.

"You're back! You did it, Jess! I'm so proud of you. And, we are all so grateful."

Jess pulled back to look into Jose's beautiful eyes, "Uh, well, almost." Jose cocked an eyebrow, puzzled.

"This world is magical and brims with Christmas Spirit. The real work is cut out for me now in my world. Belief in Christ, Christmas, and Santa are still very much, in danger of disappearing forever, as well as, the physical world—unless I can influence a change in souls." Jess looked a bit uneasy.

Jose kissed the top of Jess' head, "I believe in you. The Creator chose you for a reason. That's all the reassurance I need."

Jess beamed. "Thank you, but you just might be the teeniest bit biased," she teased. "I've got one more quick visit here. Buy the way; I will need help from all others worlds. Christmas Spirit raised from this world and others like it, transfers and helps to influence the physical world. So how about we kick that spirit up a notch! Christmas Party!" Jess started dancing and singing Jingle bells.

Jose laughed, "It's time for celebrating. I'll have it all ready when you get back."

After kissing Jose, Jess ran into the magical woods. Her heart filled with joy when she recognized the friendly tree near the home of the Lady-of-Wisdom. Jess wrapped her arms around the mighty pine and pressed her face against its trunk. "I know you can hear me. I know you're alive and play many roles in the scriptures. That's why we celebrate your brothers and sisters with lights and ornaments at Christmastime. So, I will always remember you and be grateful for you. The term 'family tree' now holds an even more special place in my heart. Thank you, my friend."

The tree's bark smiled.

The woods and its tiny inhabitants joyfully rang with the sounds of Christmas. The Lady-of-Wisdom sat in the inviting rocking chair on her porch. This time, she wore no giant hat to shield her face. Jess' heart caught in her throat and her eyes filled with tears, seeing the Lady up close now. She threw her arms around the old woman, sobbing.

"There, there, dear," the Lady-of-Wisdom cooed to comfort Jess, lovingly rubbing the girl's back. "I know, Sweetheart. I know you miss her, but I am not your Grandmau-ma. You see, in this magical world when you miss someone so deeply; as you do with your grandmau-ma, the soul you're looking at changes to the one you miss. Sadness is not permitted here, so it alters images—this is why I didn't want you to see my face the first time we met. It might have been a bit of a distraction."

Jess laughed with a bittersweet undertone, "Yes, Ma'am, you're right. I'm so happy that you're Jose aunt, Ms. Lady-of-Wisdom and that he has a family. It's just that I miss my grandmau-ma so much and I want a family too."

Ms. Sapience took Jess' hands. "I'll like to be called Auntie Sappie. A family is all of God's Creations. Once you believe in The God of all, 'I AM' you are part of a universal family who in unity believe in Christ, Christmas, and Santa Claus. I am your Aunt Sappie. Now, when the Creator separated my sister and me; we were infants, and meant to serve two very different purposes. I learned to trust Him. He sees what you need before you ask it. So, sweetheart, patience is necessary and fulfilling your mission is a must. My heart nearly burst with joy and pride when I first met you, the Chosen One, the Apprentice."

"Oh, that reminds me... I believe I have something that belongs to you." Jessica removed her necklace and restored the Book-of-Knowledge to its original size.

Aunt Sappie accepted it and smiled, "Thank you, my darling. Back where it belongs, at last. I am the Lady-of-Wisdom, and it's time I tell you about a provision the Creator has in the physical world—a provision that might help you with your upcoming challenges. We call them Earth-Angles and they are all throughout the physical world. Some are waking up with the understanding that they have a special purpose and are not mere souls. Most are still sleeping. It's time you wake them all up to help you with this challenge. Now, don't you have a celebration to get to, young lady?"

"Yes, time to amp up the Christmas magic and Joy!" Jess kissed and squeezed her newly found Aunt Sappie tightly and was off.

Jess heard the music and found Jose right away. The town was magical, and the spirit was abundant. The two filled their stomachs with tasty celebratory foods and sweet treats. Jose laid out a blanket while Jess held food. Both were taking the lotus position converted about her visit with Aunt Sappie. She was thankful that time did not exist in the magical world. Enjoying this festivities filled her heart and soul with needed familiar surroundings of love, unity, and family.

Jose thought about what Jess needed for her to influence her physical world with faith. "Jess, I think I know what you need!"

"What?"

"You need to influence the physical world of Christ, Christmas, and Santa Claus, right?"

"Yes, and?"

"Aunt Sappie had a Book... All the books of the Bible make up an entire book from the Creator. And—I was..."

Jess interjected, "Yes, I must use words and books to help them see why using Christ name for Christmas is more than important—It means their very salvation! I have to write a book! Thanks, Jose, I have to go and start."

Jose jumps up, "One more thing—before you go. Wrap up this spirit. You see it and feel it here; use your power take it with you and release it in the physical world."

"Jose, thanks for your help."

Jess stood, touched her globes and twirled her hand into the air and form a visible magical twister of Christmas spirit and sucked it up through her mouth to hold in a particular part of her torso for later.

"Now, I'm full of joy." She giggled. "I remember feeling like I knew you before when I first meet you. I am sure the Creator will reveal it to me one day. I've learned thus far that nothing is consequential."

Jose winked at her, "Let me know when you find out."

Jess wondered if Jose already knew but brushed it off and hugged him, "I'll be back to visit as soon as I can. Goodbye, Jose..."

Jess left the festivities, but Jose continued to amp it up for the sake of the physical world.

36

Finalizing Things

Jess was thrilled to be back at the North Pole. The sweater from
Grandmau-ma kept her nice and warm in the gorgeous, snowy—
but cold—winter's wonderland. She ran to the peppermint-stick
pole poking through the snow, thinking it was a magical intercom. "Hi,
it's Jess."

Nothing happened so she started singing:

"Rudolph the Red-Nose Reindeer..."

Magically, the swirls of snow blew away to reveal the beauty of the North
Pole. Rudolph jingled to her side, playfully nudging Jess with his cold,
new black nose. Jess kissed him on top of his head. "Boy, am I, happy to
see you!"

"And, I'm happy to be seen," Rudolph laughed. "Climb aboard.
Santa's been waiting for you..."

Jess jumped on Rudolph's back and grabbed the straps, taking in all the wonder around her. The reindeer dropped her off at Santa's workshop. The first person she saw was Ralph. After he welcomed and hugged Jess, Ralph ran to grab a thick, red, green and gold rope, pulling with all his might. The bell's loud ringing meant everyone front and center.

Elves scurried from every corner of the workshop, hopping up and down with excitement to see Jess.

Santa ran out from his office, "What's the emergency, Ralph?" Then, the jolly old saint saw Jess standing in the middle of a sea of elves. "HO, HO, HO!" he laughed heartily. "Jess, of course, you're back! We can tell by the renewed vigor and vibrancy of our waterfall that Christmas spirit is on the rise. But, we know we've got a way to go; so the globes are all ready and waiting for you!"

The elves parted to make a path for Jess. She hugged Santa gratefully, "Thank you so much. Are there enough for every world and realm? We need double for the physical world."

"Ah, my dear... That's the magic of Christmas... As long as you believe, that red bag will hold as many Christmas globes as you need! While the elves pack them up, why don't you join Mrs. Claus and me in the library for some fresh chocolate chip cookies and cocoa?"

"Sounds wonderful... Thank you. I think I have room. I'm only filled with joy. The Christmas magic from Christonia, held in her torso—tickled." Jess followed Santa to an enormous library—something she'd never seen. Its corridors seem to stretch into forever. But, it was still warm, welcoming and cozy, just like everything else in the North Pole.

An older man and woman were already in the library, leisurely sipping cocoa and laughing over a funny story. When Santa and Jess entered, they instinctively turned around. Tears filled all eyes.

Jess ran into the waiting arms of the old woman, both of them sobbing with joy. "Grandmau-ma! Grandmau-ma! Is it really you this time? Oh my God! You're here! I've missed you so much!"

"Yes, my Sweetpea... Yes, it's me. And, I have missed you, too. So very much—and, I couldn't be more proud of you, my Darling. I've never stopped watching over you, just as I promised."

Grandmau-ma and Jess stood there, holding onto and rocking each other for dear life.

When they broke apart, still holding each other's hands, Grandmau-ma spoke first, "There's someone I would like for you to meet, Sweetpea, your Uncle Andrew."

Jess threw her arms around her "new" uncle's neck without hesitation. Everyone laughed, dabbing happy tears.

"It's time, Jess," Santa announced.

"Yes, my Love," Grandmau-ma chimed in. "There will be plenty of time to spend together after my granddaughter saves Christmas! The last step to complete in every world and realm except our physical world. You can do this sweetheart." The three older adults all encouraged and kissed Jess.

"The globes are loaded in the bag on the sleigh. Rudolph is waiting for you right outside these doors," Santa offered.

Jess affectionately rubbed Rudolph's head and climbed into the sleigh. "Let's do this, buddy! We started together and we will finish together. First, to Uncle Bob's— Up, up and away!"

They landed in the woods near Bob's home and camouflaged the sleigh. Rudolph morphed into Rufus, shaking out, his legs. "Whoo, boy, that feels good. Haven't walked on two legs in a while."

"Uncle Bob has been asleep all this time, Rufus. He has no idea that his niece slaughtered the love of his life, Aunt Renee, and is now a headless demon roaming around hell. I can't tell him that. What do I say when he wakes up and asks where Renee and Haley are?"

Rufus hunched his shoulders. "I don't think we are the ones with the answers, Jess."

"Of course we aren't. Thanks, Rufus," Jess sighed.

Jess sat on the ground in meditation and prayer, seeking guidance. As soon as she opened her eyes, a shivering, lovely, middle-aged woman stumbled through the woods.

"Oh, thank God." She reached out for a handshake. "My family and I were visiting extended family when a horrifying storm took them all; including my husband, Odin and my only child. I've been wandering

around these woods for days. You two are the first people I've seen during this entire time."

Jess shook her hand briskly, "Hi Miss Frigga, I'm Jess, and this is my
dear friend, Rufus. And..."

Rufus interjected, "You are familiar to me, somehow. Your name
and your husband's name."

Jess saw that Rufus was, perplexed and jumped right in, "He will figure it out later. Anyhow, we were just going inside to visit my Uncle Bob.
You must be half-frozen. Let's get you warmed up and find something
to eat. Even though my uncle has been—uh—a bit under the weather, he
and his home have been cared for very well."

"Thank you so much, Jess. It's good to meet you. Not everyone
would invite a perfect stranger into their home. You're such a kind and
thoughtful young lady. And—it's very nice to meet you, Rufus."

Rufus took Frigga's hand, "Pleasure. It's pretty dark out now. If you
don't mind—we'll like you to stay over. Oh, is that okay, Jess? We can call
any other relatives that you may have to let them know you're okay."

Frigga sighed with a heavy heart, "Thank you. But, I'm afraid there's
no family to call. I was visiting my only family when that storm took
them all—I have no one else."

"Oh, Miss Frigga... I am so very sorry for your terrible loss. Yes,
please stay the night and let us take care of you for a bit. Why don't you
guys head on into the kitchen? I'll meet you there in just a few minutes.
Think I forgot something outside."

Jess smiled, knowing it was no coincidence that this beautiful
widow showed up when she did. When Rufus and Frigga headed up
the stairs to the country home, Jess turned to her favorite oak tree.
Something unusual had sprouted from one of its lower branches—
a sparkling, magical mistletoe! She carefully took it from the tree,
asked blessings from the Creator. The mistletoe ability would make
emblematic love, ward off evil from home, and act as a protector of
the loved ones in the house. After wrapping it; Jess knew what to do
next.

"Wow, you look thawed out and fabulous already," Jess remarked, walking into the kitchen where Frigga was eating a hot bowl of soup Rufus had prepared.

"Mmm, looks and smells delicious, Rufus. How about a cup of that for me?"

Jess sat down at the table. The three enjoyed the soup like old friends. "Miss Frigga," Jess began cautiously, "first, I promise that I am of sound mind. What I'm about to ask you might sound crazy."

Frigga smiled, "Lay it on me, Sweetheart. I'm pretty sure I've heard and seen it all in my time."

Jess continued, "Well, my Uncle Bob has suffered some pretty horrible tragedies himself. He lost his wife and the niece he raised. He's been in a magical sleep over the last year."

Jess glanced at Frigga for a response or reaction one way or the other. Frigga simply nodded in understanding.

"And, well, I've been given a magical mistletoe. I think that a kiss under this mistletoe is the only thing that will wake him up."

Frigga grinned, her eyes twinkling, "And, you want me to do the honors?"

"Yes, please... Would you?"

"Of course. You and Rufus have been so kind to me, how could I possibly refuse? Besides, as I said, I don't think there's anything in the world—or any other, for that matter—that could surprise me anymore."

Jess and Rufus exchanged not-so-subtle, happily stunned looks. Frigga smiled knowingly.

The three-headed upstairs to Bob's bedroom. He was comfortably tucked into the same position in which Jess had left him. Jess held the magical sprig close and said a little prayer. She handed it to Rufus, who kept it over Bob's sleeping head. Frigga leaned in and kissed Bob gingerly on the lips.

Bob's eyelids fluttered open, "Hey Jess... Rufus. And, who is this beautiful goddess?"

Frigga blushed and said, "You are too kind, Sir. But I'm no goddess."

Jess kissed Bob on the forehead, "Hey there, how are you feeling? This is our new friend, Frigga. She had issues with that storm, just as you and we were wondering if you'd be okay with her spending the night here until we can find help for her."

"We'll be right here, Mr. Bob," Rufus offered. "Jess and I already decided we're here to take care of you."

Bob sat up on the side of the bed. "Thanks, but no need, kids. It was a very enlightening rest. The Creator and all manner of spiritual guides filled me in on everything. I even had a couple of comforting visits from my Renee. Even though Haley's choices pained Renee and I—I am certain Renee is at peace and happy now. We understand God's gift of free will. We get to choose. And, I choose to do what I was asked; because I choose goodness and I will follow the light."

He turned to Frigga, "Hi, Frigga. Sorry to go on and on like that. But, I had to share what was in my heart. It's good to meet you, even under these weird circumstances. And, I'm happy to put you up for the night. Gotta admit... though, I'm kinda rusty as a host, but the guest bedroom is very comfortable. It's yours—if you like."

"Thank you," Frigga responded, blushing even-more-so. "All of you have been so kind to me. I'm at a loss for words."

Bob was back in charge of his home, "Jess, Sweetheart, I love you. But, you've got a big job in front of you and require your rest. You, too, Rufus—go home. I'm a big boy. I got this. See you in the morning."

Jess and Rudolph complied with Bob's wishes, knowing Frigga was in good hands. Jess enjoyed a good night's sleep, snuggled in her bed at Grandmau-ma's. Rufus was accustomed to the cold and slept quite comfortably on the front porch.

— ∼

Jess awoke the next morning to the intoxicating smells of bacon and coffee wafting from the kitchen. Rufus rose earlier, hit the market in town and returned before Jess even opened her eyes.

"Whoa, Rufus... Impressive... A guy who knows his way around a kitchen. Is that a Western omelet I smell?"

"Yes, Ma'am," Rufus grinned. He prepared a full plate for Jess, placing it in front of her. The table was already set with a tiny vase of fresh flowers in the middle. "The best you've ever tasted. Guaranteed. And, here's a cup of my special coffee brew."

Jess didn't realize how famished she was and wolfed down the food. Rufus laughed, "Liked it, huh?"

"Loved it. You cooked, so I'll clean." Jess suggested.

"Let's do it together. That way it'll get done faster and we can be on our way." Rufus smiled.

Just as Rufus and Jess stood, ready to step out, there was a knock at the door. It was Bob.

"Hey, Uncle Bob... Come on in, but I thought we were gonna meet you back at your place. Uh, where's Frigga?"

"I took her to the hotel in town and did you know that woman can drive? So, I let her use my old car. She should be fine now. Delightful lady—I learned the real reason behind her wondering those woods for so long. Something to do with the very thing I called her when I first woke from my enlighten slumber that you put me in. Jess, thanks for that—by-the-way. Anyhow, she was called a goddess because of her beauty and her husband Odin took part in ungodly acts, but that's a whole different tale. Wow, that coffee smells great."

"Want some?" Rufus offered.

"Sure, thanks." Bob settled himself in Grandmau-ma's favorite chair. "I'd like to fill you guys in on what I've already gotten done this morning. All a part of the plan the Creator shared with me during that long nap."

Jess and Rufus sat on the sofa across from Uncle Bob. "Okay. We're listening."

"Amazingly, there was no trace of the name of Nefari's new husband—or any of her husbands—on any of the deeds to her properties. So, all of her toy stores and properties have been legally signed over to me, her only living relative. I was informed that both Nefari's and Haley's bodies were found buried in the wreckage of one of the buildings destroyed by that freak storm last year. This felt unusual, given what I now know about who they really were. At any rate, Jess, the Creator wants me to share with you the location of every store in the toy chain. I'm pretty sure it has something to do with you moving the needle from all things materialistic back to belief in Christ, Christmas, and Santa Claus," Bob laughed, taking another sip of his coffee.

Jess leaped from the sofa, excited, "Yes!" She pumped her arm. "That's it, Uncle Bob... You're a genius! Thank you!" Jess kissed Bob on the head. "Okay, guys here's the plan. Uncle Bob, I want you to put toy globes in all your toy stores. The children will shake the globe, see the magic of the North Pole and their spirits will fill with joy. This spirit will add to the children faith in Christ, Christmas, and Santa Claus in this physical world. The Christmas spirit will grow bountifully and give this place a chance to rid itself of all wickedness for good. We must do this right away before the Christmas season so the magic would work just in time for Christmas. Let's roll!"

Bob grinned and turned to Rufus, "You got it! And, Rufus, I think we're gonna need you to turn into Rudolph right now."

They all laughed, headed for the hidden sleigh. Jess asked Rufus to say something funny.

Rufus was a bit confused. "Funny? Okay."

Rufus told a funny short story of Santa and a bush full of berries. Jess unyieldingly laughed until the Christmas magic—she held in her torso was released into the midheavens blowing to and fro throughout the realm.

Rufus and Uncle Bob was speechless.

"Whoo! I've been holding that a long time. The Christmas magic from Christonia will help this world."

Rufus said, "You do some strange things." He shook his head. "Okay to the mission. We must transport the magical mini-Christmas globes to every toy store around this physical world first."

Bob and Jess hopped in the sleigh.

Rufus laughed and said, "Who said saving the world wasn't fun." He changed to Rudolph. "Hold On!"

Jess yelled, "Yes! F-U-N... fun! Wee! Hehe!"

They all flew through the nightly skies with Christmas spirit and Santa's magic for an entire night. All the stores were filled with magical toy globes."

Bob went back home to make plans to market the globes. He knew although they were free—folks had to learn where to get them. Jess and Rudolph made sure no child was left without a globe. Jess and Rudolph also delivered globes to areas, realms, and worlds that had no toy stores; as well as to children on Santa's 'Naughty' list. Christmas spirit, belief, hope, magic, and joy multiplied exponentially... everywhere.

37

Written In The Book

After all of her deliveries and the successful completion of her mission, Jess was both exhilarated and exhausted. She stood in her beloved woods outside of Grandmau'ma's house, stared at the glorious midnight blue skies, closed her eyes and twirled around seven whole times, her arms open. "Heavenly Father," she prayed aloud, "My God! My God! The Creator of it all! The Beginning and The End of it all! The Alpha and the Omega, I bow before you, for you are Good, You are love, You are Just, and You are Patient. Thank You. Thank You for Your love, Your grace, Your protection and Your guidance. Thank you for using a regular girl like me as the instrument to fulfill Your will. Please help me, as I continue to help your children understand the link between Christ, Christmas and Santa Claus, I remain your servant, even forever. Guide me because I know so many in this physical world are still non-believers. We will always need help to keep it all together. Amen..."

The stars above her grew supernaturally bright. Jess stared at them, in awe. Instantaneously, Jess was in the mist of the midheavens with the

bright stars all around her with glorifying praise. A loving voice emanated from all around her:

"Jessica, my beloved child, in you I am well-pleased."

"Father?" Jess asked, startled, falling to her knees upon nothing. "How
is it that you speak to me... Not by Angel servants or your provision in
Christ?"

*"My child... You are a blessed one. I emptied myself as Christ to save the
physical world from their own destruction and to act as the mediator between myself and man—this is, but the same thing I have allowed my special
creation to do. They don't possess just one life form. You called your self a
regular girl."* The Creator laughed.

Jess was shocked and said within, "Does the Almighty Laugh?"

*"Yes, I Am is joyful. Therefore, I created laughter—A gift the physical
world has taken for granted. You, my child, have never been a regular girl.
I'll explain that later."*

Jess love for the Creator could no-longer be measured. "My God... How
do complete my next mission."

*"Because of the gift of free will, there will always be those who choose not to
believe. For many of them, you are their last hope. But, hearts can change.
I continue to believe in you and yours as my agent for change in generations to come. You have seen, experienced and learned things—both good
and bad—beyond your human years, my child. Remember it all. Books are
the way of knowledge for those in the physical world, and your Job is yet
done. Tell your story, some will find it hard to believe, but the earth angles
will know and help spread the knowledge. Hearts will change, and a great
awakening can happen for all in the physical realm. But, for now, rest and
enjoy the rewards for your bravery and obedience.*

The emphasis on Christ, Christmas, and Santa Clause will be abundant. As for your name—it has changed and will be written in the Book-of-Life for your faithfulness in all your forms."

Jess startled. "All my forms? I had other lives and forms as Rufus." Almighty laughs again:

"Yes, and I will reveal all your lives, deeds and forms when it is time to leave the physical realms. You will know when that time comes. You must wrap up your worldly affairs in the physical realm. You then must return to the North Pole to fulfill your destiny. There you will go by your name written in the Book-of-Life as Aseneth."

An almost blindingly shiny box appeared. In it, Jess placed the Key-of-Death, the Key-of-Hades, the Atlas, and the witch-drawn map. She kept with her both globes, the complete Armor-of-God, and the Codex bible as charms on her necklace touched them and whispered, "Thank You, Father."

The box was gone. Divinely returned to the Creator and Jess was back at her grandmau-ma's home.

38

Hopeful Outcomes & Provisions Christ

Several years passed and Jess walked about the physical realms with anew hope in humankind. The Christmas seasons were beautiful! The winter snow was bright and glistening. Playful ice skating competitions, family snowball fights took over every year with the pure joy of heart. Every home and tree was lit, up with lights and many amazing decorations. Jess thought, of her beloved trees when she saw each one. Songs like: Jingle bells, We wish you a Merry Christmas, and many more songs were sung at doors by carolers. Mistletoes hung in most homes and if you were caught standing underneath—expect a kiss. Jess smiled ear to ear while folks passed by with the magical greeting, "Merry Christmas" and "Happy New Year." Jess would chuckle thinking back to the time when Rudolph had the two heads. One looking forward and the other looking back. Although, many shopped at the toy stores and had wrapped gifts underneath their arms; due to Jess novel and the earth angels—many recognized that each blessing came from The Creator and Santa was part of those blessings. Santa's deliveries were just as important every year because only gifts from Santa retained the

Christmas magic; thus—all the children preferred Santa's toys. Santa continued to get chubby from all the cookies and milk left for him from each house he visited. His naughty list declined year after year. Every winter—man, woman, and child looked, forward to the celebration of Christ, Christmas, and Santa Clause.

Jess looked around at the physical world with joy—absolutely hopeful that the physical world would accept the provisions made by Christ. The magical toy globes for the children undoubtedly boosted the spirit of Christmas. Jess had completed her novel—telling stories of her adventures of Christ, Christmas and Santa Claus. She added a bit of Christmas magic upon all who read it and this book too—added to the increase of the spirit of Christ amongst the physical realms every Christmas. A great awakening of the Earth-Angels was Jubilant.

Jess took a walk in the woods marveling at the beauty of her favorite tree. The luminosity from heavens opened up, and Jess' past lives revealed to her with an overflow of emotions. Jose was Joseph and her name Aseneth—it all made sense. Jess loved Jose, and he was her husband once in a past life. That was the connection she felt every-time she spent time with Jose. Jess—now, Aseneth was thrilled but knew it was time for her to join her grandmau-ma at the North Pole.

She met one more time with Uncle Bob at his home for the last time. She stood on the porch with joyful tears in her eyes.

Uncle Bob answered his door and upon seeing Jess face he knew... "So, My sweet girl. It's time, huh?"

The two walked in and stood by the fire. "Yes, It's time Uncle Bob. I love you so much."

Frigga walked in and said, "What a wonderful surprise! I didn't know you were coming. I would have made you a meal to remember. Your novel has taken this world by storm. We should celebrate!"

Jess smiled, walked over to Frigga and gave her a hug that plainly stated—this was goodbye. "I am so proud that the novel is doing well, and all that read it will gain the true spirit of Christmas, but I won't be sticking around for interviews."

Frigga appeared doleful, walked over to her new husband, Bob and wrapped her arms around him. She knew how much Jess' leaving would hurt him.

Jess gave a smile and said, "Look, I'll be back to visit from time to time. You know that—right? Since money and property are of no use to me where I'm headed—I'm turning all of it over. All the money and properties that Grandmau-ma had left to me, the money from the toy globes, will go to you. The author's name in my novel will magically change from mine to Frigga's. I trust you Uncle Bob and Miss Frigga to use it all to better the world around you. Just know—all that you do with this constant fight for the physical world matters to every soul that lives in it."

Jess hugged them so tightly and said, goodbye.

Back home—she sat in her Grandmau-ma's chair for the last time then walked onto the porch. Her head turned to the heavens, and she felt the Christmas magic was abundant as God had promised but a dark cloud covered her thoughts briefly, and she also knew her journey wasn't done in the physical world. She felt the battles to come would make the previous ones feel like child's play.

Jess soon returned to the North Pole via the power of her globes. Obtaining her new God-given name Aseneth—she lived, laughed, loved and worked happily alongside Mr. and Mrs. Claus; Ralph the Jolly Elf and the multitude of other elves; her dearly loved and sweet Grandmau-ma; her witty Uncle Andrew; and her wonderful husband, Jose/Joseph. The two spent countless moments catching up on all their lives, missions and gratitude for Christ, Christmas and Santa Claus while awaiting their next assignment from the Creator, I AM...

Acknowledgements

I would like to thank God. Nothing in this life is possible without Him.
I would like to thank my husband, Eddie Floyd Jr., for his undying love and encouragement.

255

Epilogue

What If...

About the Author

April Floyd is an author born and raised in St. Louis and an exciting literary voice in the world of Erotica, dedicating each of her novels to those who want books they can't put down. She consciously chose not to drag the reader through monotonous descriptions. As you turn the pages, you will find yourself in your favorite chair with a warm blanket, enjoying her unfolding stories.

Floyd's genre appreciation goes beyond Erotica—fused with Paranormal, Drama, Horror, Suspense, Spirituality, Action, Romance, Magical Realism, and much more. Her style of writing crosses the conventional boundaries of one genre. Floyd's primary objective is to tell stories that are dear to her heart, causing her to be more passionate about her characters as they develop.

Floyd attended Nipher Middle School when she discovered her passion for writing early. Floyd attended Kirkwood High School, and it was there that she enjoyed every writing assignment. She began writing her first novel, The Look of Love. The manuscript was finished in 2005 but destroyed when a storm struck her home while her computer was plugged in. She was devastated, and she stopped writing altogether. It wasn't until she met her husband, photographer, and scriptwriter, Eddie Floyd Jr., who encouraged her to write again. As newer devices and technologies developed her husband explained everything about the proper ways of saving her work and showed her several ways to do it, with flash drives, emails, and external hard drives, and encouraged her to write again. In 2008, she began the quest of writing and attending Forest Park Community College. Her trilogies of Unique were born. Her children, Malissa, Terry, and Walter, Jr., are her inspiration for writing Unique. Her husband, Eddie Floyd Jr., was her inspiration for writing again.

Floyd started writing as a blogger for OnStL.com in 2013, promoting her hometown St. Louis.

Floyd's trilogies of Unique novels were published in February 2014 and since has held it's five-star ratings. Her books are a page-turning reflection of her passions; of issues and situations that are dear to her heart. The Unique stories entertain, educate, touch and inspire its readers. The stories are brimming with family drama—and values—love, devastation, loss, redemption, faith, comedy, suspense and a touch of erotica. Mrs. Floyd published her latest novel, THE LINK—November 2017. The concept of Christ, Christmas, and Santa Claus are Linked in a world of Magical Realism has taken hold of new readers who were looking for a new and different perspective of all three.

For more about the Author: http://www.aprilfloydbooks.com/home.html

The End

www.ingramcontent.com/pod-product-compliance
Lightning Source LLC
Chambersburg PA
CBHW050338030726
47503CB00008B/2511